Rachel felt sure she could bring down the pilot one way or another

She flew low over the clearing, mere feet above the fir trees. They could see the high-powered military craft on the runway below as it fueled up for the long flight ahead.

"Rachel—what are you doing?" Jake shouted, looking on in anxious disbelief as she banked the plane down and approached the jet from the rear.

"One way or another, we'll stop him!"

"Yeah, and stop us, too!"

The jet lurched on the runway as they passed over it, and then began to roar along the tarmac. Suddenly something slammed into their plane as a dark object shot up before them. Below them the forest erupted in an orange-and-yellow ball of flame.

"What hit us?" Jake asked, twisting desperately around to locate the jet and the source of the flames below while Rachel fought for control of the plane.

ABOUT THE AUTHOR

Laura Pender is kept very busy by a
permanent job and two young children in the
Minneapolis, Minnesota, area. Laura feels
that her spouse is a heavy contributor to all
her Intrigues. A prolific writer, she has
written for *Alfred Hitchcock's Mystery
Magazine* and many other publications.

Books by Laura Pender

HARLEQUIN INTRIGUE
62–TASTE OF TREASON
70–HIT AND RUN
91–TRAITOR'S DISPATCH

Don't miss any of our special offers. Write to us at the
following address for information on our newest releases.

Harlequin Reader Service
901 Fuhrmann Blvd., P.O. Box 1397, Buffalo, NY 14240
Canadian address: P.O. Box 603,
Fort Erie, Ont. L2A 5X3

Sky
Pirate
Laura Pender

Harlequin Books

TORONTO • NEW YORK • LONDON
AMSTERDAM • PARIS • SYDNEY • HAMBURG
STOCKHOLM • ATHENS • TOKYO • MILAN

Harlequin Intrigue edition published February 1989

ISBN 0-373-22108-8

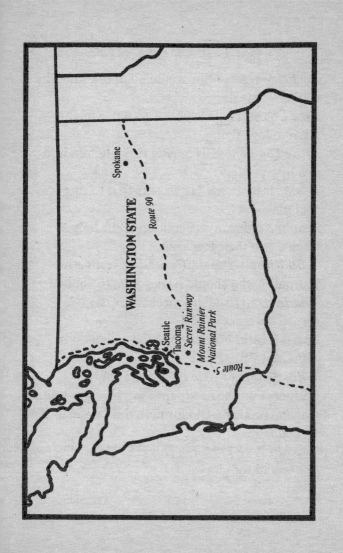

WASHINGTON STATE

Spokane

Route 90

Seattle
Tacoma
Secret Runway
Mount Rainier
National Park

Route 5

CAST OF CHARACTERS

Rachel Morgan—She would go to press despite a killer's threats.

Jake Connors—This police detective might learn to love flying.

Bruce Quinlan—His amateurism got him into deadly trouble.

Frank Ackerman—He was the first to suspect foul play.

Naomi Aaronson—A colleague, she helped track down their few leads.

Scott Kirby—The staff's brash investigative journalist who should have gotten the bullet.

Charles DeWitt—This mechanic's day off turned gruesome.

Special Agent Fowler—Was he an honest or dishonest FBI agent?

Willis Schofield—He owned the lumber business that the newspaper was investigating.

Calvin Watkins—Did his mob ties extend to the Russians?

Captain Zack Parker—This U.S. Navy pilot was *not* bound for glory.

Prologue

The April breeze blew in cold off Puget Sound as a young man in a heavy windbreaker made his way along the Tacoma, Washington, commercial pier past a freighter that swayed with a hold half-filled with lumber. He moved through the stacked crates on the dock with the determined haste of someone on his way to an important appointment. This was, in fact, the case, and he slowed as he approached another man who stood very still near the gigantic ship.

"Louie Hunt?" he asked, speaking in an uncertain whisper.

"Yeah. Are you alone?" the man in the shadows asked.

"I said I would be, didn't I?" The young man stared into the shadows, moonlight painting his earnest face a deathly bluish-white as he thrust his hands into his jean pockets. "This story is too big to risk scaring off the only lead I've got." He smiled, betraying a childlike eagerness in his round, bookish features.

"You're damn right it's big," the second man said, gruffly. "Too big for either one of us to be sloppy."

"Exactly." The young man removed a slim tape recorder from his back pocket and switched it on. "Okay, so what can you tell me?"

"I can give you the whole thing," the man said, moonlight sliding over the irregular patch of a birthmark like a small inkblot below his left eye as he looked down at the cassette recorder. "I know enough to put all of them away for life."

"Good. That's what I need." Anticipation colored the young man's face as he leaned closer to his companion. "When are they planning to make their move?"

"Next week." The man turned slightly, holding up one gloved hand for silence as he peered nervously into the shadows of the goods stacked on the dock. "You sure you're alone?"

"We've been through that, Mr. Hunt. Please, tell me what you have and we can both get out of here." There was a slight tremor in his voice.

Louie smiled crookedly, slipping his hands into the pockets of his jacket as he looked back at the young reporter. When he withdrew his right hand he held a gun. There were three muffled pops and three brief flares of light like firecrackers, then the young man jerked back woodenly. Dropping his tape recorder, he staggered and fell on the pier.

The other man returned his hand to his pocket and stood still for a moment. Then he stooped, picked up the tape recorder and pocketed the cassette. "Well, Clark Kent," he mumbled, as he dropped the recorder beside the motionless body. "I hope you liked your story."

Chapter One

Rachel Morgan, the slim young editor-publisher of the *Tacoma Banner*, felt cold in the antiseptic corridor of the county morgue and closed her pale blue cardigan in an effort to ward off the chill that stole across her neck and arms. It was a chilly, rainswept day and the cold gleam of fluorescent light reflecting from steel and tile certainly didn't create any warmth, but it had been the cold reality of her errand there that caused her to shiver. She'd never been asked to identify a body before, and it wasn't a pleasant experience.

Though she'd recognized him and said as much to the men who'd dispassionately pulled out the stainless steel tray that held his body, she couldn't really say that it had looked like Bruce Quinlan at all. The young man on the tray was gray and drawn, dimming the memory of his vitality and leaving only a shell of his physical self.

She turned, hearing the footsteps of the slim policeman who'd brought her to this sad place.

"I'm sorry to have put you through all of this, Ms Morgan, but now that you've given us a positive identification we can notify his parents." Det. Sgt. Jake Connors stopped before her, parenthetical lines of concern framing the grim set of his lips. "It's a damn shame," he said simply, his husky voice muted and weary.

"I still can't believe it." Rachel was amazed that her voice sounded so calm. "Even after seeing him, I just can't accept the fact that he's dead." She leaned her back against the white tiled wall and crossed her arms tightly before looking into the detective's face. It was a strong face that showed a capacity for great compassion as well as hard anger sparkling in his clear blue eyes.

"It's never easy," the detective offered.

"But why?" she asked plaintively, struggling with the lump in her throat. "Why did this happen?"

"I'm afraid he was just in the wrong place at the wrong time. Dockside at night isn't the friendliest place to hang out."

"I wonder if it was worth it," she said, bitterness coloring her voice. "I mean, did Bruce have enough money on him for it to be worth murder?"

The officer leaned against the wall beside her, his hands thrust into the pockets of his trousers. "I don't imagine they gave much thought to that. From the look of it, the killer shot first and went after the money later."

"What do you mean?" Rachel turned her head toward him, studying the tired expression that drew down his lean, rugged features.

"He was shot three times in the chest from a distance no greater than two feet. There was no struggle, no sign that he had time to do anything. The wounds wouldn't be straight on like that if there had been time to react."

Rachel cringed slightly, almost able to hear the shots ringing out in rapid succession as Detective Connors spoke, and he stopped when he saw how his words had affected her.

"Were you and Quinlan close?" he asked.

"Yes." Rachel sighed, pushing herself away from the wall. "Working on a small paper like the *Banner*, it's easy to get close to your coworkers."

"Well, I'll do my best to find his killer, Ms Morgan," he said, beginning to walk with her toward the door. "But you probably know crime statistics as well as I do, so I'm not about to promise anything just yet."

"I understand." Rachel smiled at him, grateful for his caring and compassionate manner as well as his honesty. "Thank you for your help, officer. Will you need me for anything else?"

"Not at the moment. If I find out anything important or have any questions, I know where to reach you."

"Yes, please do tell me how the investigation progresses."

"I will."

Rachel turned away from the man and walked down the hall to the door, stepping out into the cold gray light of a desolate, rainy day.

JAKE TURNED BACK to the coroner's office to complete his notes on the young reporter's death. The case had been a mess from the beginning and this little twist wasn't helping matters one bit.

Could it have been a robbery, as he'd told Rachel Morgan? That's what the FBI thought, but something about the circumstances nagged at him. He wished he could have asked Ms Morgan more questions about Quinlan's assignments, but the involvement of the FBI made the matter too sensitive to alert the press just now. Quinlan had been close to something, Jake believed, and couldn't have been on the pier by accident. But was he close enough to be considered a threat? No. If the FBI didn't know what was going on, how could a student reporter have stumbled onto anything?

After completing his notes with the coroner, he was on his way to his car when a lean man with short blond hair approached him. It was the head of the local FBI bureau, Agent Fowler. "You know," the man said in his usual brusque manner, "I'm not so sure Quinlan ever knew anything about it."

"You aren't?" Detective Connors stopped, crossing his arms before him. "It was you people who said he was snooping into it. Don't tell me the FBI has seen fit to change its mind, Agent Fowler."

"We think it was a robbery." Fowler smiled thinly. "The people we're after wouldn't have killed him. Not this close to the end. No, it was robbery."

"They left his tape recorder," Connors pointed out.

"So what? I've been with the bureau long enough to know a simple mugging when I see one. Quit acting like a small-town cop with hurt feelings and do your job. Until you hear something different from us, it was a robbery. Especially when you're dealing with anyone from the *Banner*."

"Is that official?"

"Yes." The federal agent turned and walked away, leaving the detective standing alone in the hallway.

RACHEL DROVE BACK to the squat brick building that housed the *Banner* offices in a humor that matched the gray clouds hanging low overhead. It was almost quitting time, and what she really wanted to do was go home and avoid the subject of Bruce's death entirely, but there were people waiting to hear from her. She still had her duties to fulfill.

She wondered how Detective Connors was able to cope with his firsthand view of such a loss. Though he wouldn't have a personal stake in the murders and robberies he investigated, the volume of grief and dismay he'd encounter as a robbery-homicide detective must wear him down. Just reporting the news grew to be a heavy load at times; how could he bear to put such events under such close scrutiny on a daily basis? Still, though his roughly handsome features had been tired, Rachel didn't see any cynicism in his honest blue eyes. All she'd seen there were kindness and compassion and perhaps a touch of anger at the young man's death.

She knew she could trust him to do everything possible to find Bruce's killer.

"I DON'T CARE what the evidence says. Bruce Quinlan wasn't the type of idiot who went for midnight strolls along the pier." Frank Ackerman, who set type and ran the presses at the *Banner*, glowered sadly at the paneled wall of Rachel's office as he rolled his thick cigar between two stained fingers. "Kirby is idiot enough, but not Bruce," he added, referring to Scott Kirby, another intern working at the paper.

"No, I wouldn't characterize him as the adventuresome type, either. Nonetheless, that's where he was." Rachel swiveled her chair in short, nervous arcs as she sat looking at Frank and Naomi Aaronson, who was a reporter and the community events editor. The three of them had gathered in Rachel's office when she returned from her unpleasant visit to the morgue. "The time of death is just preliminary anyway. He might have been shot much earlier or later than they think."

"Maybe later, but not earlier." Frank nestled his cigar beneath the walrus fringe of his mustache and puffed, angry blue smoke rising above his head. "If anything, the cold air would have speeded up rigor mortis rather than slowed it."

"Oh, Frank, must you talk like that?" Naomi shuddered visibly in her chair beside Rachel's desk. The fifty-two-year-old grandmother usually established an almost maternal relationship with the students working at the paper, and Bruce's death had hit her hard. The normally eager expression of her slightly lined face was dimmed by sadness. "We're talking about Bruce, not some derelict in an alley."

"Sorry, Naomi, but the newspaper business runs on facts, no matter who the victim might be. I thought that was relevant." Frank and Naomi were normally at odds about one thing or another, an ongoing series of friendly disagreements that seemed to be satisfactory to both parties, but neither one of them was up to arguing about this subject. "It's damn rough to think about, though."

"I thought I knew Bruce pretty well," Rachel said, "but this business has me baffled, too. Bruce just wasn't a risk taker."

"Unless he was working on a story," Naomi suggested. "He may have been a sensible boy but he was still a reporter, after all."

"He wasn't doing anything that would have taken him to the docks," Rachel said. "Especially not in the middle of the night."

"Could they have dumped the body there?" Frank asked, tilting his head back to squint up into his cigar smoke, his favorite position for thought.

"Not likely. They said there was too much blood at the scene for him to have died anywhere else." Rachel winced slightly at the thought of the blood even before Naomi's sharp intake of breath suggested a change of subject.

"What in hell took them so long in calling you about him?" Frank asked. "They didn't call here till nearly three."

"His wallet had been stolen, Frank," Rachel replied. "The only thing he had left on him was his tape recorder. It was only when they came to tow his car from a no-parking zone that they checked the registration and connected it to the body on the pier. They found his press card in the glove compartment and called us.''

"Awful roundabout way of doing business," Frank snorted.

"I suppose they didn't figure that parking violations were their prime concern at the moment.''

The trio lapsed into strained silence for a moment, each lost in his own thoughts until Rachel finally stood, saying, "I think we're done here for today. We'll have to finish off Bruce's stories for next week, but I'm not up to it at the moment. Let's go home, shall we?''

"We sure as hell won't get anything done this late in the day, anyway," Frank agreed, in his usual no-frills manner. "I'd better toddle on home." He stood and opened the office door, stopping to say, "You'll call if you find out anything new, won't you? I'd dearly like to know what he was doing on the docks.''

"Yes, I'll keep everyone up to date," Rachel assured them, as she watched both of them head out. "In the meantime, try to have a good weekend.''

"I won't make any promises," Frank called over a shoulder.

"Good night, dear." Naomi followed the burly pressman out. "You get some rest, okay?''

"I will." Rachel smiled at Naomi's motherly tone. Between Naomi's protective instincts and Frank's gruff, down-to-earth attitude toward life that so closely resembled her father's, it seemed at times that Rachel had found a new set of parents in her two coworkers. They provided a cozy feeling within her that helped dispel any sorrow.

Still, when Rachel turned out the lights and locked up the building for the night, she did so with a heavy and confused heart.

Rachel pulled her battered old station wagon into the stream of cars going home for the night and let the traffic carry her through the city as her mind followed. Why had Bruce Quinlan died? Was it simply a mugging or something of a more sinister nature? Was there anything that she could do to help solve the mystery behind the murder?

She'd learned from her father not to jump to conclusions when reporting a story, to examine all the angles before tackling the job of putting the facts on paper. He'd been an example of the complete professional, an inspiration to her growing up and again as a reporter. Now she put the Bradford Morgan axiom of news reporting to work on the case of the dead reporter. "Nine times out of ten," he used to say, "and except when writing about politics, the most obvious explanation is the most accurate. But then, there's always that tenth case that will get you."

So, if the most obvious explanation was the correct one, then Bruce Quinlan had indeed been the victim of a robbery. He'd probably been killed for the change in his pockets, and there wasn't a thing she could do to change the situation or hasten its solution. She was helpless in the face of the evidence, and that apparent helplessness frustrated her. If she couldn't bring the young man back, the least she could try to do was help avenge his death.

She took her time driving past the massive ships on Puget Sound and across the Port of Tacoma waterway as she let a myriad of questions roll through her mind. The traffic had thinned as she traveled farther from the heart of the city. Most of the commuters had turned off for their homes along the way and only a small number continued with her as she left the waterway and began the twisting drive through the trees along Dash Point Road. She drove quickly along the snaking road through the stands of pine, noticing that a yellow Volvo had remained behind her since leaving downtown. That was odd. She didn't remember ever seeing it in her neighborhood.

She drove along the quiet streets in the growing dusk, and the yellow car continued following several car lengths behind her. They were the only two cars on the street. It struck Rachel that it was a peculiar coincidence for them to have shared their route all the way from the center of the city. She slowed, preparing to turn onto White Fir Drive, and the vehicle slowed behind her, keeping its distance. On impulse, she drove past her house and turned at the end of the block. The Volvo followed her, turning when she did, keeping its speed matched to hers and maintaining its distance as they circled a couple blocks.

It was following her! A tingle of panic rushed through her body as she slowly turned the next corner. Then she pushed the accelerator down hard. The old car coughed and lurched ahead, and she turned the next corner at forty miles an hour, slowing midway down the block to see if the other car was still behind her. Yes, the yellow car turned the corner quickly and slowed to match her speed. Fear gripped her as she stared at the image in her rearview mirror. Why would it be following her? Was this connected to Bruce Quinlan's death?

There was no answer to her question, only the continuing fact of the Volvo's presence behind her.

But when she turned back onto White Fir Drive and into the driveway of her frame house, the driver just continued past her without slowing or even looking her way. Rachel sat trembling until the car turned the corner, then bolted from the car to the front door. She couldn't get the key to fit the lock too soon.

Finally, when the key slipped home she threw the door open and rushed into the dark house. With the door locked soundly she allowed herself to relax, leaning with relief against the cool wood that blocked her portal. Then she sat on the low bench by the door and peered past the sheer curtains over the sidelight window. What was going on?

The car didn't return again, and so Rachel stirred herself to motion. There was no sense waiting for bad news. She walked through to the dark living room and switched on the light.

And for the third time that day, her world was thrown into confusion. The room looked as though a bomb had gone off inside!

Chapter Two

The room looked as though a gigantic child had thrown a tantrum.

"Oh, my God!" The exclamation burst from her lips at the sight as fear and anger burst through her. "No!"

Fighting a strong desire to run from the house, she left the living room on unsteady legs and walked down the short hall to the kitchen, turning on lights as she went. In the kitchen the cupboard doors were standing open, and the contents were scattered on the countertops. Even the refrigerator stood open.

Fear took hold of her for a moment. Why would anyone want to vandalize her home? Were they still inside?

She checked each room gingerly, greeted by similar sights behind every door. Fortunately, there was no sign the trespasser was still inside.

She felt sickened as she glimpsed her bedroom. It was in the same uproar. What kind of people did such things? And why?

Why, indeed? Why, within twenty-four hours of Bruce Quinlan's death, would she be subjected to pointless vandalism? And why would that car have been following her? Could there be some link between the events? With that in mind, she hurried to the phone and dialed the Tacoma police.

"Could you connect me to Det. Sgt. Jake Connors?" she asked the police operator. She couldn't seem to get breath to speak properly at first, and even after searching the whole house she found herself turning to keep an eye on the silent room. "He's out? Please contact him and tell him that there's been a break-in at Rachel Morgan's home. Yes, at 715 White Fir Drive. There's no one here now. I'm alone. Please, tell him to hurry."

RACHEL WAS ANXIOUS for the detective to arrive and paced nervously before the window for twenty minutes, afraid to disturb things even enough to change clothes.

The waiting added fresh anxiety to her already taut nerves. She needed to get everything back into place. The sight of her things scattered around depressed her, and she couldn't stand walking through the clutter of knickknacks and stuffing strewn from the throw pillows. Tears fought with anger as she paced and waited.

Her wait finally ended with the arrival of a squad car, and she hurried to the door to let in the police.

"Good evening, Ms Morgan." Detective Connors stood on the step beside a uniformed officer who carried a stout briefcase in one hand. Connors was still wearing his white shirt and jeans but without the tie and covered by a tan twill jacket. "Are you all right?"

"I think so," she assured him. "Still a bit shocked, though. Please, come in." She stepped back to admit the officers.

"I'm glad you called right away, Ms Morgan. This is Officer Daniels," he said, passing her at the door. The other man entered with a polite nod. "We've brought equipment to take prints while we're here, too."

"Good. You can see the evidence all around," she told them as she led the way into the once-orderly living room.

"This is one hell of a shock to come home to," he said with great sympathy. "Daniels, you get to work on those prints. Try the doors and such. Where do you think they came in?" he asked Rachel.

"I haven't even looked," she replied. "I didn't want to disturb anything."

"Good idea," Officer Daniels said, with efficient abruptness. "Is there a back entrance?"

"Yes, two of them. One door leads from the kitchen to the garage and the other leads out onto the patio and the backyard."

"The patio door sounds like the most likely point of entry," Detective Connors said, his tone soft with compassion. "Let's go take a look."

She showed them the sliding doors that led out from the dining room onto the stone patio set into the cool, green expanse of yard, and Detective Connors crouched to look closely at the outside of the door.

"There you are," he announced. "They jimmied up the latch and came right in. The locks on these doors are pretty feeble. Dust this first, Daniels."

"I suppose it isn't much of a lock," Rachel said, examining the minute scratches he was referring to. "I'd never given much thought to the possibility of anyone wanting to get in here."

Detective Connors turned toward her with kindness in his calm blue eyes.

"We'll let him do his bit while you give me your statement," he said as they walked back to the living room. "But I'll be honest and tell you right away that it's unlikely the person who did this will ever be caught. Not for this crime, anyway." He opened the notebook in his broad hand and wrote something down quickly.

"I know," she said glumly. "But we might get lucky."

"I sure hope so," he said, with heartfelt conviction. "Now, about what time do you think this happened?"

"Well, I left for work at about seven-fifteen this morning," she answered, focusing her thoughts on her actions that day. "I don't come home for lunch, so that leaves the time pretty much open. I was a bit later than usual getting home today. Any time between seven-fifteen this morning and seven this evening."

"Okay." He made a note in his book. "Can you think of any reason someone would do this to your home?"

"No, I can't think of any reason."

"Have you been able to tell if anything is missing?" His eyes were friendly, consoling her.

"I don't know." Looking around, she realized it would be nearly impossible to inventory her possessions in this mess. "I don't think I could tell everything I'm supposed to have with the house in order, let alone in this state. And as I said I didn't want to disturb anything."

"That's all right," he said. "Are all the rooms in more or less the same condition as this one?"

"Yes. Would you like to take a look?"

"If that would be all right. I know it's adding insult to injury to have me traipsing around the house after this happened, but they might have left some kind of clue."

"I understand."

She led the detective upstairs and on a tour of the trashed rooms on the second floor. He made a few notes, saying little about what he saw, though he called the other man up to take prints from a couple of areas. As she guided him, Rachel allowed herself to take a closer look at the mess that was her home. Something wasn't right about it, something that she couldn't put her finger on. Leave it alone, she thought, and you'll figure out what it is.

"Do you have any medical condition that requires prescription drugs of any kind?" he asked her, leaning against the back of the couch in the living room.

"Me? No, nothing like that. Do you think this was caused by someone looking for narcotics?"

"Maybe." He shrugged, putting his notebook away in his hip pocket. "What about money? Do you keep cash in the house?"

"No, I'm afraid I rely all too much on my plastic," she said, with a small smile. "And I don't have any kind of valuables, either."

Detective Connors didn't say anything for a moment but subjected the living room to the careful scrutiny of his observant blue eyes, pursing his lips in thought. Then he turned his gaze back to her as though about to say something, but he looked past her instead calling, "Daniels!"

"Yes, sir?" The other man entered the room quickly, his case in hand.

"Let's wrap it up here." Connors turned back to Rachel. "We'll have to take a set of your prints now, if we may."

"Why is that?" She watched him closely. Why did she have the impression that he was leaving something unsaid?

"It wouldn't do us much good to send your prints off for identification, would it?" He smiled broadly, with a slight tilt of his head. "You're under no obligation, you understand, and the prints won't go into any file except the report on this robbery."

"By all means," she answered, returning his smile. "I want to do everything we can to clear this up as quickly as possible."

They both joined the uniformed officer, who had set up an ink pad and a print card on the coffee table. He helped her to ink her fingers and leave her marks in the squares printed on the card while Detective Connors looked on. When the process was finished, Officer Daniels snapped the case shut and left the house with a courteous goodbye.

"Will you be all right alone tonight?" Detective Connors stood near her, looking down with a protective gaze. "I can arrange for a car to keep an eye on things."

"I'm all right," Rachel said, with more conviction than she felt. "You've done plenty for my peace of mind already."

"You should fit your back door out with a better lock," he said. "They make some good ones for that kind of door, but they're not usually standard equipment."

"You don't suppose they'd come back, do you?"

"No, I doubt they'll be back." He placed one hand on her shoulder, giving it a small, encouraging squeeze. "When you've had a chance to go over your belongings, you can make a list of anything that is missing and bring it to me on Monday." He moved the comforting hand away, its warmth lingering.

"Thank you, Detective," Rachel said, following him to the door. "I thought at first that this might be connected to Bruce's death. Do you think that's possible?"

"I couldn't say for sure," he answered, his broad forehead wrinkling slightly. "Anything is possible, of course, but these are two very different types of crime." Then he smiled gently, his face softening as he looked at her. "The lock seems to be intact, but you should tie that patio door shut with some wire. Tie it shut, and double-check the other locks in the house. Until we know more, you should take extra precautions."

"Precautions against what?"

"You would be best advised to take precautions against any possibility." He held her eyes with his serious gaze for a moment. "There's no sense making it easy for the criminals."

"No, there isn't. I'll check into a new lock."

"Good. Bye now."

"Goodbye, Detective." She watched as he opened the door and walked down the sidewalk, moving with the smooth strides of someone comfortable with his body. Then she closed the door and returned to the living room, vague dissatisfaction nibbling at the edge of her thoughts. But what she was dissatisfied with she couldn't begin to say.

JAKE CONNORS RODE IN SILENCE as Daniels drove them back downtown. He watched the houses and trees flowing past the car windows with a pensive frown marring the straight lines of his face. *I should have told her more,* he thought. *But if I did, I'd only have started her thinking, and that could be more dangerous than leaving her in the dark.*

"Sir?" Officer Daniels spoke carefully, his own face set in thought. "What about that break-in? Didn't it look kind of, well, a bit odd?"

"Yes, it did," Jake admitted. "But for the moment you're going to treat it like a normal break-in. Probably just kids up to no good. Got me?"

"Sir?" The young officer's confusion registered clearly in his voice.

"It was just vandalism. Nothing unusual. Nothing odd. Nothing worth gossiping at the station about. Right?"

"Right." Daniels fell silent, worry knotting his brow.

"Drop me off at the federal building," Jake said, after a moment. "I've got some business with the FBI." Then he turned his attention back to the city moving beyond the window and rode the rest of the way in silence.

ALTHOUGH SHE KNEW there wasn't any more that could be done right then, Rachel felt a need to take some kind of action in the matter after the officers left. It wasn't in her nature to take a passive role in things, and there had to be something she could do to fight off this feeling of total helplessness. But all she could do was pick up the pieces and put the house back together. She knew that she wouldn't find that anything was missing. It seemed to be just senseless vandalism, and that notion wasn't the least bit satisfying.

Rachel spent the entire evening cleaning the house, which was largely a matter of putting things back where they belonged and throwing out the few things that had been broken. It was well after midnight that she went up to bed. But even after her evening's exertion she found it hard to sleep.

Though Detective Connors was obviously concerned and would certainly do his best to solve the crime, she still had the impression that he'd been about to tell her something earlier but had changed his mind. Perhaps he did think there was a connection between the incident at her home and the young reporter's death but didn't want to scare her by sharing his suspicions.

Could there be a connection? And then there was the matter of the yellow car that had followed her home. Could the death, the strange car and the break-in all be mere coincidence?

Now, in the stillness of her dark bedroom, the yellow car loomed in her mind. But how? She didn't know anything about Bruce's personal habits, especially any that would have taken him to the dock. Unless—yes, unless Naomi had been right, and he had been working on a story when he was shot. That would be a clear link between everything. Or would it?

As sleep finally began to fall over her, Rachel came to the conclusion that Bruce must have been working on something that she didn't know about, something that took him down to the docks in the middle of the night. Something that ultimately got him killed.

Chapter Three

The morning sun glittered on the snowy heights of Mount Rainier as Rachel piloted her sturdy, single-engine airplane toward the summit of the mountain. The spring sky was crystal blue and the carpet of pine trees thousands of feet below her rippled like a green ocean disturbed by the light morning breeze.

Rachel had learned to fly while a student at Northwestern University in Evanston, Illinois, and since then she'd found it helped her thoughts and clarified her outlook when a dilemma faced her.

She took her Piper Cherokee up shortly after nine on Saturday morning after filing a flight plan for a short pleasure trip taking her toward the Cascade Mountains and down on a southern loop to Olympia and home to Tacoma.

Rachel switched on a cassette recorder lying on the seat beside her. "Note," she said, projecting her voice over the steady drone of the plane's engine. "See if we can check Bruce's usage of reference materials from the University library. If he was investigating a story, he'd have used the library for research. Put Naomi on that right away."

She was flying southwest along the Puyallup River as she fought to channel her outrage at the young man's death into an investigation to find the culprit. But the more she thought about it, the angrier she became. Bruce was a kind, soft-spoken young man who would never harm anyone. His death was too unjust to go unavenged.

"Send Scott out to the dock to nose around," she continued. "Have him find out about security there, incidences of theft, smuggling, whatever he can find out. Double note: make absolutely certain he conducts his investigations in daylight and in public. Take no chances."

Scott Kirby, an energetic senior, was the student who would most need constant reminders to proceed with care. He showed a certain brilliance for investigative reporting, but along with his instincts for the heart of a story he seemed almost totally without concern for his own personal safety. He'd created a local splash only a couple of weeks before by getting a firsthand account of illegal cost cutting used by the company building a high rise downtown. Of course, he'd gotten the story by trespassing on the work site late at night and other questionable, if not illegal, methods that could have gotten him jailed, at the very least. Rachel didn't expect him to be any more cautious on this story just because the danger was personal injury rather than criminal charges.

And that was the confusing part of the mystery. Of the two interns, Scott was the one Rachel would expect to put himself in danger, and he was the one most likely to start an investigative story without telling her about it. Yet it was Bruce, patient and careful Bruce, who apparently had been killed for a story.

Had Bruce's youthful zeal led him into a dangerous situation? Though a good reporter would surely follow up any lead that came his way, a seasoned professional wouldn't have kept the story under wraps and continued without telling someone what he was doing. Was that what he had done? Had he followed the path that led to his death for a good grade in a journalism class?

She switched off the recorder, thinking of other areas that should be explored. The next week's issue was set, so they were safe to devote their full energy to the story of Bruce's death, and she was determined that the *Banner* would do everything possible to bring the killer to justice.

Rachel began making her turn. The movements required to keep an airplane moving through the air were second nature to her after nine years as a pilot. She pressed the right rudder pedal slightly and moved into her turn smoothly. She watched the majestic white mass of Mount Rainier slide to her left as she flew parallel to the Cascades. She continued the turn until she was heading due west and then adjusted the controls to bring her back to level flight.

The plane shuddered slightly as she returned the yoke to neutral position, pressing it forward slightly to level out the nose. It behaved as though it was hitting a crosswind, and Rachel moved to counter the effects by adjusting the rudder a bit. Suddenly, the plane vibrated along the entire length of the fuselage and the nose began to swing hard to the right.

Rachel knew immediately that the rudder had become stuck, and she pressed down on the left rudder pedal hoping to free it. The pedal sank loosely to the floor, and the plane continued to turn.

She'd turned nearly one hundred and eighty degrees already, losing altitude fast. The rudder had to be jammed.

"Tacoma tower. Come in Tacoma tower." Rachel spoke calmly into the microphone as she sought a landmark to fix her position on. "Tacoma tower, this is Rachel Morgan in Piper Cherokee Delta Niner Zero Three Zero Charlie requesting clearance for an emergency landing. Over."

Mount Rainier was visible ahead and slightly to the right. She was traveling west northwest now and still turning right.

"Cherokee Delta Niner Zero Three Zero Charlie, this is Tacoma tower," a calmly professional voice came crackling over the radio. "What is the nature of your emergency? Over."

"My rudder is jammed to the right," she replied. "Rudder controls have gone slack and I'm fighting an extreme right yaw. Over." Perspiration beaded on her brow as Rachel held the yoke tightly to the left and the plane bucked through the air at an angle of about thirty degrees.

"Can you maintain level flight? Over."

"Negative, tower. I'm banked steep left and barely holding course. I may have trouble leveling out for landing. Over."

"What is your current position? Over."

"About twenty miles due south at eight thousand feet. Over." She'd lost a thousand feet, but was maintaining her new altitude. If she could get the plane to continue on a straight path to the airport, she felt certain she'd find a way to get it down. But landing was a future concern—flying in a straight line was the problem right now.

"Would you prefer clearance at McChord? Over." He was referring to the air force base south of Tacoma.

"Sure would, but only if I can't get back to you." The last thing she wanted was to deal with the air force security personnel who would swarm the plane if she put it down on a military strip. At the moment, however, she would take what she could get. "I think I can bring it back home. Over."

"Bring it on in, then. We have you on radar." He paused for a long moment, then came back. "McChord has advised that landing on their field should be undertaken only in the case of extreme emergency. Over."

"I'll make it." The plane had drifted farther south, but she twisted the yoke to the extreme left and began to make headway against the turn, bringing the nose back around to the left by rolling the plane into a forty-five degree bank. "Turning left now, tower."

"Do you require emergency equipment on the runway?"

"Negative. I think I can level it out long enough to hit the runway without tearing the wing off." The airfield was only a couple of minutes' flying time away, but her muscles already ached from holding the yoke in place. "Could use someone to tow me off the runway, though. I should be there in five minutes or less."

"Roger. You have clearance for runway seven, heading three sixty. Do you copy? Over."

"I copy, tower," she answered breathlessly.

"Roger, Cherokee. Good luck."

Rachel held the yoke to the left, and the sharp angle of the plane overcame the resistance of the rudder to pull her around to the north. Then she turned the yoke right until the plane stopped turning, continuing on a straight, though somewhat unsteady path toward the airport. The sideways angle of the wings gave Rachel the impression that she was sliding down a hill as she continued losing altitude flying past the Air Force base and over the southern fringe of Tacoma.

"Piper Cherokee, we have ETA of approximately two minutes. Over." The air controller sounded calm and detached, as if this were just a training exercise.

Rachel thought for a second about the what-if situations her flight instructor had put her through in college. He'd even covered this situation by jamming the rudder control to her right using his pedals and asking her to fly them out of the forced turn. What if your rudder was jammed; what if you lose the flaps in the left wing; what if you encounter wind sheer in mountainous terrain? What if? *This is what if,* she thought.

"I have you in sight," she said into the microphone.

The airport seemed terribly close, the runway far too narrow to contain the bucking beast she was about to drop onto it. She slowly decreased her air speed and brought the nose down, descending toward the long strip of mottled concrete. She held the wings angled dangerously as she approached, keeping the plane on a straight course toward the open runway.

"Five hundred feet," she said, reading the altimeter.

"You'll have to level out, Cherokee," the calm voice warned her.

"Roger."

Her hands were slick with sweat as she gripped the yoke securely, and her jaw ached from unconsciously gritting her teeth. Landing the plane would require every last bit of skill she had, if she wanted to walk away unscathed. If she leveled the plane out too soon, the rudder would begin pulling her around to the right and she could hit the runway diagonally. That would surely cause her to flip onto the left wing. But if she pulled out too late, she'd scrape the left wing tip on the runway, sending her into a cartwheeling crash. And she'd only been aloft a short time when the rudder jammed, so the plane's wing tanks were full of highly flammable aviation fuel. Fortunately the wind was calm that morning, so she didn't have to contend with it, too.

"Two hundred feet," she said, still holding the plane at its dangerous angle. She was descending rapidly toward the rows of approach lights standing up from the grass at the end of the concrete strip.

"Level out, Cherokee."

"Fifty feet."

The runway rushed up only feet below her left wing tip, and she twisted the yoke to the right and pushed the throttle in to cut power to the engine. The plane hit hard and bounced, then began slipping to the right as she lowered the flaps to slow her movement. It shook and bounced across the stained runway surface, the vibration increasing as it continued twisting to the right. But the plane finally came to rest diagonally on the runway, and Rachel allowed herself to take a deep breath.

"Good job, Cherokee," the controller said. "We have a tow truck on its way to get you."

"Thank you." Rachel turned off her radio and sat back in the seat. Then she allowed a smile to steal onto the perfect oval of her face. Now that was a fine piece of flying, even if she did admit it herself. But then, with the emergency over, a weak-limbed feeling overcame her as if all the fear she'd avoided in the air had come down on her in one blow. *My God! I could have been killed!*

"Is there a mechanic on duty?" she called to the man getting out of the truck that pulled up before the airplane. "Is Chuck here?" Getting out of the plane on her unsteady legs seemed an almost impossible task, but she made it to the ground.

"Not today, ma'am." The burly man in grease-stained coveralls pulled the heavy cable back from the towing arm of the truck, straining it back toward an eye-hook mounted on the underside of the fuselage beneath the engine. "That was one hell of a landing, lady," he said, snapping the hook in place and walking up to tighten the cable between the plane and the truck. "Thought for sure we were going to be picking you up in pieces when I saw you coming in cockeyed like that, but you pulled her out like a pro."

"Thank you." Rachel smiled broadly. "I don't know you, do I?" She joined him at the truck.

"I'm on weekdays, usually, but Chuck called in sick this morning. Harry Peterson," he said, extending a greasy hand across the taut tow cable. "I'm head mechanic with this chicken outfit, but I don't see much of you weekenders. Hop in the truck. Let's give them back their runway.''

They towed the plane back to the hangar, and Harry heaved a heavy tool chest the size of a small metal bureau beside it. Then he selected a wrench and began removing bolts holding the skin of the airplane in place over the rear of the fuselage. Rachel helped him gently lower the curved metal covering to the pavement.

"Probably a bolt gave way," he said, kneeling to look up at the cables and rods that connected the mechanical pieces to the cockpit controls. "Metal fatigue. Yup, here's your culprit."

Rachel sat on the pavement beside him, craning her neck to look up into the guts of the airplane. A cable hung loose on the left side of the plane, and the tie-rod it should have been connected to had jammed against an interior brace.

"One little bolt? Is that all that holds it?"

"No, there's a couple," he said. An expression of concern crept onto the older man's craggy features as he reached inside and removed two bolts from the free end of the rod. "Say, this is screwy."

"What?"

He slipped out from under the plane and stood examining the bolts in the sunlight. "This isn't right at all."

"What are you talking about?" Rachel stood at his side, eagerly squinting at the bolts glittering in the palm of his hand.

"It wasn't metal fatigue," he said. "Look at that." He held up one bolt, showing her the broken end which had been sheered mechanically.

"Somebody cut these bolts," he said seriously. "See that? He cut them almost all the way through, leaving enough to hold them together until you had a chance to get into the air. Looks like they left about two millimeters at most."

Rachel stared at the small bit of metal lost in his broad hands as a shiver of fear shot through her body. The bolt had, indeed, been cut and there was no longer any question about Bruce Quinlan's death being connected to the newspaper. He'd stumbled onto something, and now she was a target for his killers. Why?

"You'd better call the cops, lady," Harry said. "Somebody around here is trying to kill you."

RACHEL'S FEAR HAD HARDENED into anger by the time she'd finished talking on the phone to the police and the local office of the Federal Aviation Administration. Someone was going to pay for all he'd done, if Rachel had to bring him to justice herself.

"Call the cops?" Harry entered the hangar office.

"Yes, they're calling for a detective who's already working on some problems we've had," she explained. She'd called specifically for Jake Connors, giving the police switchboard operator only minimal information. The connection between Bruce's death and everything that had happened to her was crystal clear now, and she felt it was important to bring him up to date on everything.

"I've taken a look at the rest of the tail assembly, and I'd say that somebody out there wants you dead," he said, gruffly. "They sure weren't messing around with this business. They cut the bolts on the trim tab and elevator controls, too. If they all would have failed like they were supposed to, you'd have dropped out of the sky like a gutshot goose."

"Damn them!" Rachel exclaimed. "Do you think Chuck is connected to this?"

"Could be." Then he paused, a hard look on his face. "Dammit, he must be. We try to keep the same mechanic on the same planes so they'll know about previous service work. If anyone else was working on your plane, it would have looked suspicious. I don't know him that well, except to say that he's a good mechanic. But he's really the only one who would have had the opportunity. I'd sure as hell pass his name on to the police."

"I may go visit Chuck personally. I was just lucky the rest of the bolts didn't break," Rachel said. "And I don't want to rely on luck when I'm in the air."

"Do you think you know who's behind this?" Harry asked, sitting on the edge of the desk.

"Wait a second, that's my question."

They both turned toward the hangar, where Detective Connors stood just outside the open office door wearing jeans and a faded Princeton sweatshirt. Rachel smiled as he stepped into the cluttered room and extended a hand toward her.

"Good to see you again, Ms Morgan," he said. "You called for me?"

"That was fast," Rachel said, shaking his hand. His hand was firm and lightly callused, the hands of a man not unaccustomed to physical work but not one who earned his living by it.

"I was in the area when I got the call on my car radio." He released her hand and shook hands with the mechanic. "All they said was that you had plane trouble."

"That's an understatement," Harry said. "Especially with the guts of that plane chopped up like they were."

"So the problem wasn't an act of God?" Sharp concern darkened his gaze, but he kept his tone professional.

"Not unless God is using a hacksaw to get his point across these days," Rachel said.

"All right, then, why don't the two of you bring me up to speed on this business."

Detective Connors leaned against the door frame as they related the incident, taking notes in the dog-eared notebook he carried in the hip pocket of his jeans, but Rachel couldn't help but notice that his special attention seemed to be directed at her person rather than her story. If his appraising looks had been in any way furtive she might have been angered by his attentions. But he was so boldly open and obviously approving that she felt a certain pride and returned his gaze in kind. And she had to admit that he was a man worth looking at.

When the story was done, however, he returned his focus to the matter at hand and accompanied them out to look at the crippled airplane.

"What about the flaps and that stuff?" Detective Connors ran his hand along the left wing. "Any tampering?"

"Haven't looked at that, yet." Harry tapped a wrench against the wing lightly. "Doubt they'd go that far, though. They probably wanted it in the air when hell broke loose and messing with the wings would make it too likely that the plane never got off the ground. If it crashed on the runway, there would be too many big pieces left."

"Makes sense," Jake said.

"I'm going to look up your service records, Miss Morgan," Harry said, as he began to walk back to the hangar. "It wouldn't hurt to know if any special work was logged on it."

"So that brings us back to the original question." As the other man hurried away, the tall officer turned toward Rachel, his straight dark hair fluttering in the light breeze. "Do you have any idea who did this?"

"No, I don't know who or why, but I can make a few guesses about the what." Rachel crossed her arms tightly, staring into the man's eyes. "It's got to be connected to Bruce Quinlan."

"Quinlan?" His lips tightened as he pronounced the name, the warmth drained from his eyes. "I don't follow you," he said carefully.

"Bruce must have been on the docks following a lead on a story. Once we find out what story he was working on, we should be able to bring his killer to justice," Rachel stated confidently.

"I don't know. His wallet and watch were missing, so it looks like simple robbery." The smile that spread across Detective Connors' square-cut features as he looked at her was tight and he spoke in a suddenly abstract tone. "I'm afraid your reporter was just in the wrong place at the wrong time. I don't know what to make of the tampering with your airplane, but there's no provable connection at this point."

"Can't you see the connection?" His reaction to her theory caught her off guard. It had never occurred to her that the policeman might not agree with her findings, and even though her instinct was to trust his cool competence, she found his offhand dismissal unsettling.

"I'm just saying that we have no proof." Connors seemed to be picking his words very carefully, and Rachel again had the impression of things being left unsaid.

"I can't think of a single reason for Bruce Quinlan to be down at the docks unless he was following a story," she told him, fighting to control the frustration rising within her. "He lived on campus. His friends are on campus. Why would he be taking a stroll along the pier in the middle of the night? Does your robbery story provide any reason for that?"

"No, but surely there are several likely explanations. It may be that we'll never know why he was there. I'm sorry, but that's the way it works sometimes."

"I can't accept that. Say, what about his recorder?" she asked on sudden inspiration.

"Recorder? Nothing special, it was just lying on the dock beside him. It must have bounced out of his pocket when he fell."

"Yes, but what was on the tape? Didn't you listen to it?"

"There was no tape. We would definitely have checked it if there was."

"No tape? Then the killer took it!"

"That's kind of a stretch, isn't it? I use a tape recorder to make notes to myself, too, but I don't always have a tape in it," he said.

"Yes, but you carry a notebook, don't you," she pointed out. "Bruce didn't carry one unless he expected to copy printed material. He never used one for an interview, only his tape recorder. And he always kept a tape loaded and ready just like he always carried spare batteries in his pocket."

"He did have batteries in his right pocket," Connors mused, as his eyes lit with interest. "All right. You might have something there. So what was the story?"

"I don't know," she admitted.

"But if he was there on a story, why don't you know what it was?" He looked at her kindly, as though hoping to find a common thread to bind their reasoning together.

"Bruce was working for me as part of an apprenticeship program at college," Rachel explained. "If Bruce thought he had a lead on something big, something that would not only be good for his grade but for the paper as well, it's possible that he wouldn't tell anyone about it until he had it all wrapped up and ready to be set in type."

"The boy was a real go-getter, was he?"

"Yes, but not really the kind of person I'd expect to follow a story to the pier in the middle of the night," she admitted, crossing her arms over her mint green windbreaker. "He was generally more careful than that, but there's always a first time. And just because I was his editor doesn't mean I knew everything he was working on."

"Is that standard practice for your newspaper?" the detective asked, and his broad smile spread to his clear blue eyes.

"No. But a big story, carefully researched and written, could get him a higher grade, and I'm sure he would have wanted to spring it on his professor and me as a completed story."

"I don't know," he began.

"Well, the police can believe any theory they wish," Rachel cut in. "But the *Banner* is going to conduct its own investigation into his death."

"Now wait a minute!" A frown clouded the man's open features as he spoke. "This is a police matter, Ms Morgan, and you can't interfere."

"I'll be reporting a story, not interfering."

"But, you'd—" Then he smiled slightly, saying, "Okay, we'll look into it."

"It seems like the least you can do," Rachel pointed out.

"But you'll stay clear of it. Right?"

"Wrong. It's still a story, detective, and you can't stop us from reporting the news."

"I won't have some reporter messing up my investigation!"

"I'm not going to mess up anything! Do I look that incompetent?"

"Hold on!" The detective raised his hands as if in surrender. "There's no reason for the two of us to argue about this. I'm the cop and you're the reporter. That means that I've got the authority to conduct searches, collect evidence and make arrests. Not you. Your job is to report the news, not create it."

Rachel grew angry. "Wait a minute. We're talking about one of my employees who may have been killed on newspaper business. I will do whatever I can to find out who killed him. Surely the best thing for us to do is cooperate on it."

Jake paused a moment. He realized she had a point. If he was to get anywhere in this investigation, he'd need her. But he didn't want to concede as much openly yet. There was even more at stake than she realized, and he wouldn't have been able to live with himself if he did anything to encourage her to put her own life in jeopardy. But if he didn't give some encouragement, she might feel compelled to go off on her own without telling him. For her safety, they had to find some common ground.

"Yes, it would be better if we cooperate," he said softly. "So where would he have kept the notes for this big story?"

Rachel perked up. "I don't know. I don't believe they're at the paper. At least, I don't remember him working on anything other than the assignments I'd given him."

"Was it his practice to hide his notes?"

"Of course not. Both Scott and Bruce did a lot of their actual writing in the dorm. That's probably where the notes are."

"Okay, we'll get a warrant and search his dorm room." With a knowing nod, he walked toward the hangar, stopping with his hand on the knob of the office door. "I can't stop you from running your newspaper as you see fit," he said, his hand gripping the knob tightly. "But be careful."

He was watching her closely, his blue eyes passing quickly over the auburn tresses pulled back in a banana clip and lingering a moment on the straight line of her nose before reuniting with her thoughtful brown eyes.

She smiled. "Don't worry, Mr. Connors. I have your card."

"It's Jake."

"Jake, then."

He turned the knob and pushed the door open, walking in to join Harry, who was seated at the desk inside. "Say, did you find that anything was missing from your home?" he called over his shoulder as they entered.

"No, there isn't anything missing."

"Well, then, I guess my next step is to visit your mechanic, Mr. DeWitt, who is presumably at home on his sick bed. Where does he live?" he asked Harry Peterson.

"Give me your notebook." Harry fished a pen out of his shirt pocket. "I'll write it down for you."

"I'm coming with you," Rachel announced, her tone leaving no room for argument.

"Damn reporters," he said, with apparent sincerity. "Okay, since I'm not going to be able to talk you out of it, I might as well have you where I can keep an eye on you. Let's go." Then he took the notebook from Harry and said, "I assume the FAA inspector will be around soon. I'll leave it up to you whether you take that wing apart yourself or wait for them to get here."

"I'll leave it, if it's all the same to you," Harry said, grinning. "Those boys get awfully snooty if you mix into their business too far."

"Great. I'll send a man out to get a formal statement from you."

"Thanks for everything, Harry." Rachel shook the older man's hand firmly.

"You'll get my bill." Harry laughed, and turned back toward the plane as they walked away.

THEY ARRIVED at Charles DeWitt's address just in time to see the firemen rolling up their hoses and loading their equipment onto their trucks. The small ranch style house was still swarming with firemen and police officers, who performed their rituals before a small crowd of neighbors.

From the front, the house looked undamaged, but the northwest corner was blackened, the wall burned through and the roof stained black by the smoke that curled upward.

"A neighbor spotted the smoke," one of the firemen replied, when Jake asked what had happened. "The guy must have been smoking in bed."

"When did it start?" Rachel asked.

"About nine-thirty this morning. We're lucky it didn't spread through the house."

"What about the occupant?" Jake jammed his hands into his pockets and stared at the house.

"He didn't stand a chance," the fireman said, as he turned to walk back to the truck. "The room went up like a torch."

Rachel stood silently beside the detective as two men in white emerged from the house carrying a stretcher between them that held the victim wrapped in a soot-streaked sheet. She shuddered as they scrambled to the waiting ambulance.

"This is too much," Jake said softly.

"What's that?"

"In light of all that's happened, I can't believe that this fire was just an accident." Jake spoke seriously, watching her with deep concern. "The mechanic who normally works on your airplane couldn't have died in an accidental fire on the very morning that you almost got killed by sabotage. I don't buy it."

"So you think it was Chuck that wrecked my plane?"

"Yes, or he was paid to look the other way."

"And it must tie in with Bruce's death," Rachel insisted.

"Circumstantial evidence seems to support you. Whoever is behind all of this is playing for keeps," he said, a worried frown darkening his features. "And after this morning we know that they have no more regard for your life than they did for your reporter's. If I were you, I wouldn't stick my head too far out into the open. Nobody's luck lasts forever."

Chapter Four

"What was Bruce Quinlan supposed to be working on when he was killed?"

Detective Connors stretched back in his chair as they sat with their coffee in a downtown restaurant. He was watching Rachel closely, his fine blue eyes constantly probing hers as he weighed the truthfulness in her words.

"His assigned business story for the next issue was about small boat builders and how they're faring economically these days. He'd begun looking into the lumbering industry for the next issue, too, and those are the only assignments he got from me."

Rachel frankly enjoyed his concentrated attention, and allowed herself to study him in return.

"Doesn't sound especially dangerous," he commented, sipping his coffee.

"No. So the only thing I can think of is that he had fallen onto something on his own."

"Would he really go out on the docks at night after a story that hadn't been assigned and without telling you about it?"

"I wouldn't have expected him to, but that's the only answer I can think of. You see, Bruce was taking a double major in journalism and business administration, so his principal focus as a reporter was on finances. If he was doing anything special, I would have expected it to concern something along those lines. But a reporter is a reporter, and he was no less a reporter than Scott Kirby is.''

"He was after a good grade, and ended up getting in over his head.'' The police officer stated grimly.

"That's my guess. I'm planning to start my staff working to find an explanation on Monday.''

"That isn't wise,'' he said thoughtfully. "I realize that you feel you have a big stake in the matter, but it wouldn't do to start stirring up more trouble.''

"I think I've already run into *more* trouble, don't you?''

"Yeah, and you found that without even trying.'' He cocked his head slightly, looking at her with deep concern grazing his eyes above his open, friendly smile. "Look, whoever rigged your plane probably thinks that you knew about Quinlan's story. They want to stop anyone privy to his information from making it public. If you start nosing around and asking a lot of questions, you'll be making it obvious that the paper is continuing to pursue the story. You'll be forcing them to make another attempt on your life. Next time, they might succeed.''

"But there's no guarantee that they won't try anyway.''

"No, but I don't think they'll want to raise any more of a fuss than they have to. One murdered reporter is just another statistic. But two murdered reporters, both of them from the same paper, is a crime wave. Official attention would naturally turn to a news story as the reason for the murders.''

"But what about my plane?''

"They were hoping for a one-two punch. A reporter is murdered and his publisher dies in an aviation accident the next day. Until the FAA report came in on the crash, it would be looked upon as a coincidence.''

"Until the report comes in," she mused. "The FAA would take about a month to release their findings, I suppose. So whatever is going on must be a short-term concern, if they aren't worried about discovery a month down the road."

"What do you mean?" Jake asked quickly.

"If I had died in a plane crash, you probably would have written it off as coincidence and continued investigating Bruce's death as a robbery. Only after the FAA confirmed that the plane had been tampered with would the two events have been connected. Obviously, the people responsible planned to be well away from here before the connection was made."

Jake didn't say anything, but smiled sourly and stared into his coffee.

"What?" Rachel reached out to touch his hand lightly, tilting her head to catch his eyes. "Is there something you're not telling me?"

"What do you mean?"

"I have the distinct impression that you're holding back on this."

"I am?" His expression grew pained, as if silently asking her to let her questions go.

"Yes," she said, ignoring her inclination to drop the subject and accept him at his word. "Come on, you're a very transparent liar."

"Why do you say I'm lying?" His blue eyes clouded briefly with hurt but held no denial.

"Because I can tell you're not telling me something about this case. In fact, I think you knew yesterday that the incident at my house wasn't simply vandalism. It was a search, wasn't it?"

"Why do you say that?"

"Because they didn't break anything. They made a holy mess, to be sure, but they didn't cause the kind of damage they could have. I think they were searching for something—maybe Bruce's notebooks—and covering it up with the mess."

"No, they weren't as destructive as they could have been. But that doesn't mean it was a search," he said. Rachel thought she saw a flicker of enjoyment in his eyes as he spoke, though what he might find enjoyable was beyond her.

"Why don't you just tell me what's going on?" she insisted.

"You're giving me a lot of credit, aren't you? And, if I know so much about what's going on, why don't I just trot out and arrest someone? It would sure cut down on my paperwork if I just used all this secret information I have to end the case right now."

"You don't have to get smart about it."

"And you don't have to read more into my words, or lack of words, than exists. Please, Ms Morgan, newspapers have a hard enough time getting the simple facts straight without trying to become mind readers, as well."

"And if the police would just tell us what's going on, we wouldn't have to be mind readers."

"Free exchange of information is a wonderful idea, but it rarely benefits law enforcement. The papers get a new headline to feed to their readers, and the cops are left to pick up the pieces of their blown investigations." Jake's temper softened and he paused, frowning, as he sipped his coffee.

"Are you speaking in a general sense, or specifically about this investigation?"

"You're the mind reader," he said, shrugging. "I'm sure I'll find out your interpretation when I read the next issue of the *Banner*."

"We don't make up news at the *Banner*." Rachel fought the indignant anger that pounded at her chest. She didn't want to argue about publishing ethics and, after all, it was her questions that had set him off. With that in mind, she changed her approach slightly. "You know, I wouldn't report anything you didn't want to see in print."

"Maybe not, but by the same token I can't reveal information that I don't have." He smiled again, reaching toward her hand but arresting the movement awkwardly. "Let's get back on track, shall we?"

"I'd like that," she said softly. "After all, the point is to find out who killed Bruce Quinlan."

"Yes, and to find out why he was killed as well as keep you safe until we do." He looked at her seriously. "You know that a ransacked house and sabotaged airplane don't look promising."

Rachel paused. "I can't very well do my job if I hide under a rock."

"Rachel, look," he insisted, leaning toward her across the table with a pleading look in his eyes. "Your life is in danger, and you might only get in the way of the police." Then he stopped abruptly, seeing the set look in her face. He sighed. "Damn, I don't know why I waste my breath. I've already lost that argument, haven't I?"

"We have a common goal," she said, returning his smile warmly. "It just seems logical that we both pursue it. Besides, I probably wouldn't be able to stop Scott from getting involved, so it's better that I make it official so I can ride herd on him."

"Is that Scott Kirby, the kid who broke into the construction site a couple weeks back?"

"The very same. He's our investigative go-getter this semester."

"He ought to be jailed for his own good," Jake stated. "But I suppose that's how the big stories are broken."

"I wouldn't recommend it," Rachel said. "No, he's a good reporter, but far too impulsive. It might have been Scott's bad influence that pushed Bruce into mishandling things."

Jake sighed. "Okay. Do you think he might have come across something from the financial end that eventually led him out into the real world?"

"Sure. I don't suppose Bruce would have gotten very fired up about anything else. It would have to involve a large organization since something's been pulling the strings the past two days."

"That's what I was thinking. What was his lumbering story about?"

"Economics. How the business is these days, the employment situation, information along those lines. It was meant to be an overview."

"What about mob influence?" he asked, sitting forward. "Did he ever mention running across anything like that?"

"No, not Bruce." Rachel laughed. "He was more level-headed than that. Scott is the boy who finds gangsters under every rock. Is there a mob influence in Tacoma?" she asked seriously.

"I thought you were a reporter," he scoffed gently. "Of course there is. Nothing like the East Coast, of course."

"So, what's our next move?" Rachel sipped her coffee, watching him over the rim of the cup.

"Our move?" He frowned, his brow lowering over his thoughtful eyes, then he let a smile seep through his official demeanor. "Okay, if I keep you informed of my progress, will you at least stay in your office and do your reporting on the phone?"

"I can't guarantee that, and you know it."

"I thought so. All I can do, then, is get an officer assigned to keep an eye on you."

"You think I can't take care of myself?" Rachel spoke in a teasing tone, finding that she was enjoying this conversation with the handsome policeman no matter how grim the subject.

"No, what I think is that you may have trouble seeing them when they come after you the next time. After all, if your luck had gone the other way today, we'd be scraping you off the side of a mountain right now."

"Ouch! That's not a pretty way of putting it."

"Do you want to be dead?" He spoke grimly, all levity leaving his rugged features. "You've got to keep Bruce Quinlan and Chuck DeWitt in mind. Freedom of the press may keep me from restraining you, but it won't hold water with the people we're dealing with. If they don't want something reported, they'll stop the presses permanently."

"All right, you've made your point." She stared out at the busy street beyond the restaurant window for a long, silent moment, then composed her face in a smile and looked back at the man seated across from her. "But I don't want to be tripping over a policeman every time I turn around."

"You won't be. I'll have a man keep an eye on you from a distance, so he can watch your back. If he's any good, you'll never know he's there."

"I can't object to that."

"I'm glad we found something to agree on, Ms Morgan."

"I am, too, actually. And my name is Rachel."

"All right, Rachel," he said, smiling. "And don't forget to call me Jake."

"Okay then, Jake, what do we do next?" An errant flutter of excitement moved through her as they reached a new level in their formal relationship. "What about the rest of the *Banner* staff?"

"At this time, I think we can assume that the rest of the people at the *Banner* are in no danger."

"Why can we assume that?"

"Because of the speed with which they've acted. If they were going to try anything against them, they'd have done it by now. I'd guess that Quinlan only came across his big story recently and wouldn't have had time to spread it too far."

"That makes sense, though that doesn't exactly get me off the hook, does it?"

"No, I'm afraid you're still in the thick of it. They might logically assume that Quinlan told his buddy, Kirby, too."

"Scott is in California right now. He'll be back on Monday."

"Do you have a number where he can be reached?"

"No. He's backpacking somewhere, but I don't know where."

"He's probably safe enough, then. Can you think of anyone who Quinlan might have told about his story?"

"His roommate at school, I suppose, but I don't know who that is."

"I'll find out. He might know something."

"Have you turned up any witnesses to the murder yet? Was there a night watchman on the dock Thursday night?"

"Yes, there was, but he was investigating an unlocked door in a warehouse at the other end of the dock. We've checked the times he stopped at his punch stations and his story checks out."

"Whose warehouse was open?" Rachel asked, her interest piqued by finally getting some facts about Bruce Quinlan's death.

"It's rented by the Pandora Exporting Company." Jake smiled broadly. "Pandora is owned by Schofield Enterprises."

"Is there any link between Schofield Enterprises and organized crime?" she asked quickly.

"You don't miss a trick, do you?" Jake laughed. "No, we have not established any link between Schofield Enterprises and the mob."

"But that doesn't mean there isn't a connection."

"No, it doesn't," he admitted, still smiling. "But Schofield has been under investigation before and come out of it smelling like a rose."

"Why was it investigated?"

"There was nothing sinister about it, Rachel. The firm bought a computer company contracted to do classified work for the Defense Department. It was checked out as a matter of course along with everyone else in the new management. It passed with flying colors."

Rachel scowled, tapping one long fingernail against the edge of her cup. "Did the watchman find anything unusual in the warehouse?"

"No, just an open door. They'd just shipped out their inventory, so the warehouse itself was empty."

"What was the inventory?"

Construction equipment. They shipped everything overseas last Tuesday."

"That sounds innocent enough, but it's still awfully handy that the watchman was busy at the precise time of the murder."

"A handy coincidence, that's all." Jake finished his coffee. "Those things do happen, you know."

"Sure, but I think I'll make a few phone calls."

"Just as long as that's all you do. No unapproved field trips, okay? You check in with me."

Rachel bit down on her tongue and tried to smile. No way would she agree to checking with him before making every decision. "I'm not stupid, Jake," she said calmly. "I won't go looking for trouble."

"You won't? Don't hand me that lie, Rachel. All reporters look for trouble." Jake stood, smiling, and slid his chair in to the table in a gesture of helplessness. "In the meantime, I'm going to hunt down Quinlan's roommate. Where will you be for the evening?"

"Either at home or the paper. The university library is closed on Saturday nights, so I can't do anything there. But why do you want to know where I'll be?"

"I'm going to send someone to watch you. And I want to know where to get in touch with you quickly."

"Do I have a curfew?" she asked, rising.

"Yeah, be home by ten-thirty, young lady, or you'll be grounded for a week," he said, smiling as he extended a hand to escort her from the restaurant.

"That sounds awfully strict."

"Just trying to keep you healthy."

RACHEL HAD SOME OF HER OWN ideas about how to stay healthy and after Jake took her back to her car she set about to ensure her own safety.

Since they thought she already knew the nature of Bruce's story, she felt that her best defense would be a strong offense. With this in mind, she called in some favors from several reporters at the *Tacoma News Tribune* and obtained some information about the Pandora company and its connection to Schofield Enterprises. Then she called Calvin Watkins, the president of Pandora, at home.

"Yes?" A thin, reedy voice answered her call. He sounded impatient with the interruption.

"Calvin Watkins?" she said.

"Yes, this is he. What can I do for you?"

"This is Rachel Morgan of the *Tacoma Banner* and I'd like to get a statement from you about your warehouse, if I may."

"Our warehouse? Has something happened? A fire?" He spoke with clipped urgency, biting off the words in alarm with a hard, East Coast accent.

"No, I was referring to last Thursday night," Rachel continued. "A man by the name of Bruce Quinlan was murdered on the docks at approximately three in the morning. It seems rather strange that the watchman would be detained investigating an unlocked door at your warehouse at the very moment a murder was taking place. Would you care to make any comment?"

"An unlocked door at our warehouse?" He seemed confused for a moment, and Rachel's hopes that he might be connected to the murder sank. "My God, woman, you don't really think that has anything to do with the man's death, do you? I'm sure if you checked the records you'd find that many warehouses have had doors left open over the years and any inference drawn from such a coincidence would be highly suspect. Printing such inferences would surely be grounds for legal action," he snapped.

"I wasn't drawing any conclusions, sir. I just wanted to cover all the bases." Rachel spoke soothingly. Once Watkins knew what she was talking about, it didn't take him long to start threatening lawsuits. She didn't need the worry of dealing with an angry businessman on top of everything else. "I'm sorry if I misstated myself."

"Yes, well, I suppose it's understandable since the man was one of your own." Mr. Watkins was calmer now, his voice modulated to a dissatisfied nasal twang. "Have the police come up with anything about the incident?"

"No, sir, we're still in the dark."

"Whatever was he doing on the pier at that hour of the night?" Watkins asked. "He was a financial reporter, wasn't he? It hardly seems like his proper turf."

"He was working on a story, sir," Rachel replied quickly.

"Well, I won't take up any more of your time. Sorry to disturb you on a Saturday."

"Not at all, Miss Morgan. Good day."

He hung up with a firm click, leaving Rachel sitting with the receiver held loosely in her hand and wondering how he had known that Bruce was primarily a financial reporter. Coincidental knowledge? It hadn't been mentioned in the brief account the *Tribune* had run that morning. Her suspicions had almost been laid aside before he made that one offhand remark, and now she would have all she could do to check up on the man before she got any rest that night.

"YOU PEOPLE BETTER BE A BIT more open with us if you want cooperation." Jake stood in a brightly lit office in the federal building. He crossed his arms resolutely across his broad chest and coolly appraised the blond man seated at the desk. "I can't conduct a proper investigation under these restraints."

"We're not ready to open this business up yet, Connors." The man returned Jake's cold gaze in kind, lines of suspicion radiating from his hard eyes, his thin lips set into an officious scowl. "It's a national security matter, and that takes precedence over a local murder."

"Like hell, Fowler." Jake leaned forward to rest his hands on the desk and bore his eyes into the other man's. "If our cases overlap we should pool our resources, not hide things from each other. The FBI can't withhold evidence regarding a murder."

"We're not withholding anything." Fowler pushed himself up to his feet. "We surely don't know any more than you do."

"Then why all the secrecy? Why can't I tell Ms Morgan what little background I have on the case?"

"Mainly because you don't have any background. Besides, you should know what will happen once the press begins to even suspect the broader issue. Do you want to hand your case to them on a silver platter?" Fowler's eyes narrowed as he spoke, tightening to a flinty gleam of antagonism.

"You're an ass, Fowler." Jake's voice held menace and he scowled. "You're going to mess up both our cases, the way you're playing it."

"Nonetheless, this is the way I'm playing it."

"Dammit!" Jake stepped away from the desk, clenching his hands impotently. "Nobody believes that it was a robbery."

"They would if you had stonewalled the issue, instead of giving in!" Fowler snapped.

"No. Rachel Morgan isn't dumb enough to believe that lie, and I don't think that it's a good idea to continue with it."

"I didn't ask you to think, Connors, just follow through on my orders."

"You don't give me orders, Fowler!"

"You're the liaison, Connors. You're supposed to cooperate with us. You've got her asking questions, now that you gave up the robbery story."

"She was already asking questions. Bruce Quinlan was a cautious person, a bookworm. She knew damn well that he wouldn't have been on the pier in the first place without good reason. She was about to start her own investigation into the matter, and I wouldn't have been able to offer her any protection if I had stuck to that robbery line.''

"Well it's done now, isn't it?" Fowler sat in his chair, running his fingers back through his short blond hair. "You're sure she has no idea what story he was working on?"

"Yes, I'm sure. She's as much in the dark about that as I am about your investigation, and neither one of us likes it very much."

"What about Kirby?" Fowler ignored Jake's remark, picking up a pencil and drumming it on a stack of typed papers. "Was he in on Quinlan's story?"

"I don't know. He's backpacking in California someplace, so I don't think he was in on it. Why?"

"Nothing. It just seems that dockside meetings are more his speed."

"Is Scott Kirby our connection here?" Jake asked suddenly. "Not Quinlan, but Kirby?"

"I don't know."

"Bullshit!"

Fowler paused a moment, regarding the angry detective quietly, then he dropped the pencil and sighed. "I'll make some calls. Maybe I can get authorization to bring you up to speed."

"When?"

"I don't know. Don't be so damn impatient, Connors. You local cops always think you're the center of the universe, don't you?"

"Just make your calls and get back to me," Jake snapped. Then he turned and strode from the room, slamming the door behind him.

IT WAS SHORTLY AFTER EIGHT o'clock on a Saturday night, and all the major resource centers were closed. But there was one way Rachel could check up on Calvin Watkins and the Pandora company at any hour of the day. The computer they used to compile stories and set type at the *Banner* was connected by telephone modem to a variety of business and news data bases throughout the country. She could probably get everything she wanted by simply placing a few calls from the newspaper office. So, she grabbed her jacket and went out into the night, driving back to the center of the city in search of the answers to her questions.

She knew something was wrong as soon as she opened the door to the newspaper office. It was only a vague impression at first, but then she heard a noise within the building. If one of the staff had come back, they would surely have turned on some lights. So who was there?

Rachel crossed the reception area without turning on the light, poking her head cautiously into the hallway beyond and listening carefully. Yes, she heard voices and thrashing around in the offices. Rachel stepped back, fear knotting her stomach, freezing her limbs as she pressed her back against the wall beside the door. She couldn't be caught, and yet she couldn't let them go without trying to see who they were.

She crept closer, cursing herself for deciding not to run while trying to get into a position where she could look through the open door into the moonlit room.

"We're done here." A man's hoarse whisper. They came from her office, and the doorknob was turning.

Fear gave her feet wings and she jumped away from the man emerging from her office, running down the dark hallway past the layout room.

"Someone's here!" A man shouted behind her. "Let's move."

Footsteps thudded on the floor as she reached the door at the end of the hall and threw it open, then staggered into the echoing press room. They were behind her as she hurled herself past the offset presses and the rolled newsprint waiting for the next week's edition.

The press room was shrouded in twilight black, the few small windows not admitting enough moonlight to relieve the hazy gloom. Rachel took advantage of the murky darkness to crouch behind some stacked cartons while the intruders approached and shuffled past.

"Forget it. They're gone now." The man spoke sharply. "Let's leave before they call the police."

She could hear the outside door opening, and the darkness lifted slightly. Peeking out from her cardboard sanctuary, she watched three men slip through the door. The last man, with a stocky build and blotch below one eye, stood for a moment in the open doorway, moonlight illuminating his face. He scanned the large room slowly, but he didn't see Rachel in her hiding place. Finally, he closed the door.

Rachel collapsed against the rolled paper in relief.

Chapter Five

"I can't figure out what they'd want here." Frank Ackerman scowled at his computer terminal in the layout room. Rachel had called him right after she'd spoken to Jake, feeling that it was important for him to know what had happened. He arrived shortly after the first squad car. "Nothing's been tampered with."

"It's been more than this, I'm afraid," Rachel began, and regaled the older man with all that had happened to her and how she believed it related to Bruce's death. When she finished, he reached out to grasp her to him with one arm in a fatherly hug.

"This is a hell of a mess," he said. "Neck deep in trouble and not a clue why. You say he was reporting the lumber business? Maybe I'll get in touch with some of my friends in lumbering and see if they've heard any gossip."

"Any little bit of information might help, Frank. I just wish I had an idea what area to concentrate on. He could have been digging into almost anything."

"We'll find out what it was," he said, confidently. "But not by sneaking in to get a close look at people skulking around in the dark. Damn, girl, you could have gotten yourself busted up."

"Yeah," she admitted, an abashed smile on her face. "I was telling myself that even as I did it. But I couldn't just let them get away with it, could I?"

"Sure you could," the older man told her, with a smile. "At least, anyone but you could."

Rachel laughed, slipping her arm around the man's neck and hugging him affectionately. "Why don't you take off, now? I only called because I felt you should know right away."

"I'm glad you did. And call if anything turns up missing."

"Good night, Frank."

Rachel stood watching him walking away, then turned back toward the policemen who were busy dusting the knob of her office door for fingerprints as they continued working methodically toward the back of the building.

"It looks like they were trying to be discreet this time," Jake said, as he emerged from her office.

"Maybe they were in less of a hurry this time," she said. Rachel leaned one slim hip against Scott's desk and watched him approach. It was a great relief to have him there in charge of the investigation, and his proximity calmed her fears considerably. He was so calm and competent that she couldn't help feel safe with him.

"We can only hope they remain discreet, and don't turn violent again." He looked at her somberly, his square jaw set with obvious concern as he studied her face. "You say the guy had a mark below one eye?"

"Yes, probably a birthmark—though I couldn't be certain from that distance."

"Dark hair, medium build and a birthmark. You didn't see any of the others.

"No."

"You do your typesetting on computer. What about data storage? Is there any way to tell if they've been in your files?"

"I doubt they have. We use a data storage service provided by the store where we bought the equipment. It's all just back issues, anyway. We keep them on file with the service and on floppy disks in the office safe. The safe wasn't tampered with, at all."

He pinned her with his questioning gaze. "Is there anything about this that you haven't told me?"

"No, why should there be?" Something in his tone put her on guard, a note of deep-seated suspicion that hadn't been there before.

"There shouldn't be," he said. He pushed a stack of paper on Scott Kirby's desk back a bit and sat on the edge. "But if you've got any other special stories cooking that might have a bearing on the case, I should be told about them."

"What kind of paper do you think we run?" she asked, with a small laugh. "I mean, we do the best we can, but don't have the resources to go off on investigative binges. Half our space is still taken up by classified ads, and half our reporters are university students!"

"I'm sorry, Rachel, but I'm a cop," he protested. "You'll have to expect me to ask some cop questions every now and again."

"And I guess I read more into it than you intended. I'm a bit on edge from all of this."

"You'd hardly know it to look at you," he said, admiration coloring his voice. "You're a tough woman to crack."

Anything else he may have wanted to say was cut off when Scott Kirby came barreling through the door.

"Rachel!" he shouted, making his way to them. "I heard about B.Q. on the radio and hopped the first flight up here. What the hell is going on?"

"We don't know yet, Scott. You didn't have to come back, you know," she told him. But she knew better than that. Nothing on earth could have kept him away from a friend in trouble or a story waiting to be written.

"Of course, I had to come back. I'm a reporter," he said, laughing. Then he pointed at Jake, and asked, "You one of the cops?"

"Guilty as charged. You must be Kirby." Jake stood, looking down on Scott with a smile. "Do you know if Quinlan was working on anything out of the ordinary last week?"

"What? You think he was working a story when he got killed?"

"It's possible," Jake said. "Did he mention anything to you?"

"Sorry, not a word. Of course, I don't suppose he would have told me. I think Bruce was jealous after that construction story I did. Besides, he had a fierce sense of competition when it came to grade point averages, and Kaminski grades on a tight curve. Most of his stuff involved such dry topics that he didn't have a chance to do anything sensational."

"It looks like he found something sensational, all right," Rachel said. "It's just too bad he didn't have a chance to report it."

"Then I guess it's up to us," Scott said.

"Hold on, son," Jake glowered at the young reporter. "You're not going to get messed up in this."

Scott gave the policeman a sour look. "I'm sorry, but I can't sit back—"

"Mind your manners, Scott," Rachel cautioned. "You're talking to a policeman, you know."

"Yeah, I guess I am. You got a name?" he asked Jake sharply. "I'll need your name for my story."

"Scott, a good reporter can get the information without being rude," Rachel said.

"Connors," Jake replied, turning to look at Rachel with a wry smile. "Det. Sgt. Jake Connors. Need help spelling any of it? If you call me Jack, I'll have your car towed."

"I got it. Do you prefer Jake or Jacob?"

"They're both my name," the policeman said, still looking softly at Rachel.

"Okay, Scott, give it a rest for now," Rachel said. She felt drawn by the feeling of Jake's eyes on her, her own gaze moving to rest on his strong face. The story you think you're going to write can wait till morning."

"I thought I might run out to the docks tonight," Scott said. "Maybe get some pictures."

"No, you are not going to the docks," Rachel exclaimed, fixing him with a stern gaze. "Especially not at night."

"But night would be the best time," he countered. "I'd be more likely to run across someone who was there on Thursday night."

"Or they might run across you," Jake pointed out. "Rachel is right—stay away from the docks, for now. Besides, I've got a more important assignment you could take care of for me."

"Do I get to be a junior deputy?" Scott crossed his arms skeptically.

"No, just a reporter. Do you know Quinlan's roommate?"

"Yeah, he's a twerp."

"Well, we haven't been able to track him down," Jake said. "Why don't you find him and find out if Quinlan ever talked about doing a special investigation of some kind. He might have talked to him about it."

"Sure, he might have told his roomie. I'll get on it." He turned toward the door and started out without another word.

"Try to be discreet, Scott!" Rachel called out as he disappeared through the door.

"No problem!" His reply echoed down the hall and was punctuated by the slam of the front door.

"Bright kid," Detective Connors remarked. "You might want to hang on to that one."

"No way." Rachel shook her head thoughtfully. "He'll get snatched up by some big daily as soon as he shows his scrap book at the city desk. Scott is destined for the big time."

"And your paper isn't big-time?" Jake stepped closer to her, enveloping her in his aura of protective warmth.

"It's a money-maker, but it isn't big-time," she admitted thoughtfully. "But it's my money-maker and I'll be damned if I'm going to let some creeps mess with it, without a fight. So, what happens now?" Rachel looked up into the gentle depths of his eyes.

"We'll check out the prints they got here tonight, and see if they match anyone on file. Your intruders probably wore gloves, but sometimes we get lucky. I think we'll increase patrols in this neighborhood, as well as by your home. Our most important task is, of course, to find out what Bruce was onto that got everybody so riled."

"I have a feeling that we don't have much time," she said softly. She'd become entranced by the rugged lines of his face and the way the muscles flowed beneath the skin in concert with his changing thoughts and emotions. It was the face of an athlete, a man more at home in the woods or on a sailboat on the bay than behind a desk at the police station.

"No, we don't." He shifted his gaze to include the room around them, then brought it back to her face. "I think you should have better protection than I mentioned before. I want someone by your side, at all times." He spoke softly, and his eyes were gentle and contemplative.

"Don't worry, Jake. I can take care of myself."

"I'm sure you can." His tone had lost all of its official edge, and he spoke as a man concerned about a woman. "But I'm not willing to take any chances."

"No, Jake, I appreciate the offer, but I can't have some cop living with me. I just won't have it." A small electric tingle fluttered in her stomach, and she fought the impulse to reach out and touch him.

"Please, Rachel, I can't afford to lose you," he said, leaning closer.

"It wouldn't be any picnic for me, either," she said. "But I don't want some stranger hanging around all the time. Let your people circle the house if you want, but I'm not willing to sacrifice my privacy entirely, because of this. That would be giving in to the pressure."

"This is no time to be stubborn," he insisted, leaning back.

"I don't care. My life has been disrupted enough, and I'm drawing the line."

Heavy footsteps sounded in the hall and they both stepped back almost guiltily as a policeman trooped through the door.

"That's it, Sergeant," he said, not noticing their reaction. "Anything else?"

"No, pack it in for now." Jake's voice crackled with authority as he walked around her toward the other man. "I'll be out in a minute."

"Yes, sir. Good night, ma'am," he said, walking away.

"I'd better be going, too," Rachel said.

"Would you like me to follow you home?" Jake asked as they left the layout room and walked down the hall.

"You needn't bother." Suddenly Rachel felt infinitely tired, as though she hadn't slept in weeks, and all she wanted to do was get home and fall into bed. "I think they're done with me for one day."

"Probably," he admitted. "Drive carefully, okay?"

"I will." They stepped out into the cool night air, and Rachel locked the door to the building. "Will you be around tomorrow?"

"Of course." He touched her arm lightly.

"Good, I'll call if I think of anything new," she said, trying to cover her disappointment when he removed his hand. "Good night."

"Good night, Rachel. Lock up tight tonight." Then he turned and walked resolutely toward the patrol car waiting on the street.

Rachel drove home, torn by conflicting thoughts and emotions. She could feel herself slipping into the warm embrace of desire as she remembered the sound of the detective's voice, and she didn't know if she liked the idea. Jake Connors presented a tantalizing challenge, in ways she couldn't count. She worried that he might step up his demands that she play it safe and not pursue the story. His warmth and her professionalism warred with one another. She had to know the truth. And, more importantly, the thought of a dead college student—someone within her care—lay like ice in her mind.

Chapter Six

Sunday morning was cold and wet. Sheets of rain swept across the city, descending from the black clouds that rolled in low over the roiled waters of Puget Sound. Rachel was awakened early by Jake calling to say that he had work to take care of out of town and would be gone most of the day. He assured her that he would stop by in the evening to make sure she was all right.

Assuring him she'd be around, she finished her cup of coffee and drove to the newspaper offices. She'd only just gotten started with her task at the computer terminal when Scott Kirby entered.

"What's our assignment, boss?" he asked, pulling a chair up to sit across the desk from her.

"This week's issue is set except for a small piece I'm going to insert about Bruce," she told him. "But we haven't done a thing for next week. Did you have a chance to look for Bruce's roommate?"

"Yes, but he was a big zero. He did say that Bruce was awfully pleased with himself for the last week, but he wouldn't breathe a word about what was going on. He also gave me several files from Bruce's effects. His parents wanted you to have them."

"So I've gone through them and there's nothing really legible—just notes. But I'll comb through them more thoroughly later... after I follow some other leads."

"You better remember this, buster," Rachel said, standing. "You don't go off on any of your little trips without clearing them with me from now on, right? I should have booted your butt out of here after that construction story."

"But you didn't because it was such a dynamite story that you couldn't bring yourself to get tough." Scott grinned.

"That's about it," she admitted. "But I'm not going to be so nice the next time you pull something stupid. You've got the naval maneuvers to write about for this week and next, so you should be able to keep out of trouble on that story, anyway."

"Actually..." Scott began, then he stopped, looking away with a grin.

"Actually, what?"

"Nothing much. I just got some first hand photographs out at the base, is all. Great shots, and they'll help fill the story out."

"And how did you get them?"

"I took a tour out at the naval yard last week. No big deal, but they had that Trident in dry dock scrubbing her up for the big show. See? No big deal."

"Did you bother to get permission for your photographs?"

"Permission? Come on, Rachel. They'd hand me a couple eight-by-ten glossies of the submarine rolling through the bounding main and show me to the gate. My pictures will give our readers a sense of scale for the damn thing."

"You sneaked your camera in, didn't you?"

"Of course I did. They don't like people taking pictures in there, you know. I hid it inside a heavy coat and went through with the sixth grade class from Truman elementary school. Their teacher's aide is a friend of mine, so she let me tag along.''

"That was illegal, stupid and pointless,'' Rachel said, stuffing her hands into the pockets of her jeans. "You don't even know if the maneuvers have anything to do with submarines.''

"No, I sure don't. Nobody does.'' Scott raised one eyebrow pointedly. "They've kept the whole thing under such tight security that the best anyone can do is guess what the big deal is. Did you know they've got another fleet of ships sitting off the East Coast and nobody knows what they're doing, either? It's damn unusual for them to run such large military games without blowing their own horn about it for weeks in advance, so I figured that anything I could get would help us out.''

"No, you just wanted to see if you could do it. We don't need pictures, just a simple story.''

"And simple is what you'll have, too. They're going to run their little test next Thursday and then hold a press conference to say that everything went smoothly, and the dailies will scoop us with even that much,'' he protested. "But, they won't have pictures of sailors scrubbing down a Trident submarine. It really gives you a sense of how huge the thing is. Whether they have anything to do with the maneuvers or not, the pictures will help fill pages if we don't come up with anything about Bruce.''

"But the pictures are illegal and we don't dare run them,'' Rachel pointed out. "That was a federal offense, Scott. Not a misdemeanor, but an honest-to-God felony. You could get life for espionage. And if I use the pictures, Lord knows what they could do to us.''

"But, Rachel—''

"Never again, Scott,'' she said, vehemently. "I'm not going to have you get yourself killed, too.''

SHE WASN'T ABLE TO FIND much information about the Pandora company that afternoon. It was a new company, apparently started sometime within the last year and purchased by Schofield Enterprises shortly after beginning operation, but that's where the information stopped. She was getting nowhere fast and felt vaguely threatened alone in the silent newspaper office. Finally, that prickling feeling drove her out entirely, and she went home tired and disappointed at making no headway.

"THE KID MUST NOT HAVE TOLD anyone about his story, otherwise they wouldn't be floundering like they are. And you can bet the broad at the newspaper would have told Connors about it."

The small man in the back of the limousine listened to his companion with silent attention, as the car cruised along the sound. He nodded without speaking and looked out over the water ruffled by the wind, then he turned to look at his companion in stony appraisal.

"We've managed to alert her now, haven't we?" he said. "And the policeman will return with more concrete knowledge than he had before. I think that if we eliminate her, that will stall them enough for us to be done and gone."

"But Connors has a guard tailing her now."

"No matter. Now that we've started it, we must see it through."

"But there's less than a week now," the other man stated, a thin whine of apprehension weakening his gruff voice. "What harm can she do this late in the game?"

"Too many games are lost in a ninth inning rally, my friend." The small man returned his gaze to the waters of Puget Sound. "Deal with the woman. I want her out of the way."

And the car continued on toward Tacoma, entering the city just as Rachel was driving home.

THE STORM CLOUDS had cleared away by eight-thirty. Rachel had finished washing the dishes from her light supper, and had put on a raincoat over her heavy sweater to leave the house. She loved going for long walks, especially after a rain. The clean, scrubbed smell of rain mixed with the tang of the sea to help clear her mind, putting her at ease.

She walked down the quiet streets toward the bay, thinking. All the anxiety would be over soon, and her life would settle down again. She was sure of that. But, what would her life be like after this period of uncertainty was over? Did she want Jake Connors to be part of it? It was foolish to think about such things just because he seemed to show an interest in her. Yet she felt that he was the type of strong, dependable man she wanted to know.

She walked onto the long dock jutting out into Commencement Bay, nearly half of its sailboats already back in their slips for the summer, and stood looking at the gently rippling waters. *This water has touched the shores of Japan*, she thought, *and Australia*. The feeling of immensity, of being part of a larger world, soothed her as she stood watching the placid movement of the waves. She loved nights like this with a thousand stars twinkling overhead like the benevolent eyes of watchful angels and the ocean lapping the pilings of the dock below her feet.

Standing on the dock, Rachel took the time to examine her life from a different point of view.

She had never thought too much about her future. Was she content to devote her life to a newspaper, substituting the satisfaction of a headline and a few paragraphs of crisp prose for a husband and family? No, she wasn't. It wasn't that she thought of those things as being mutually exclusive. They certainly weren't. But she knew herself well enough to know that without some kind of prodding she might remain focused on her work and never make the effort to find the life she wanted. She was a lot like her father in that way.

Her father had almost let his dream slip away. Locked into his own workaholic pattern, he'd been content merely talking about returning to the beautiful Puget Sound area. He kept his dream of owning a small paper locked away, only taking it out occasionally when he and her mother talked about the carefree future days "when their ship came in." He treated it almost like a joke. And after her mother died and he'd moved west to achieve his dream, his one regret was that he hadn't done it sooner. He regretted having to live his dream without his wife at his side.

"You have to make your own mark the best way you can," he'd told her once. "Even if it falls flat, if you've done your best and worked your hardest you haven't failed." It was something he'd told her since she was a child, and she'd grown up believing it with all her heart. It was the advice that shaped her life. But in the uncertain days immediately after his heart attack he'd amended his advice somewhat. "Don't put it off," he said. "If you have something to do, go out and do it. Don't dream about it for twenty-five years. Don't put it off or you may lose the chance to get it done."

Yes, that was the simple truth. She didn't regret the time or energy devoted to her work, and she knew she'd be devoting a lot more in the future, but she wouldn't allow herself to use it as an excuse to put aside the other part of her life.

The air grew cooler as she stood in the darkness, too cool even for her coat and sweater. It was time to go home, time to rest for another day. She turned and walked inland along the edge of the street, savoring the clarity the vast ocean had imposed on her mind. Streetlights cast a cold glow on the wet pavement, creating a darkly sparkling world out of her neighborhood, an unreal, beautifully ominous world.

She slowly became aware of a sound behind her as she walked, a motorized hum accompanied by the soft crunching of gravel. It was a car, driving slowly and seeming to draw nearer from about forty feet back. A chill skittered up her spine as she realized that it was indeed a car, and it was following her with its lights out. She didn't dare turn to look, almost afraid it would pounce if she did. She knew what she'd see—the man in the yellow Volvo had grown tired of watching from a distance.

The heavy sound of the vehicle seemed to echo along the street like the evil purring of a large hunting cat. Fear moved her body as a drunken puppeteer would move his wooden-limbed doll, propelling her awkwardly forward in a stiff, mechanical gait. She felt herself shivering, every muscle tensed against the imagined impact of a ton of steel.

She was approaching her corner, just half a block from the safety of her home, but she didn't think she could make it. The Patersons' lawn, on the corner of the block, was treeless and wide open. It offered no protection from a speeding car, so there was nowhere she could run that they couldn't be upon her in seconds. Her mind raced, as she searched for a means of escape and found nothing to hide behind. There wasn't even a car parked by the curb.

Rachel kept walking toward home. A light-colored car approached slowly from the direction of her house as she neared the corner, still walking along the side of the street. As it came closer, she recognized it. It was the yellow Volvo! It was ahead of her, picking up speed as it neared the corner. Who was behind her?

Could this be the policeman that Jake said would be watching her? Had she been unnecessarily afraid of danger from behind while the true danger was approaching in front of her?

Rachel turned quickly, trying to keep both cars in view at the same time. Behind her was a large, black automobile, the streetlights intensifying the evil appearance of its obsidian bulk. Marked or unmarked, it was no police vehicle. Its headlights flared on abruptly and she froze, blinded by the glare and unable to move as the engine roared and the hot eyes of the vehicle swept toward her.

"Oh, God, no!" She threw her hands up, stumbling back farther into the street, and slipped to one knee on the slick pavement. Then the yellow car squealed as it accelerated, jumping the curb onto Patersons' yard and roaring toward her. She could only scramble backward as one car bore down in front of her, and the other rocketed in from her left.

With a hideous squeal, the yellow car skidded to a halt before her and the black limousine roared around it to her right. Rachel pushed herself up and sprinted away from the stopped vehicle, running blindly back toward the bay.

"Rachel!" A man shouted behind her, and she fought to run faster. "Rachel! Wait!" The voice closed in and she could hear steps running behind her, gaining quickly. She ran onto the grass of someone's yard, hoping to make it to the front door, hoping for enough time to ring the bell. But a strong hand grasped her shoulder, spinning her, and she fell to her back on the wet grass with her pursuer on top of her.

"No!" The word rasped out of her constricted throat as she raised her hand to strike the man holding her down. "Leave me alone," she cried."

"It's me, Rachel. Me."

She slowed her hand, staring at the shadowed face above her as she recognized her assailant's voice. It was Jake Connors.

"Jake!" She threw her arms around him in joyous relief. "My God, I thought they were going to kill me!"

He said nothing, hugging her tightly in return. But then he released his hold and stood suddenly, "That's a pretty likely scenario," in a subdued tone, as he helped her to her feet. Still, his eyes were taut with concern and didn't leave her face as she brushed herself off. "Are you all right?"

"Fine, I guess. But where did you come from?" she asked, shaking in the aftermath of her terror.

"I was on my way to your house when I saw you at the corner," he replied. "I'm afraid I've blown my chance to crack the case, however. I didn't get the license number."

"Where was that protection you said you'd give me?" she asked.

"Dispatch called them away to investigate a reported burglary in the neighborhood. I heard it on my radio on the way over."

"What about that yellow—" she began to ask, then stopped when she saw the Volvo sitting diagonally in the street where it had stopped before her. "Wait! The yellow car is yours?"

"Of course, it's mine," he said without pause.

"Damn you!" She stepped back and stared at him in anger. "You were following me on Friday? You were the one? How dare you? You—" Anger seemed to tear the power of speech from her as she stormed away.

"Please, Rachel," he said, following behind her. "I was worried about you."

"Why? According to you, there was no reason to be worried back then! If you were so concerned about me, you could have let me in on the secret!" She kept walking, passing the idling car. "Why don't you go write a ticket or something!"

"Wait, Rachel! I thought you knew it was me when you led me around the block like you did. I didn't realize you didn't know."

But she walked away without turning back. Behind her, she could hear the car shifting into gear and turning on the roadway. He passed her and was waiting in her driveway when she reached the house.

"I came to talk to you," he said, smiling, as she walked past to her door.

"Tell me one thing." She turned on the step and confronted the man standing below her. "Do you believe I'm totally helpless?"

"No. I never said you were."

"Then why treat me like a child? Why follow me around playing bodyguard without telling me it was you back there? You had me scared half to death."

"Won't you let me come in and explain myself?"

His rugged features had assumed a look of dismay, and he stood plaintively with his hands at his side as if waiting for a judge to pass sentence on his life. Rachel's heart leaped within her chest as she looked at him. How could she refuse him the chance to explain?

"All right, come in," she said, turning to open the door. "There's no sense in my acting ridiculous about it."

"Thanks, Rachel." He walked past her into the living room and stood with his hands hidden in the pockets of his leather flight jacket while he watched her with calm, innocent eyes. "I did have some rather serious news to give you tonight."

"What? Have you learned anything new?" Though Rachel stood with her arms folded resolutely across her chest, she was already over her surprised anger with the detective. It was quite apparent that he had been honestly concerned with her well-being on Friday.

"Not about Quinlan's murder, no. But I did have an interesting meeting with the FBI today." Jake took his hands out of his pockets and unzipped the fleece-lined jacket. "Did you assign Scott Kirby to report on the upcoming naval maneuvers?"

"Yes, I did. He's got a short background piece this week and a follow-up next week," she said, and, suddenly the reason for his meeting with the FBI seemed quite clear. "Do you mean that—"

"Exactly," Jake said, quickly. "Mr. Kirby seems destined for trouble, I'm afraid. Your little yellow journalist was seen taking photographs at the naval yard last weekend. That got all of you listed as possible security problems for the upcoming maneuvers and put Kirby on an FBI watch list."

"My God! He only just told me about it this afternoon," Rachel said, unbuttoning her coat and throwing it off. "I told him we couldn't use the pictures."

"You're right about that. Since they were illegally obtained, you could have a few problems if you used them. But, of course, that all depends on what's in the pictures. For our purposes, all that matters is that Kirby and, to a lesser degree, the rest of the staff at the *Banner* have been under loose surveillance by the bureau since they identified Scott as the man taking pictures."

"Does this have anything to do with Bruce?"

"I don't really know." He looked away for a moment then, seeming somewhat embarrassed. "All I know is this. When we finally identified Bruce Quinlan's body on Friday, and before you'd come to make a positive ID, the department got a call from the FBI to keep our public statements about the case to a minimum. They wanted us to play it like a simple robbery while conducting our investigation into the crime."

"The FBI instructed you to lie to me?"

"No, they—well, I guess that's one way to put it," he said, uneasily. "But it's not entirely fair, either."

"Nor was it fair to withhold the truth from me!"

"Please, Rachel, we customarily withhold certain facts about ongoing investigations if those facts might be useful in unearthing the culprit later. This wasn't really any different than that."

"But to have insisted so strongly that it was just a robbery is beyond what was asked of you!"

"Oh, please," he scoffed. "I've worked on too many cases where promising leads have gone up in smoke because the press let information out prematurely to feel terribly sorry about withholding something from your paper on this one. The FBI doesn't want anything to come out that might sour their own investigation. That's all."

"And, when the FBI says jump, all you ask is how high!"

"Maybe it looks that way sometimes." His gaze simmered at the point of anger but he fought the emotion back, quenching it with a sour smile. "But I was concerned, so I followed you home on Friday. I didn't know what it was about, but if the FBI thought it was serious enough to interfere in our work I figured that it warranted my keeping an eye on you. I thought about stopping after I blew my cover and thought you knew it was me behind you, but I couldn't have maintained the robbery story if I admitted giving credence to your theory. The fact is that neither our department nor the FBI wants anyone to stir things up right now."

"Oh, Jake, I shouldn't have gotten so steamed about it. I guess I've been a reporter too long not to get excited when I smell a cover-up of any kind." Rachel sat tiredly on the long couch before the fireplace.

"It goes with the territory, I'm afraid," he said softly. "I'm not exactly disposed to trust reporters, myself, but that doesn't mean I find it easy to lie to them."

"Please, Jake, take off your coat and sit down. This isn't an inquest."

"Thank you." He walked out and hung his jacket on the coat tree in the entry hall, then returned to sit on the other end of the couch. "As long as I'm coming clean, I should probably give you as much as I know. The FBI has reason to believe that one of the service personnel involved in the upcoming maneuvers is working both sides of the fence, but they don't know who it is or what he's planning.

"When Scott started taking pictures, it looked like a solid lead, but that didn't go any farther than the paper so it pretty much died there. Then last week Bruce Quinlan made a couple of phone calls to the naval station wanting information about the mission and the pilots who'd be flying during the maneuvers. They flagged his name and ran a check and came right back to the *Tacoma Banner*. Now Quinlan has been murdered, several attempts have been made on your life, and your home and office have been searched. Suddenly the paper is at the center of everything."

"You found out about this just today?" Rachel felt a strange chill creeping over her as they spoke. It was as if talking about the case made the danger all the more real.

"Yes, that's what the meeting was about." He spoke in a soft, serious tone, keeping his eyes on her face with careful attention the whole time.

"What was Bruce asking that was so terribly sensitive?"

"Just what I told you. But his questions ran directly to the heart of the security breach that the bureau is looking into." Jake leaned back on the couch, tiredly. "They haven't told us what kind of information they have, just that they think something is up. The exact nature of the maneuvers themselves is classified, so they're awfully tight about releasing anything."

"They think that Bruce was working on a story about some kind of espionage?" She watched him closely, appraising the comfortable way he sat with his long legs stretched out and crossed at the ankles and one hand resting on the arm of the couch. He was so much more relaxed, now that the truth was out.

"Yes, that's about the size of it. And that's why we were supposed to be quiet about it. They didn't want to scare anyone off before he can be caught."

"And what was the department supposed to do about Bruce's death?"

"Conduct a normal investigation. Following you home was part of that. And being at the airport yesterday was, too. I'd called for you at the paper and when Frank said you were flying I went out to check on you."

"So, that's how you got there so fast. Did you know it was me making that goofy landing?" she asked.

"Not till you were down and I could see your identification numbers."

"Why didn't you come over to the hangar right away?"

"I don't know much about airplanes," he laughed. "I thought maybe you always landed that way. Besides, I had a cover story to protect."

"And then you came when I called."

"I try to make it a point of always coming when I'm called."

"But why are you telling me the entire story now?" As much as she appreciated being told the truth, she didn't want Jake to be at odds with his orders.

"That's what the meeting was about today. The FBI man wanted to keep you out of it entirely, but naval intelligence and our department believe it's too late for that. We out-numbered the bureau and decided to tell all.'' He cast a warmly appraising glance toward her, one eyebrow raised. ''It's obvious that you aren't going to let go of this thing until you've either gotten to the bottom of the mystery or been murdered. It seems more reasonable to give you what little we have so you can make educated decisions rather than jump blindly into trouble. Quinlan was moving on blind instinct when he stumbled onto the same trail the FBI is following. He caught hold of something big and fol-lowed it, getting too close because he didn't have enough facts to be careful.''

''That's possible.'' The new information opened a whole range of possibilities in Rachel's mind. If Bruce Quinlan had uncovered an espionage ring, that would have been a story far too good to pass up. And announcing his discovery to Rachel would have been an open invitation to Scott to steal the story out from under him. But where could he have found a spy ring?

''Do you think he was killed by a foreign agent?''

''No, the bureau is pretty certain that we're dealing with domestic espionage. The Russians wouldn't run the risk of their people getting captured.'' Jake nodded thoughtfully. ''But I don't have enough basic information to form an ed-ucated opinion. The FBI only tells us enough to hold up our end of the bargain and not a bit more. And neither the bu-reau nor naval intelligence is willing to release any of the information that explains why they believe spies are in-volved in this operation.''

''Wait. Did you say that the FBI was watching Scott?''

''Loose surveillance,'' he explained. ''Nothing active, just keeping an eye out to see if he came near the naval yard again.''

"What about Bruce?" Rachel leaned toward him, sliding her arm along the back of the couch as she waited for his answer.

"I don't know." He pursed his lips and sat staring at the cold grate in the fireplace. "Special Agent Fowler is in charge of their investigation in Tacoma and he said that Quinlan wasn't being followed, but I don't know if I buy that. It seems as though there's something about his death that Fowler isn't telling us."

"But they can't withhold information about a murder, can they?"

"They can do anything they want to do if it affects national security, and it wouldn't be the first time they've been less than honest with local law enforcement. Agent Fowler is the guy who wanted to continue shutting you out of this story."

"Then maybe they know who killed him!" Rachel exclaimed, leaning excitedly toward him. "You've got to get them to release their information!"

"It's a delicate situation for us," Jake said seriously. "It isn't so simple as coming out and asking them to tell us what we assume they know. If there's anything to be told, they'll open up after the maneuvers. After all, that's the whole point of the secrecy."

"Fine, and the killer will be miles away, probably safely overseas by then," Rachel scoffed. "Can't you do anything faster than that?"

"No, I'm afraid not. My hands are tied pretty tightly on this one."

"Well, mine aren't."

"Rachel!" Jake's voice was stern with warning. "You keep your nose out of FBI business. I as much as promised them that your paper would be willing to keep the secret once you understood the nature of things."

"You promised? For me?" Rachel stared at him, shocked.

"Would you rather I continued dragging my feet and telling you half-truths? Think about it, Rachel. The paper doesn't come out until Wednesday, and the maneuvers are on Thursday. Besides that, what are you going to print? '*Banner* reporter *may* have been killed because he stumbled onto a nest of commie spies, but then again, we may be wrong?' That would be one hell of a story."

"I know. But it's not just another story that we're talking about here. A boy was killed, Jake."

"Yes, and we will get all the cooperation in the world in solving the murder once the maneuvers are over. For the moment, however, the government is trying to find out if the traitor works for them. I think we can pretty much assume that the person they are after is the same one who killed Quinlan, so their success will be our success, too."

"You're right. But they want to catch their man redhanded, so they'll wait until he actually tries to do whatever he's planning. What if they miss him? Oh, Jake, this is awfully frustrating. We've got to find out who killed Bruce." Rachel fell back against the couch in angry despair. There didn't seem to be any way to attack the problem that would insure success. "It's not that I argue with the government's need to keep their tests secret," she said. "But it isn't fair that national security should conflict with finding a murderer. If the man who killed Bruce was indeed connected to some kind of espionage, he'll surely leave the country once the maneuvers are over."

"It's a problem, all right." Jake looked at her closely, studying her strained expression with a look of tender concern. "I think the best we can do is concentrate on the most immediate matters, Rachel. The interests of national security have closed us off from finding the killer right now, so we'd better focus on trying to keep you alive till everything is finished."

"Keeping me alive? I'm sorry, Jake, but I don't think that's our main priority. That was a pretty crude attempt tonight."

"Tampering with your airplane wasn't crude at all, Rachel. That was deadly serious and professionally done. And they did a pretty good job of getting rid of Charles DeWitt. Don't treat this problem lightly."

"I'm not treating it lightly. Believe me, Jake, I'm scared to death. But I know they're out there, and I can keep an eye out for them."

"Like you kept an eye out tonight?" Jake touched her hand resting on the back of the couch tenderly, a light caress. "They could have run you down easily."

"But they didn't."

"No, they didn't. Maybe they were only interested in scaring you. But, maybe my arrival scared them off. Maybe they fully intended to kill you in the street."

"We'll never know for sure, will we?" Rachel said, looking into the gentle depths of his eyes and hoping the tenderness she saw there was more than a police officer's concern for her safety.

"No. I hope we never find out how serious they are." Jake's voice was soft, a caressing murmur that indicated personal concern. "But you've got to realize that you're not dealing with some corporation trying to keep a secret. This is serious business, with life in prison as reward for getting caught, so they aren't going to be gentle with anyone who gets in their way. Now, they haven't tried to harm anyone else on the paper, only Quinlan and you. So they must assume that Quinlan reported his knowledge to you alone. They believe you know enough to expose their plans, but maybe you haven't figured it all out yet. They must stop you before you put it all together. And they'll surely put all their resources to work for the sole purpose of killing you.''

The thought of someone out there determined to kill her sent a chill through her colder than the winter wind off the sound. And to have all this attention focused on her because of information that had died with a college senior on a barren dock made the threat seem all the more serious. It was totally impersonal, a decision made not in the heat of anger but with cold, precise thinking. These people neither hated nor feared her; they simply wanted her out of the way.

But it wasn't part of her nature or the nature of her profession to succumb, to be defeated. And no matter how much it scared her she had to press on to find Bruce's murderer.

Chapter Seven

Rachel rushed into the office at eight-thirty Monday morning, determined to make some kind of progress in the case. She strode down the short hall past her own office and leaned through the open door of the layout room. Frank Ackerman was busy inside. "I need the computer as soon as possible, Frank," she said. "And could you send Scott to see me when he shows up. I'll be in my office writing our obit for Bruce. And hold the front page, there'll be a new headline, and we've got to leave space for the obituary. The rest stays the same. Say, do you know when Bruce's parents are coming for the body?"

"Tomorrow, sometime," Frank replied.

"Good. I'd like to give them my condolences when they arrive."

She turned and walked quickly to her office, seating herself in a chair before her typewriter to begin work on her intern's obituary. It wasn't a pleasant task, but she was spurred on by the new depth revealed by Jake's information.

Jake had promised to call off the officers assigned to watch her house. He'd tried to persuade her to allow a policewoman to stay with her, but again he had failed and he left only after securing her promise to double-check the locks on all the doors and windows before retiring for the night. He had, however, arrived prepared with a padlock which he had attached to the patio door with a steel hasp. And after he'd gone Rachel saw him drive past on the street twice before she went to bed. How many times he passed after that, she didn't know, but she had a cozy feeling that he'd made many rounds before returning to his own home for the night.

Rachel knew he was right about protecting herself, but she couldn't give up her freedom by allowing a police officer to tag after her throughout her working day. She wasn't the type to enjoy having someone looking over her shoulder, no matter what the reason. But as she typed out the meager statistics of Bruce Quinlan's short life, the finality of death struck her deeply. Those people were killers and it was only foolish to turn help away when it was offered so sincerely. Well, she thought grimly, as she removed the sheet from the typewriter, I guess I'm stuck with being foolish because I'm sure not going to let anyone interfere with my life. Neither armed guards nor mysterious hit men in black cars would deter her from continuing with her life as she saw fit.

"Knock, knock!" Scott Kirby came through her door and kicked it shut behind him. "Big news, chief," he announced, tapping a spiral-bound notebook on his leg.

"In a minute, Scott." Rachel looked up at him severely. "You weren't quite as sly at the naval yards as you thought. In fact, you were quite sloppy."

"How's that?" Scott regarded her blankly, cocking his head slightly in confusion.

"They saw you take those pictures, Scott. The FBI has had their eye on you."

"Really?" He grinned broadly, his eyes twinkling with amusement. "Must have had them worried."

"A bit, yes. And you've got me worried." Rachel stood and walked around to the front of her desk. "Two of the many things you have to avoid in the real world are sloppiness and illegality. Sloppy reporting leads to mistakes, and illegal methods of news gathering can destroy your credibility. You have to be absolutely beyond reproach professionally if you are going to be any good at all. Do you understand what I'm saying?"

"Sure I do."

"Good, because your cloak-and-dagger methods could have gotten this newspaper shut down."

"They can't shut down a newspaper, Rachel," he scoffed.

"Of course not. But we can't put out a paper from behind bars while we're waiting for our trial to come up. Come on, Scott, you must realize that taking those pictures could be seen as an act of espionage. Treason, Scott. And no newspaper will risk hiring a reporter who puts himself and his newspaper in jeopardy for a bunch of photographs that he didn't need in the first place. I don't like having to play stern mother with someone your age. Don't make me have to do it again or I'll see to it that my displeasure is reflected in your grade."

"It won't happen again," he said quite seriously. "And I suppose that means I should get rid of the pictures."

"That might be a good idea," she agreed. "The negatives, too. Now, what was your big news?"

"I went back through B.Q.'s stuff. This time I came up with a couple of interesting papers that made some sense." He opened the notebook and removed two wrinkled sheets of typing paper. "He wrote down some names. Nothing concrete, but they tie into the pier. See?"

Rachel took the papers and studied them closely. The pages were both covered with squares and swirls drawn with a ballpoint pen around a few boldly printed words. Apparently Bruce had started an outline but had given it up for his habitual, absentminded scribbling while thinking the story over. Before he gave up the task, however, he'd listed several interesting items.

The first heading written on his list was "Pandora" and below it, "Calvin W." and "Arnie C." Secondly, he'd written "Business Concerns?," with "Heavy machinery and concrete" and "Fuel tanker" listed under that. The last item on the list said simply, "Not Schofield set-up."

That was it for the first page, and the second page said only "Calvin Watkins" several times, amid the maze of aimless lines.

"I didn't know if this stuff was any help or not, but it's all he had in his room that looked even remotely like a lead. What do you think?" Scott sat on the edge of Rachel's desk drumming his fingers nervously on his knees.

"I don't know for sure, Scott." Rachel leaned against the edge of the desk holding the papers before her. "It does seem to confirm my suspicion that the Pandora company has something to do with the mess, but that would seem to fly in the face of the FBI investigation."

"How so?"

"I tell you what, Scott, I'll send you after the FBI." She laid the pages aside excitedly and stood facing the young reporter. "Just find out if they have any statement about Bruce's death. Don't pressure them, just ask and see what the official line is."

"I don't understand," he said. "Murder is a state crime, not federal. Unless you think they know something and aren't sharing it."

"Just go and talk to them," Rachel answered, with a smile. "I want to find out what they say. The agent to see, if possible, is Special Agent Fowler."

"I get you, boss." He hopped down eagerly, striding to the door. "I can lay my freedom of the press rap on them and see how far it gets me. I'll check back later."

"Okay, Scott."

Rachel took the two sheets of paper around and sat behind her desk. Who was Arnie C. and why had Bruce noted that something was not a Schofield set-up? What wasn't? She could probably get most of her answers by going directly to Schofield Enterprises, but she didn't want to take that step without obtaining as complete a background as possible on Calvin Watkins and Pandora. Laying those papers aside on the desk, she took her article about Bruce and hurried down the hall.

"I need that computer as soon as possible," she said, handing him the typed page. "Here's the obit and headline."

"Student's death linked to newspaper vandalism," he read, raising one bushy gray eyebrow. "Really, Rachel? I hope you've got some kind of proof to back this up."

"Solid hunches, is more like it," she admitted. "But they're solid enough. It's in the story."

Frank glanced over the page briefly. "Come on, you don't name any sources," he said, looking up at her. "Who says there's a connection?"

"I do, Frank. Let's print it up and see what happens."

"You're the boss." Frank turned back to his work with a smile as Rachel walked out of the office.

Frank had come to the paper from the *Tacoma News Tribune* when Bradford Morgan first began operations, and he'd become quite accustomed to the Morgan family penchant for the dramatic. Though the paper had started as little more than a classified ad sheet, Brad Morgan had done his best to find something interesting for the few pages devoted to news. And he was a firm believer in the power of a banner headline to bring in the readers. Since the institution of the student internship program, there had been a dramatic increase in the space devoted to hard news. But the boldly printed accusing headline had been something they'd steered away from even as Rachel had struggled to rid the student writing of unsubstantiated accusations and broad contentions. But now it seemed that Bruce's death had brought out the Morgan family's penchant for hyperbole in Rachel, and Frank wasn't a bit surprised. In fact, he found it mildly amusing that she would plunge into her father's style of head-on journalism with such gusto.

If Frank had known all the facts surrounding the death of their student reporter, he wouldn't have found any humor in it. But Rachel saw no reason to alarm him more than she had. More to the point, she didn't want anyone else trying to tie her down with good advice about her health. She already had a police officer for that job.

Jake called shortly before noon. "Did you send Scott Kirby down to talk to the FBI?" he said. He sounded distracted, tired, and Rachel had an image of him sitting half-awake behind a cluttered desk wearing that old Princeton sweatshirt and drinking coffee from a Styrofoam cup.

"Yes, as a matter of fact, I did."

There was a pause on the other end, and then he said, "Well, he must be acting his usual self, because Agent Fowler has already called here to complain about leaks and false accusations. He's all but accused them of withholding information. What did you tell Kirby, Rachel?"

"Nothing. I just asked him to find out what the FBI had to say about Bruce's death. Nothing more than that."

"Well, they can't get rid of him and seem to think it's our job to remove bothersome reporters from government offices."

"You must have been right about them, then," Rachel declared. "They wouldn't be so annoyed with a simple question if there wasn't something to it."

"Lay off them, Rachel," he said. "You're not helping anything by sending that news hound after them."

"I told him not to pressure them."

"But you must have known that he would."

"Maybe I did." Rachel smiled, tapping one finger on the desk as she spoke. "Maybe now that someone has opened that door, you might start asking them some questions yourself."

"You don't have to tell me how to do my job," he said.

"So don't tell me how to do mine. I sent a reporter out to do some research for a story. That's all I did."

"Okay, me cop and you reporter. I wouldn't leave Scott over there too long, or he's liable to get himself locked up on general principle."

"Has he got them that mad?"

"He's got Fowler that mad, and that's good enough," Jake said. "Are you free for lunch?"

"Probably, though I can't be sure right now. By the way, Scott found some interesting information in Bruce's dorm room."

"Did he find the roommate?"

"Yes, but he didn't know anything. He gave Scott some of Bruce's stuff, however, which Bruce's parents thought would be helpful," she said. "They indicate quite clearly that Bruce was investigating the Pandora company. There was no mention of spying, only some comments about earth-moving equipment and a fuel tanker. Do you know of anyone named Arnie C. who might be connected with Pandora?"

"The name doesn't ring any bells, but then I haven't gone over their payroll."

"Bruce listed him and Calvin Watkins in his notes," Rachel went on. "And he mentioned something about the company not being a Schofield set-up. I don't know what that means."

"Maybe the feds know. I'll give them a call."

"Maybe you should tell them that it was Scott who found the notes. They might be more willing to talk to him if it helps them out."

"Sure, they'll talk to him, all right," Jake laughed. "They'll talk all night in a small room with a bright light."

"I think I'll call him off."

"Good plan. Gotta run now, but I'll give you a call around eleven-thirty about lunch."

"I'll talk to you then," Rachel said. "And, Jake?"

"Yes?"

"Thank you for driving by last night," she said softly. "I felt better knowing you were out there if only for a while."

"My pleasure, Rachel." The detective hesitated over the words as his voice dropped to match her confidential tone. "I don't plan to lose you."

"You won't," she assured him. "Goodbye."

Rachel hung up the phone feeling a pleasant warmth lingering within her chest. But she didn't have the time that the subject of Jake Connors deserved. There was work to be done, and the time to do it was growing shorter by the minute.

Rachel hurried down the hall to the layout room. "I've got to do some research," she said, standing impatiently behind Frank's chair and squinting down at the electronic representation of their front page.

"Don't take too long," he said, clearing the screen and removing his disk from the computer drive. "What are you looking for?"

"I may have an idea how to get information about the Pandora Exporting Company."

"Pandora?" Frank rolled his chair around and looked up at her, with a smile growing beneath his drooping mustache. "A friend of mine over at Washington Lumber says that Schofield just bought that company not too long ago."

"I know, but I don't have any facts."

"Well, what I heard was that Schofield Enterprises was apparently threatened with a hostile takeover and buying Pandora had something to do with a proxy battle. I was asking if anything unusual was happening in the lumber business lately and that's all he could think of. I didn't think it was much, either. What do you know about them?"

"Hunches, mostly." A gleam of triumph stole into Rachel's eyes, as she looked down at the man in the chair before her. "The guard was busy checking an unlocked door at the Pandora warehouse when Bruce was killed."

"That's not much basis for a story," Frank warned her.

"The story isn't specifically about Pandora. I'm looking for a link to them now," she said, pulling a chair up to the keyboard. "With any luck, we may be able to find out what Bruce was working on when he was killed."

After Frank left, Rachel engaged the telecommunications program from the hard disk in the computer and called a local network that would connect her to a data base containing information on Washington state corporations.

After entering several more commands, Rachel was rewarded by a screen full of information under the heading: SCHOFIELD ENTERPRISES, INC. She scrolled through several screens filled with information about Schofield's various holdings before finding Pandora buried between Pacific Mills and Pascal Semiconductor. The file said only that North Chemical had purchased the Pandora Exporting Company from Calvin Watkins in August of the previous year. The stated reason for the purchase was to form a holding company, but as of yet the company held only Schofield stock.

It struck her as odd that someone would purchase an export company in order to use it as a holding company when they could set up their own new company for far less. They'd owned the company for nine months and had done nothing with it but rent a warehouse and purchase some secondhand construction machinery for sale overseas.

Calvin Watkins had apparently stayed on as president of Pandora, but there were no other officers listed. Rachel didn't have a strong enough background in financial reporting to know if this arrangement was normal or not, but it did strike her as peculiar. She also took note that Pandora had bought the heavy machinery in September and had held it over the winter, finally shipping it out just last week.

The machinery had been purchased from Northland Construction and Demolition. On a hunch, she searched the file for the company and was rewarded with the name listed among Schofield's holdings. Well, that was one way to use a holding company. Schofield bought the equipment from itself.

Rachel exited the business data base and called up the UPI clipping service, a data base set up by the news wire service to provide background information for subscribing newspapers. She asked the system to give her anything it had on Calvin Watkins and sat back to wait.

The data base signaled that it was searching its files, taking several minutes, then flashed on an item about Watkins's sale of Pandora Exporting to Schofield. It was a very dull story.

But maybe the lack of information on Watkins was the most deadly news of all. The man certainly hadn't operated in a vacuum before becoming president of a company. And it took a certain amount of power and money to keep your name out of the paper entirely. Perhaps calling to talk to him the other evening hadn't been the wisest course of action for her. She could see now that the action against her had increased drastically after the call, for she'd surely confirmed his suspicions about her by talking to him in person.

To find your way through a maze you must start at the beginning. Where was the beginning of this maze? Bruce had been writing two stories at the time of his death: an article on small boat building, which couldn't possibly be connected; and a piece about the lumbering industry. Was there a link between that and Watkins? Of course there was! Schofield Enterprises held vast interests in both the lumber and paper businesses, and Pandora was owned by Schofield. It was a weak link, but a link nonetheless. Now, where did Bruce first become interested in Watkins and Pandora?

Rachel left the UPI service and returned to the Washington state business information directory. She looked in the obvious place first, checking the holdings of Washington Lumber Developers and Pacific Mills, Schofield's primary timber concerns. And, when that lead led to nothing, she moved through the many smaller companies Schofield owned that worked in the lumber industry.

It proved to be a harder task than she'd at first imagined, but at last she found what she thought was the slim connection between Pandora and Bruce's lumber story. It seemed that Pandora owned a small stand of timber south of Tacoma. It was a connection, but a nebulous one at best. How could that have interested him? She'd probably never know.

There must be another connection that would explain everything. Rachel continued her search with fresh excitement. Somewhere in this mess lay her answer.

"Calvin Watkins has underworld connections," Jake stated over lunch. "He's been on the edge of several FBI investigations but never the prime suspect, and he's known to have friendly relationships with several California mobsters."

"My God, Jake, he has to be connected to this mess!" Rachel reached to grab his hand in her excitement, wanting to hug the man for beginning to answer the questions her research had raised. His hand was warm in her grasp, and the replying pressure of his fingers sent small shivers through her as she stared into his happy blue eyes. Then she collected her enthusiasm into a demure smile and fought down the womanly urge playing within her. "Did Agent Fowler finally come through with some information?"

"No, but I did my own search through the law enforcement data banks regarding Pandora and Watkins. We've got a few things that you might not have access to."

"Like what?"

"Rachel, this stuff has to be off the record," he said seriously.

"Off the record?" Rachel, in chagrin, swallowed her journalistic urge to protest. She didn't want to manufacture antagonism between them over what was a slight issue at this point.

"Anything we might suppose about Calvin Watkins and his connection to the maneuvers is still just an unproven suspicion." Jake greeted her reaction with calm acceptance, carefully explaining his position as though hoping she would excuse him for playing by the rules. "I can't just hand over information from police and FBI files so that you can put them in print."

"I wouldn't print unproven information," she said, still holding his hand.

"No, but you might hint at it. And even the hint might be enough to blow months of investigative work."

"Is there an ongoing investigation into Watkins's activities?"

"There's always an ongoing investigation into mob figures. He's on the list, so they keep tabs on him."

"So, what does that mean to me? A moment ago you acted like you wanted to tell me about him, but now you're hiding behind official secrets. Why?"

"Because I don't want you to walk into a libel suit by printing anything prematurely—especially if you plan to connect Watkins to espionage in any way."

"The paper comes out on Wednesday, Jake," Rachel told him. "It's too late to work up a full story now."

"Like hell," he laughed. "You don't start printing till tomorrow morning, and if you think it's important enough, you can rearrange the whole paper overnight."

"Okay, we'll keep it off the record," Rachel said, allowing herself to squeeze his hand again. "The story isn't the important thing right now, anyway. Finding Bruce's killer is our main task."

"Right. So we're agreed that this is just between us?"

"Cross my heart."

"Good enough for me," he said, and he withdrew a folded sheet from the inner pocket of his sport jacket. "Here's what I've got. Mind you, it's only a beginning. And it doesn't show any connection to the upcoming maneuvers."

He gave the typed sheet to Rachel, who read it hungrily.

"Arnold Carbellino," she read, looking up at Jake with excitement brightening her eyes.

"Most likely the Arnie C. mentioned in those notes Scott found," Jake replied. "Mr. Carbellino is an old pal of Watkins, and his company, Death Valley Express Aviation, sold Pandora to Watkins last July. Carbellino was under investigation for laundering money at the time. He has a long history of involvement with gambling and racketeering. The charges against Carbellino were eventually dropped."

"So, Calvin Watkins leads to Arnold Carbellino, who leads into the bowels of organized crime in America," Rachel exclaimed. "Something like that would surely have piqued Bruce's interest, but what would take him to the pier in the middle of the night?"

"It's a start, anyway," Jake said. "And I found out something else that might have caught his attention, though I'm not sure if it means anything. Pandora Exporting purchased an aircraft hangar in Baker, California from Death Valley Express Aviation shortly after Schofield took it over."

"And Death Valley Aviation is Carbellino's company."

"Exactly."

"But knowing that doesn't solve anything, does it?"

"No, but it might be the avenue that Bruce Quinlan took into the story he was doing," Jake said, gazing into her eyes. "As I said, it's a place to start."

"This is great." Rachel found herself returning his gaze with increasing ardor, unable to look away from the lively depths of his clear blue eyes. "What's our next move?"

"You go back to work getting your paper out, and I keep checking around for clues to Quinlan's murder," Jake said. "Keep a low profile, won't you?"

"Please, Jake, I can take care of myself," she protested, though without the vehemence she might have had earlier.

Jake laughed, reaching out to touch her hand. "You go ahead and do your job as you see fit, but please let me worry about you a little bit."

"I wouldn't mind that, Jake." No, she wouldn't mind that at all.

And Rachel found a primal stimulation in this man that would outlive any story, any matter of business that had previously occupied her attention. A living spark of compassion passed through his touch. He was someone she could devote the rest of her life to if given the chance. She wanted to be certain she would have that chance.

YOU'RE GOING TO MAKE A FOOL of yourself, Jake. Falling for a reporter against all your instincts and conscious desires is the worst thing you can possibly do.

Jake left their lunch date feeling a confusion of emotions that struggled within his mind. Rachel Morgan was the most exciting and self-confident woman he'd ever met, and the most beautiful. But her very self-confidence was one of the reasons Jake felt compelled to warn himself against her. She was secure enough to follow her own instincts professionally and personally, and that could lead to trouble.

Still, Jake was finding that his better judgment was losing the fight against the memory of Rachel's silky skin and the warm pools of her dark eyes. All he could think of was protecting her against the still-unseen threat. All he wanted was to love her.

Chapter Eight

"I'm Special Agent Carl Fowler, Miss Morgan. I've come for the information you spoke of with Detective Sergeant Connors." The man in the blue suit had come in practically on Rachel's heels as she returned from lunch, and now he stood in the door to her office holding out a leatherette case for her to examine his identification. "Two sheets of paper, I believe?"

"Yes, I've got it here." Rachel walked to her desk and opened the top drawer, removing the crumpled papers. She handed them to the agent. "Is there some significance to any of this?" she asked, wearing an open smile.

"That's not for me to say, ma'am." He folded the papers lengthwise and slipped them into the inner pocket of his jacket. "Do you have any copies?"

"Of course I do." Rachel's smiled faded. "You don't want them, too, do you?"

"Yes, if you please." He held his hand out, his face set in a blank mask of official secrecy.

"I had no idea that this was such hot stuff." Rachel took two more sheets of paper out of the drawer and gave them to the agent.

"How did you come into possession of these documents?" he asked, slipping the copies into the pocket with the originals.

"Why? They weren't illegally obtained." The man's professional zeal was beginning to grate on Rachel's nerves.

"I wouldn't know about that," he said. "But we'd like the opportunity to talk to whomever obtained them for you."

"Gee, the name slips my mind," she answered, returning his stony stare.

"It would be much easier if you'd cooperate with us, Miss Morgan. We can always get a warrant."

"Get one." Rachel crossed her arms resolutely, staring the agent down.

"All right." He turned and walked out the door, saying, "Goodbye, Miss Morgan."

"Have a nice day," she called to his back.

When he'd gone, Rachel withdrew another set of copies from the desk drawer and sat looking at them again. Was there really something important about this mess, or was the bureau trying to throw her off the track by sending her after useless information? The exchange with the agent had left her wanting more information but having no place to go get it from.

"Who was that scowling fellow who just left?" Naomi Aaronson knocked and entered Rachel's office, concern stamped on her face.

"An FBI agent," Rachel said, raising one eyebrow in comment. "He came to get the notes Bruce's roommate had given to Scott.

"That was fast work, wasn't it?" Naomi said, her motherly features taut with thought. "You only just got those notes."

"Yes, but Jake said he was going to call them about the notes when I told him this morning."

"Jake, is it?" Naomi smiled gleefully, watching Rachel carefully. "You and the young officer seem to be getting along quite well now."

"Oh, Naomi, don't start your matchmaking now," Rachel scoffed, laughing. "We've all got better things to do than worry about my love life."

"You're right, dear," the older woman said, though the knowing twinkle remained in her hazel eyes. "I'm sure you're much too preoccupied to think about such things right now."

"Yes, and though we're making some progress, I don't have much hope of finding our answers soon enough to do any good. Where on earth can we go to find out what Bruce was working on?"

Naomi pursed her lips thoughtfully, then smiled with excitement. "I think I know where we might find out something! Bruce mentioned a cousin working for some computer company in Seattle, and I think it's owned by the same corporation that owns one of the lumber mills he was checking into. I'm sure he was talking to him about his story one afternoon last week."

"How can you be sure of that?" Rachel straightened up eagerly. Finally someone had some positive information about Bruce's story.

"He said he'd put in a couple of lengthy long-distance calls to his cousin to get some background on a story."

"And his cousin works for a computer company?"

"Yes, but I can't think of the company's name right off hand. He said it was owned by Schofield Enterprises."

"Thank you, Naomi. You don't know how much help you've been." Rachel stood restlessly. "I'll have to get in touch with his parents to get his cousin's name, I suppose.

I've heard they're taking his body home to Iowa tomorrow and I don't imagine this is a very good time for it, but it can't be helped. He didn't tell you his cousin's name?''

"No, just said it was his cousin who worked for a computer company. No, it was a computer chip company.''

"Pascal Semiconductor,'' Rachel said. "Okay, I've got some work for you to do. Go to the college library and see if you can find out what kind of research Bruce was doing in the last couple weeks. He practically lived in the library. I need the information as soon as possible. All right?''

"I'm on my way.'' Naomi turned and opened the door. "But what is all of this for? I saw Scott downtown on my way here, and he said you've got him going after the FBI for something. What's going on?''

"Maybe we're just spinning our wheels, Naomi.'' Rachel came around to walk the woman to the door. "But, if we can figure out exactly what Bruce was after, we might have more than a story. We might be able to catch his killer.''

"Us? My, the newspaper business gets more exciting every day.'' Naomi paused in the doorway, studying Rachel with an uncertain smile. "Well, I'm off, dear.''

"Good luck,'' Rachel called, as the door swung slowly shut. Then she turned to the phone to call Bruce's parents who'd arrived from Iowa. This would be the most painful part of the whole sad case.

"LYLE QUINLAN?''

"Yup, that's me.'' Bruce's cousin spoke in a friendly, no-nonsense tone that brightened Rachel's spirits considerably after her conversation with Bruce's parents. "What can I do for you?'' he asked.

"My name is Rachel Morgan, and I'm calling about Bruce,'' she said. "I understand that he had been in contact with you as research for a story he was doing for my paper.''

''Ms Morgan? Well, it's nice to almost meet you. Bruce spoke highly of you.''

''We thought quite highly of him around here, too.''

''Yeah, he was a good kid. So, you don't know what his story was about?''

''No, he was assigned to work up something about the lumber industry, but it appears that he found something more interesting to report on. Do you know what it was?''

''Calvin Watkins,'' the man said, without having to give it a thought. ''I don't know what he was after, really, but he was terribly interested in Watkins.''

''How is he connected to you?''

''Watkins worked with accounting here about two years back. He was here as a troubleshooter of sorts—you know, trimming off excess fat and all that—and he was here only a couple months.''

''What did Bruce want to know about him?''

''Odd stuff. Mostly wanted to know how much Watkins had to do with research and development here. Especially our government work.''

''Did Watkins have anything to do with it?''

''Sure, he had control of the money for everything while he was with us. A real slasher, too. He cut us to the bone in all departments till we could barely meet our contract obligations. The brass decided we didn't need to save money so badly that we should cut our own throats, so they saved themselves about forty grand and let Watkins go.''

''Did he have any direct contact with research?'' An idea was beginning to shine dimly in Rachel's mind. ''Especially government research.''

''He shouldn't have, but I couldn't say for sure. He sure was around here often enough, and all I do is test the finished products. I don't suppose it was any different in R and D."

"What kind of work are you doing for the government?"

"That's classified," he laughed.

"But it's possible that Calvin Watkins managed to become a bit more intimate with the research in that area than he should have been?"

"Anything's possible." He cleared his throat. "And just between us, Watkins was an awfully slick piece of work. Personally, I never trusted the guy."

"Did you and Bruce talk about anything else?"

"No, just Watkins. He wanted to know about research, too, but I haven't kept my job here by babbling about the work."

"You know, I have a strange feeling that they're about to test your company's work this week," Rachel said quietly.

"Gee, I wouldn't know about that," he said, with somewhat exaggerated innocence.

"Thursday," she added. "Yes, I believe this Thursday is a good day for a test, isn't it?"

"You're an awfully accurate guesser, Ms Morgan," he said, again. "I'll have to go now. They just brought in a new batch of chips for testing."

"Yes, I'll let you get back to work. Thank you for helping me out. And don't worry, I won't use your name in print."

"I didn't tell you anything, Ms Morgan. Good luck on your story."

Rachel hung up the phone with a satisfied smile radiating on her face. Somehow, in doing background on Schofield Enterprises, Bruce had found something that connected Watkins to the upcoming naval maneuvers and his death had been the result. So, what was Calvin Watkins doing that would affect the maneuvers? And how was it connected to Pandora, heavy machinery, concrete and a fuel tanker?

"YOUR BLOODHOUND CAN GET TO BE a real pain in the neck."

Jake laughed as he tilted the wooden chair back against the wall of Rachel's office and kicked his feet out straight ahead of him on the floor. He laced his fingers behind his head and regarded Rachel with hooded eyes.

"Is Scott too much for you to handle?" Rachel studied his face as he sat across from her, memorizing the tiny wrinkles that radiated from the corners of his eyes and the parenthetical creases that formed beside his lips when he smiled.

"Oh, we could handle him well enough, I suppose. It's just that we wouldn't be able to keep him locked up for very long on a charge of pestering the police department."

"I didn't send him out to bother the police."

"I guess he got tired of hanging around with the federal boys, so we were blessed with his presence downtown for a couple of hours after lunch. If snooping is what set the bad guys off against Quinlan, then Mr. Kirby might find himself in trouble, too, if he keeps the pressure up."

"I hadn't thought of that," Rachel said. Yes, she thought, his was a face she could live with. A well-used face, it had obviously known both happiness and sorrow and had gained character from the experiences. "But then his assault on the police department should only prove that we don't know where to look for the answers."

"I hope so. Because I already have you to worry about and I'm not all that eager to worry about Kirby, too." Then the concerned smile left his face as his features composed themselves into a more blankly official look. "Back to more immediate concerns, however. I found out some interesting things about your friendly mechanic, the late Chuck De-Witt."

"What is it?" Rachel brought her thoughts back into focus on the matter at hand, leaving her eyes to the pleasant assignment of watching him rock on the back legs of the chair.

"He was a gambler," Jake said, dropping the chair onto all four legs. "And he was in debt to the tune of four big ones, payable in full as of about two weeks ago. His bookie was a guy named Jerry Barker, who has been linked with a gambler named Arnold Carbellino. And you know how Carbellino comes into the picture."

"He sold Pandora to Watkins, who sold it to North Chemical."

"Exactly," Jake said, grinning. "So do you know the circumstances surrounding the sale of Pandora to Watkins? Or do you have any idea how long it was in business before it was sold?"

"I haven't dug that far yet. Surprise me."

"Two months. The company was incorporated in California in June by Arnold Carbellino, and he sold it to Calvin Watkins for an undisclosed sum the first week of July. Now, Watkins ran Pandora for a little over a month, and they didn't export a damn thing in that time from what I've been able to find out. All they did was buy stock in Schofield Enterprises. It looks to me that the whole reason they started the company was to sell it. Lord knows why."

"And Carbellino was under investigation on organized crime charges," Rachel said triumphantly. "That should give the FBI a good, solid lead for their spy search."

"No, it doesn't hold water with Fowler." Jake shook his head slowly. "First off, though they're willing to concede a possible link between Pandora and organized crime, there's no discernible link between the sale and espionage. Secondly, Watkins has never been anything but a model citizen. And, most important, the Mafia doesn't sell secrets to communists. Next to the Daughters of the American Revolution, they're generally the most patriotic organization in America. The bureau has pretty much decided to just hang on till the gig on Thursday and wait for someone to try pulling something fancy.''

''For crying out loud!'' Rachel slapped her hand on the desk top in exasperation. ''Do they, or do they not, suspect that Bruce's death had something to do with the maneuvers?''

''Of course, they do. And the fact that Agent Fowler came trotting over here to get those papers confirms the opinion that they haven't told all in that department.''

''But if they know something, they should be moving heaven and earth to follow every lead they turn up. What's wrong with them?''

''Not enough manpower. They have to provide protection for the maneuvers on both coasts, you know.'' A frown crossed his rugged features as he spoke. ''Besides, the painful truth is that it's not their business to capture murderers for us.''

''It's amazing any laws ever manage to get enforced if that's the way you people go about your business,'' Rachel proclaimed. ''Isn't there any cooperation between the local and national level?''

''Usually, yes, but we're into national security here and that's a blank wall.''

''All right, then,'' Rachel said, standing. ''It's up to the local authorities to find out what's going on. What is your exact assignment in this mess?''

"I am now assigned to you," he replied, with a wry twinkle in his eyes. "And I consider it to be a very important assignment."

"My very own policeman? How long do I get to keep you?"

"Officially, until we're reasonably certain that you're out of danger." Then he stood to meet her. "Of course, I'd like our working relationship to be as friendly as possible. Maybe you'd like to make it easier for me to keep an eye on you."

"That sounds fair." Rachel smiled up at him, a taut, warm feeling welling inside as she stood close to him. "I don't want to be tough on the police."

"Good. Would you accept an invitation to dinner?" He placed a hand on her shoulder, stroking the fingers up to brush her cheek tenderly as he gazed into her eyes.

"I'd love to." She felt the warmth of desire growing within her, felt it and savored it, though she knew it must remain unfulfilled for now.

"Rachel!" They stepped apart quickly as Scott Kirby threw open the door and rushed in, calling her by name. "Oh, sorry, I didn't know you were with anyone," he said, then continued heedlessly, "The FBI isn't talking, but between them and the police and various sources in several city offices, I picked up a couple of interesting things. Should we be talking with him here?" he asked, nodding his head toward Jake.

"It's his case," Rachel said. "You can feel free to tell him what he already knows."

"Well, there's something fishy about the way Schofield bought Pandora. The guy who started the company was under investigation for racketeering, and he originally sold it to Watkins for about eighty-five thousand dollars. That sure ain't much for a whole company. But here's the fun part. Watkins turned around and stuck Schofield for a million to buy the company, even though they had done no business. They did own some land south of Tacoma, however. I don't know how much or what it's worth, but I'll find out. I've got an appointment to interview Schofield an hour from now."

"One million?" Jake bit his lower lip in thought. "Where did you get that figure?"

"Various sources," Scott said, looking to Rachel warily. "I don't really want to start naming names."

"No, I'm not interested in names, kid," Jake told him. "I'm just curious how accurate the amount is."

"It's accurate, all right." Scott grinned, leaning against the wall. "I triple-checked it."

"Why on earth would he pay so much?" Rachel looked from Scott to Jake, receiving no answer, and then continued. "There doesn't seem to be any legal reason. I think there are a couple of questions that Mr. Schofield should answer."

"I'll be talking to the man, himself, soon," Scott said, eagerly. "And even if I don't get a straight answer, I'll sure get something that can be verified."

"Sorry, Scott, but I'm going to keep your appointment for you," Rachel said.

"Neither one of you is going," Jake cut in. "For God's sake, Rachel, is this how you keep a low profile?"

"No, this is how we report the news."

"But, if you start asking Schofield questions about Watkins, the first thing he'll do after you leave is to call the man up and ask him what's going on. You might as well paint a target on your back!"

"For crying out loud, Jake, the target is already there! Besides, I plan to use a bit of subtlety. That's why I'm not letting Scott go," she added, with a laugh.

"Now wait a second, I can be subtle if I have to," Scott protested. "I did all the legwork on this. It's not fair to take the interview away."

"You're about as subtle as a train wreck," Jake told the reporter. "If you two are determined to do this, then I agree that it's better that Rachel conduct it."

"I'm sure it's not fair, Scott, but I'm doing it anyway," Rachel said. "You can write it up for the paper, byline and all. But I have to talk to Schofield myself."

"But—"

"No objections. This is how newspapers are run in the real world," Rachel cut him off, adding to Jake, "And no more objections from you, either. There's too much at stake to back off now, but we have no idea if Schofield himself knows anything about it."

"Come on! A million dollars for a practically worthless company? Of course, he knows something is up."

"See? You've got the man convicted already, Scott," Rachel told him sternly. "I can't have you going in there like that."

"Okay, I'm out of it." Scott crossed to the door in sour resignation. "But I sure don't appreciate having my work pulled out from under me, even if it is by my boss," he said, as he pulled the door shut behind him.

"You'll be careful, won't you?" Jake asked somberly.

"Yes. Besides, Bruce's notes said it wasn't a Schofield set-up. He doesn't pose any threat to me."

"All right, then. But our people will be around to watch over you."

"They won't be hanging around Schofield's office, will they?"

"No. It would just make matters worse, if you had a parade of cops trooping after you into the office."

"Don't worry, it's just an interview," she said soothingly.

"Yeah, sure," Jake said. "I'd better be going, too. We'll have to start our own trace on that sale, though it'll take a bit of talking to convince the captain that it's necessary. I'll get on that right away."

"Must you rush off?" Disappointment tinged her voice as she watched him turn the doorknob. "I was rather hoping, well, that we could go over the questions I'll need to ask Schofield."

"Come now, you don't need my help in that department." He smiled. "Besides, I want to get my work out of the way so I can keep that date tonight."

"Well, in that case, you'd better get going." Rachel smiled slyly. "What time should I expect you to call?"

"Seven," he said, leaning against the open door. "I might stop by here later if I have time, though."

"I'll be waiting."

Lonely desire tore at her heart as she watched the door swing shut behind him, a desire that combined with the tingle of anticipation she felt at her upcoming interview with Schofield. Both feelings promised fulfillment to the two sides of her nature, woman and reporter, and she felt that both would be rewarded soon.

Chapter Nine

The black car circled the block, a man with a birthmark under one eye watching sourly as Rachel got out of her car and walked up to the door of the office building. After she'd gone inside, he picked up the car phone and dialed.

"Calvin Watkins, please," he said, when his call was answered. "Oh? Okay, I'll talk to him later. No, no message."

He hung up the phone angrily, then leaned forward to bark to the man behind the wheel. "Take me back to the other car," he said. "Then come back and keep an eye on the broad. We're going to have to take care of her."

The black car continued sedately down the street, just another vehicle lost in the stream of traffic.

THE EXECUTIVE OFFICES of Schofield Enterprises occupied the fifteenth floor of the Foster office complex overlooking the bay. It was a pleasant steel and stone building that one of Schofield's companies had constructed two years earlier, with small shops and an outdoor café installed on the main floor. From what she could see on her way to the elevators, the Foster building merchants were doing very well.

Rachel was at Schofield's office a couple minutes after four.

"May I help you?" the receptionist in the richly appointed room enquired efficiently.

"I believe that Mr. Schofield has an appointment with Scott Kirby from the *Tacoma Banner*," Rachel answered. "I'm Rachel Morgan, the editor of the *Banner*. Scott was called away, so I'm here to conduct the interview."

"Ms Morgan." The woman's brow furrowed slightly as she regarded Rachel analytically. "It's a bit irregular," she said tonelessly. "But I suppose it's all right. He's in conference at the moment, but he should be finished shortly if you'd care to take a seat and wait."

"That's fine." Rachel took a place on one of the soft couches and glanced through a news magazine while she waited.

She couldn't concentrate on the articles, though, and just paged absently through the magazine as she let her thoughts drift. This interview with Schofield could be a big mistake, but she didn't feel threatened. In fact, she didn't feel that Schofield was a threat to her at all, though she couldn't say why she had that feeling.

She wasn't exactly sure what she would ask the industrialist once she joined him in his office and, according to Scott's explanation, her impetuous intern had been a bit more blunt in stating his purpose for the interview than Rachel would have liked. He'd asked for the appointment to talk specifically about Schofield's connection to Calvin Watkins and the Pandora company, so she didn't have much leeway to gain his trust by misdirecting questions. Like it or not, she would have to go at it head on and hope the direct approach would provide a useful clue.

She'd spent fifteen minutes in the silence of the reception office, leafing through a magazine, when her thoughts were interrupted by the opening of the door to the receptionist's right. A short man with thinning black hair slicked back along his narrow skull emerged smiling. Rachel took note of how his smile had little effect on the flat, opaque look in his gray eyes. He looked at Rachel with a glance so cold and penetrating that she dropped her eyes quickly to the open page on her lap and pretended to study it. The man moved past the secretary with a slight nod and continued out the door.

"Good day, sir," the woman behind the desk said, obvious distaste showing in her voice. Then she turned to Rachel, saying, "Mr. Schofield will see you now."

"Who was that?" Rachel asked, rising.

"Mr. Watkins," the woman replied, mouthing the words as though they were laced with cyanide.

"Oh, yes. He runs the Pandora Exporting Company, doesn't he?"

"Yes, I guess you could say he runs it," she answered sourly, then she stood and opened the door with a smile. "He's all yours."

"Thank you."

Willis Schofield's office was situated on a corner of the building with two walls of glass. Sunlight spilled into the austerely furnished room. His office furnishings were modern, featuring a lot of glass and stainless steel, with a couple of oak pieces to add color to the mint walls and gray carpeting. Two softly cushioned tubular chairs faced the large oak desk. Rachel walked up to the chairs and faced the tall, silver-haired man who rose to greet her.

"Rachel Morgan," she said, extending her hand. "I'm from the *Banner*."

"Hello, Miss Morgan." He took her hand firmly, with a seemingly genuine smile. "I was under the impression that I would be interviewed by a young man."

"Yes, Scott Kirby. I'm afraid that I stole this interview away from him, sir. I hope you don't mind."

"Not at all, Miss Morgan. Please, sit down," he said, motioning toward a chair as he took his place behind the cluttered desk and sat studying her in a disconcertingly direct manner. "I read your paper quite often, and I've always found your reporting to be perceptive and interesting. You've improved and expanded it quite a bit over the years."

"We try," she said. "Do you mind if I record the interview?"

"Not at all. Anything to avoid the possibility of misquotes is perfectly acceptable. And from what your reporter said when he called for the appointment, I have a feeling that I should be especially on guard this afternoon." He spoke with a disarming smile and seemed quite comfortable at having to answer questions about the overpriced company.

"What Scott lacks in tact and diplomacy, he makes up for in instinct," Rachel said, as she took the small cassette recorder out of her purse and laid it on the desk between them. "And we have come across some information that seems odd to us. It concerns the Pandora company and some of the people associated with it." She started the tape and took out a notebook and pen, mainly to give herself something to do with her hands. "Do you mind talking about the company?"

"Not at the moment, but I imagine I'll regret it before the interview is over." He smiled broadly, holding his eyes on her face.

"I hope you won't regret it, sir. I've heard that you paid one million dollars for the company, even though it was worth only a fraction of that amount."

His smile grew a bit pained and he paused before answering. "A million, plus change," he said after a moment. "If I remember the figures correctly."

"Did you know that Calvin Watkins paid only about eighty-five thousand dollars for the company to begin with?"

"Yes, I think that figure is accurate." Schofield smiled, seeming to enjoy the slight confusion that crept into Rachel's eyes. "But Pandora Exporting, as a company, is nothing. It's only a name on some corporate ledger."

"But why did you pay so much for it? Did it have something to do with a takeover attempt?" she added, remembering Frank's information.

"You're quite well informed, aren't you? It was a matter of stock," he said, as if that explained it all. "Pandora Exporting held nearly eight percent of our voting stock."

"You bought the company to gain control of the stock?"

"Exactly. It's a simple story, really. We didn't want it to get around at the time, but we were facing a serious takeover bid from a competitor and Pandora's stock gave us the edge."

"I see. But why buy the company?"

"That was the deal. Watkins had us over a barrel and he knew it. His price for the stocks was that we buy the whole company and give him a five-year contract as president. Either that, or he would sell to the competition."

"All or nothing."

"Right. It's a rather silly way to do business on the face of it, but we had to have that stock." He dropped his hands, folding them calmly in his lap before the slight paunch that pressed at his belt.

"How many people does Pandora employ?"

"Twelve, I believe. I must beg ignorance as to the inner workings of the firm. It's not one of our major holdings."

"But does the company actually do anything? I mean, was it simply a shell to hold a bunch of stock certificates, or does it do business?"

"Yes, it exports heavy machinery. Pandora acts as a brokerage house, locating equipment for overseas buyers and arranging for purchase and shipment abroad. They do have some timberland south of here, too," he added. "We're always looking for land to increase our pulp timber stands."

"But Pandora was purchased by a chemical company. Why was that?"

"Economics," he said. "We wanted to keep our vulnerability quiet until the deal was closed, Miss Morgan. It wouldn't do for us to fend off one vulture only to alert a whole flock to our struggles. North Chemical will lease the timberland to Washington Lumber for logging, if it proves to be feasible."

"What about Pandora? Are you going to develop it into a going concern?"

"No, we'll phase it out of operation. I have no real need of an exporting company of that nature."

"Weren't there plans to use Pandora as a holding company?"

"No. It was just a stock deal."

"Where is the land Pandora owned?"

"There are several acres east of Ashford between the Puyallup and Nisqually rivers."

"So your plan is to liquidate Pandora Exporting?"

"Yes. I believe their last contract was to buy earth-moving equipment from Northland Construction and Demolition and ship it to the Philippines. The deal fell through, however, and it took quite a while to unload it."

"Does Pandora have any use for concrete or a fuel tanker?"

"Not that I know of, though I believe there was a fuel tank truck included in the used equipment they obtained for shipment."

"None of this sounds very suspicious the way you've explained it, Mr. Schofield."

"It's not suspicious, at all." He spread his hands out in a gesture of all-inclusive openness. "So why would you want to devote a newspaper article to it?"

She paused for a moment, studying his open features before forming her response. Should she stick with tact or just lay her cards on the table? What would her father have done? That was easy—he'd have gone straight ahead and gotten the information in the most direct way possible. And unless she'd misjudged the man before her, it was the best method here, too.

"The article isn't directly about your purchase of the company, sir," she explained. "It's just part of a larger question we're looking into. One of our reporters, Bruce Quinlan, was killed on the docks last week. And he was investigating Pandora Exporting, Mr. Watkins and a Mr. Carbellino, who sold Pandora to Watkins, at the time of his murder. He didn't leave many notes about the story he was working on but since we suspect that his story is connected to his death I felt it was important that we do all we could to follow up on it."

"Do you honestly suspect someone connected with Pandora to be responsible for the man's death?" Schofield's smile faded entirely, concern darkening his features.

"We've tried not to form any solid opinion, but the possibility hasn't been ruled out yet. What do you think?"

"Me?" The question seemed to have caught him off guard, and he lost his even composure to obvious surprise and confusion. "I don't know Mr. Watkins very well," he said thoughtfully. "And I know nothing of his employees, so I couldn't begin to hazard a guess."

"And you don't want to defend them, either?"

"I don't know that they need my defense, Miss Morgan. And, for that matter, I would never defend a murderer in any way. If I knew that any of my company employees was connected to something like that, I would be the first to call for the police."

"Then it might interest you to know that the FBI also suspects someone at Pandora with complicity in the death." Rachel wasn't entirely certain why she told him, but she believed him when he said he had no knowledge of any wrongdoing at the Pandora Company. "They are looking into the possibility of a foreign government being involved."

"That's absurd." He smiled again, but not as openly as before. "But I suppose they've had stranger notions over the years."

"They're just playing it safe, I think." Rachel put her notebook away and relaxed in her chair. "What about Mr. Watkins's connection to Pascal Semiconductor?"

"I didn't realize that there was a connection."

"Yes. About two years ago he was hired as a consultant to help the company trim its costs."

"Two years?" He smiled thoughtfully. "Pascal is another recent acquisition, Ms Morgan. It was having financial difficulties and we purchased the company rather than have it relocate overseas. I would assume that hiring Mr. Watkins was the old management's last-ditch effort to bring their costs into line. I'll grant you, however, that it strikes me as odd that Calvin would have moved from financial consultant of one company we purchased to that of owner of another."

"Odd? But not criminal?" The man was comfortable to talk to, and it was easy to pose difficult questions to him.

"I couldn't say that it's criminal." He took a pen from his desk set and wrote a quick note on a small pad. "But I'll check into the matter. Off the record, I don't have much use for Mr. Watkins. He's a hard man to deal with. Though I can't see where Mr. Watkins could have profited unduly by his actions, you've made me curious."

"Can I call to see what you find out?"

"Certainly." He smiled. "I won't be able to ask Calvin himself, however, because he's just left on a business trip. He'll be back on Friday, but if I come up with something before then I'll have my secretary call you at the paper. All right?"

"That would be fine, sir. More than I expected, in fact." Rachel returned his open smile. "You've been very helpful."

"I'm glad to help. So, is the FBI looking for spies?"

"I couldn't really say, sir. But the facts seem to point that way." Rachel switched off the tape recorder and tucked it away in her purse. "Well, thank you again for your time, Mr. Schofield. I hope I haven't kept you away from your work too long."

"Not at all." He stood with her, coming around the desk to escort her to the door. "I've gotten to the point in my career where I welcome distractions. The place really runs itself by now, anyway."

"May I quote you on that?" she asked, smiling, as she stood.

"You'd probably better not. I've got too many vice presidents sniffing at my job and I'd rather not encourage them." He took her elbow lightly, walking to the door. "So, was the interview worth stealing from your Mr. Kirby?"

"Oh, yes, entirely worth it. But then I've got a personal stake in the matter."

"Really? What is that?" He paused with his hand on the knob, as he regarded her with friendly interest.

"I'm a pilot," she said, watching him closely. "And the day after Bruce Quinlan was murdered, someone sabotaged my airplane. My house was also ransacked."

"My God!" he exclaimed. "That's terrible! And you believe that the same people who presumably silenced your reporter are trying to do the same to you?"

"That's what the police think. But I have no idea what they think I might know." She looked at him with a wry smile. It was clear that the man wasn't feigning his surprise about her news. "Good afternoon, sir." She extend her hand.

"Good day, Miss Morgan." He shook her hand heartily. "And, please, if there's anything I can do feel free to call on me personally."

"I'll do that."

"Good," he said, as he opened the door. "And take care of yourself."

"I will, sir."

WHEN SHE RETURNED to the newspaper at five-thirty, Rachel took some time to read over Scott's background article about the upcoming maneuvers. Given the tactics he'd already employed, she wanted to check the final version before they went to press.

She needn't have worried. It was pretty much as he'd predicted, a rather trivial listing of the small fleet of ships that had gathered off the coast in support of the Nimitz-class aircraft carrier, *Eisenhower*. Incidental to this was the information that two of Washington's native sons were assigned to the *Eisenhower* as pilots. Captains Dale Medvid, of Spokane, and Zachary Parker, from Seattle, were named as possible participants in the maneuvers.

The paper that week was another example of the *Banner*'s solid and satisfying reporting, but in the light of their current investigation it struck Rachel as being somewhat boring. There had to be something more to life than just reporting other people's plans and problems and selling classified ads.

"You about done for the day?" Frank dropped into a chair beside the desk and looked at her with concern.

"Yes. You were right about that takeover attempt." Rachel patted his arm affectionately. "Good reporting."

"I'm no reporter," he scoffed. "I'm just an old printer who's been around long enough to have a few contacts of his own."

"No matter, it was good solid information. It helped quite a bit."

He scowled in rebuttal of the compliment as he studied her face with fatherly concern. "Do you mind another bit of help in a slightly different area?"

"Not at all."

"From what Naomi tells me, you and that policeman have begun to see eye to eye on things," he said, somewhat haltingly. "He seems like a nice young man, but you might be headed for trouble with him."

"How so?"

"He's a cop. Now I know that cops and reporters sometimes get along real well. They joke with each other and drink together and put on a good show of being buddies. But I don't know any cops and reporters that date each other, nor any who would. You know what I mean? The jobs don't mix, honey, because neither one can afford to get into a situation where he trusts the other completely. They can't afford to share secrets. You know what I mean?"

"Yes I do, Frank, and I appreciate the advice." The sight of him giving her his embarrassed counsel filled Rachel with such love and admiration that she couldn't help but smile. Her father would have told her the same thing, just as she'd been telling it to herself all along. "Naomi may be exaggerating a bit," she said. "I wouldn't say she's entirely wrong, just a bit ahead of the story."

"Yeah, I figured she was reading more into it than was there, but she's not a gossip and she's not stupid. I figured maybe I should say something now before you get hurt."

"I'll take your advice to heart, Frank. But I'll have to just let things run their course and see how it comes out. Okay?"

"That's fine, honey." Frank stood, clearing his throat abruptly. "I just don't want to see you hurt. Now you go home and get some rest. And keep an eye out. We don't want to lose you."

"You won't. Good night."

Feeling tired by a long, seemingly pointless day, Rachel locked up the office and got into her battered old car. No matter what Frank might think, dinner with Jake would bring a refreshing change and the possibility of a new beginning. In the face of all uncertainties, the possibility of lasting love was the most exciting thing that life could possibly offer.

The traffic on Dash Point Road wasn't very heavy for a Monday evening, and Rachel found herself driving faster than usual in her haste to get home and dress for the evening. She slowed the car down, with a smile, preferring to arrive in one piece rather than five minutes earlier.

The gray Ford sedan behind her, however, wasn't willing to drive more slowly and it moved out to pass as soon as she slowed down, only to pull back as a car approached from the other direction. Once the road was clear, the sedan pulled out and accelerated rapidly, pulling abreast of her worn old station wagon. But, instead of continuing to speed on past her, the sedan swerved suddenly, slamming against the side of her car with enough force to bounce her toward the stand of pines beside the twisting road.

Too alarmed to cry out, Rachel hit the brakes and twisted the wheel. The sedan slipped ahead but swerved again in time to clip her front bumper, sending her into a spin toward the edge of the road again. Rachel fought the spin, turning the wheel and pumping lightly on the brakes to the sound of the harsh squeal of tires on the pavement. When the car stopped sliding with a convulsive jerk, she fell forward against her shoulder harness and then backward as the car bounded forward again.

The gray sedan had circled around and was approaching with increasing momentum. Rachel hit the brakes, freezing momentarily as she watched the car bearing down on her. Then instinct took over and she jammed the gas pedal to the floor and lurched to meet the speeding car like a knight at a joust. She passed within inches of the other car and sped on down the road toward the safety of home. But her older vehicle was no match for the sedan, and it caught up with her after the first curve, taking advantage of its maneuverability to nose up past her left side.

Rachel stared straight ahead, concentrating on the road as she gripped the wheel with a force that knotted the muscles in her shoulders. She didn't dare look at the car that was gaining position beside her, couldn't bear to watch it move up for the final slam that would send her flying off into the fir trees waiting down the slope to her right. A left curve was coming up, and Rachel braced herself for the impact of metal on metal that was sure to come.

She hit her brakes just before the curve, but it was too late. The sedan hit her car just behind the driver's door, and she skidded across the narrow shoulder to hit the ridge of dirt. The car nearly flipped over as it bounced up and descended the thirty degree slope, to slam into a Douglas fir with a final, bone-jarring jolt. She was thrown against the restraint of the harness.

The world seemed to waver for a moment, shivering against the blue haze that floated past her eyes. Her left shoulder ached horribly, and her fingers were cramped from the strain of gripping the wheel as she took stock of her situation. Though she'd been traveling about forty miles an hour when she left the road, it seemed as though she'd emerged from the ordeal largely unscathed.

Or, had she?

Sudden terror gripped her as she jabbed at the seat belt release and frantically threw the door open, falling into the coarse grass covering the slope. It seemed like hours since her car had left the road, but they hadn't appeared at the top of the hill yet, hadn't come to finish their work. Maybe she still had time to escape into the woods.

Tires squealed above her, and a car door slammed. She took enough time to spot the bulky figure of a man in a dark sport coat appear over the rise and start down before turning and stumbling into the stand of trees. Then there was another sound, like the tires of another car screeching to a halt, and someone shouting out a command. Rachel turned her head, slipping down on one hip on the damp hillside, and she saw the man above her scramble back to the roadway. There were two popping sounds, and the roar of a car leaping away. Then, there was the sound of footsteps in the gravel at the side of the road.

Chapter Ten

Jake was almost to the *Banner* office when he saw Rachel's car slipping out of the lot and into the heavy evening traffic. He honked, but couldn't catch her attention, so he joined the flow of traffic behind her. A gray sedan ran a red light to stay behind Rachel at the next intersection, and Jake craned his neck to see around the cars between him and the cross street as they drove away. "Damn," he said, aloud, his hands tensing on the wheel as nervous anticipation grew like a current of electricity humming through his body. Finally, the light changed and he followed as quickly as traffic would allow.

He'd lost sight of them, and had almost given up hope as he sped along Dash Point Road, only to come to a screeching halt when he'd rounded a turn. He saw the gray car parked at the roadside, a man just beginning to descend the bank beside the unmistakable track left by a car skidding off the road. Jake was out of the car before it had stopped completely, drawing his gun.

"Hold it there!" he shouted at the man, raising his gun to fire.

The other man turned and ran up to the waiting sedan, throwing himself into the open door even as Jake fired twice at the vehicle. The car roared away, and Jake didn't hesitate to run toward the break in the grass and start down.

He ran propelled by a vision of her mangled body lying in the wreckage of her car. Driven by fear that the worst had come to pass and that the headstrong reporter was gone from his life, he raced on.

"Rachel!" he shouted urgently. He spotted the vehicle. Thank God, it was still upright. There was still hope. "Rachel!"

"I'm here!" And then she was scrambling up from behind a cluster of bushes, climbing the slope toward him. "I'm all right!"

He discarded the gun that refused to fit back into his holster as he ran to her, throwing it and his policeman's sense of propriety away as he reached her and embraced her.

"I just missed you at the paper," he said breathlessly. "I saw you drive away. They picked you up downtown, but I got caught in traffic and couldn't catch up in time. Oh God, Rachel, I thought for sure I'd blown it. It was so close!"

Rachel huddled within his arms, shivering from shock and fear and utterly unable to say anything for a moment. All she could do was hold herself against him and thank God he was there.

"I'm all right," she said at last. "I'm all right now."

"This is it." Jake's breath was hot against the hair on top of her head when he spoke. "I'm not letting you out of my sight again. Never, never letting you out of my sight. I almost lost you." He pressed his lips hard against the crown of her head as he tightened his arms around her and stood rocking slightly in the tall brown grasses at the foot of the hill. "I just can't face the thought of losing you."

And Rachel felt secure in his arms and secure in the feeling that her enemies weren't the only ones playing for keeps.

Everything would be all right. They could beat them together.

SO MANY QUESTIONS. Uniformed policemen with notebooks and measuring tapes and cameras and impatient but understanding eyes swarmed around her with questions. They wrote down their notes and measurements at the roadside and continued their repetitious array of questions at her home upon the arrival of the detectives from both the police and FBI. Who, what, when, where, why and how—they were the same crucial questions all good reporters learned to ask, except this time Rachel was on the receiving end. And no matter how well-intentioned the questioner was, it was an aggravating, frustrating experience to attempt to answer them when she was still so much in the dark herself. With Jake in attendance to act as a buffer, however, things went more smoothly, and finally—over two hours after Jake first called on the police radio in his car—the official legions departed, leaving them alone.

Her car remained where it had come to rest against the fir tree. It would remain well concealed by darkness till morning, when a tow truck would be dispatched to retrieve it. So with their plans for the evening necessarily aborted, Jake established his protective presence in the house by going to make coffee while Rachel retreated gratefully to the shower upstairs.

When she came down, dressed in a comfortable cotton blouse and jeans, Jake brought the coffee out on a tray. "I would imagine that secretly you're a little bit pleased about your near-miss out there," he told her, pouring a cup of steaming liquid. He'd retreated a bit from his burst of worried affection on the hillside, but still retained an affectionate gleam in his eyes. "After all, when the dust has settled down you'll be able to set Tacoma on its ear with the account of your experiences."

"Is your opinion of the press so low that you think we like getting run off the road if it makes the story spicier?" Rachel fought against the annoyance that leaped within her at his teasing words. It was just a joke, after all, but the basic view the joke expressed annoyed her and emphasized Frank's earlier words.

"I don't mean to suggest that it was fun, but come on," he said, his laughing eyes studying her face with close attention. "It won't hurt will it? You can admit it."

"No, it won't hurt the story a bit." She took a deep breath, smiling up at him from the couch as he handed her a cup. "But it doesn't help anything, either. At this point it doesn't look like we'll ever know what's going on here."

"Come on now." Jake sat beside her, inches away. "As much as I'd like you to stay out of trouble, I don't want to hear you lose your positive attitude. I'll admit that we don't have anything that will stand up in court yet, but look at the progress we've made. We've already found Calvin Watkins's connection to known criminals and to Bruce's death. I'd say that ties it all into a nice, manageable bundle."

"Bundle of what? That's the question. I mean, have we picked up a nest of spies or just ordinary mobsters? Or are we barking up the wrong tree entirely?"

"It would be one hell of a coincidence if the two breakins, two murders and three attempts on your life are totally unrelated," he said, laughing.

"Have you proved that Chuck DeWitt's death was murder?"

"Yes, ma'am, we have," Jake told her, beaming. "Coroner's report indicated that he was killed by a blow delivered to the back of the head. The theory is that he was placed in the bed unconscious and a lit cigarette was dropped on the sheets beside him. Besides, the room went up too fast not to have had some help. The evidence seems to point to gasoline."

"Well, I can't argue with that," she said, placing her cup on the table before them. "It all fits together, and all we're lacking is the name of the glue."

"We may have help on that soon, too." Jake turned toward her on the couch, unconsciously shifting one leg up till his knee almost touched her leg. "Our vice boys busted Jerry Barker, DeWitt's bookie, last week. It was through some of the papers that were seized then that we linked the mechanic to Barker and Barker to Carbellino. Now, if gambling debts were what tied them all together, it's possible that there are other players listed in his betting slips as well. I've been going through the papers today and I'll finish it up tomorrow."

"I got a few crumbs of information from Schofield this afternoon." Rachel stared into his eyes as she spoke, exploring their intelligent depths. It was hard to concentrate on the facts of the investigation when those eyes promised such excitement.

"What did you find out?" he asked, breaking eye contact shyly—as though he'd caught himself staring at her.

"They bought Pandora because it owned a block of Schofield stock, and he needed it to fend off a takeover attempt."

"I hadn't heard anything about Schofield being threatened by a takeover bid," Jake said. "I thought it was in good shape, financially."

"It is, as far as I know. Most forced mergers don't get any publicity until they're complete. Anyway, Calvin's price for the stock was that they buy the whole company and keep him on as president for five years."

"And they agreed?"

"Apparently it was worth the price." Rachel spoke slowly, smiling into those knowing eyes as she let her own eyes wander over the strong terrain of his face. "They got some timberland in the deal, too, but only a small parcel. I also found out that Schofield had no idea that Watkins had a previous connection to Pascal Semiconductor. He said he'd look into it. Only time will tell whether he checks it out or not."

She felt like it was another woman telling the detective about her afternoon's activity, a woman whose ability to think of facts and figures hadn't deserted her in the face of the man's enchanting aura. She might have passed by Jake Connors innumerable times on visits to the police station, might even have spoken briefly to him at some time and, distracted by her work, not paid attention. But when he entered her life in such an absolute manner, coming to occupy the comprehensive role of protector, confessor and friend, she was able to actually see him. She wanted to see more. It wasn't that she felt she needed his protection or his collaboration. She just wanted him near, involved in her life. How far? She wasn't sure of that yet. For now she'd be content to know that she had a chance to be with this man, to know more about him, to know her own desires. And if the fates were otherwise cruel, they were at least allowing her this chance.

"So you believe Schofield is innocent?" He had moved closer as she spoke, as though he was as irresistibly drawn to her as she to him. He made no overt move to act on those emotions.

"Yes, I'm sure of it. If you could have seen his face, you'd be sure, too."

"Good." He smiled broadly, and the full-blooded glow of sunset gave his face a handsome, tempting hue. "We don't need any more complications than we've got."

It felt good to be with him, warm, cozy and safe. It was as though they'd known each other for a long time, old friends who suddenly found themselves feeling an attraction far beyond friendship. A tingle of heightened anticipation surged within her, a longing for their relationship to live up to her inner wishes. He managed to relax and excite her simultaneously, creating a delicious blend of vibrant emotions that flowed through her senses. A conversation with Jake Connors was like a taste of chocolate that leaves you wanting more.

"I hope you realize that I'm not going to leave you alone tonight," he said softly. His hand slipped along the back of the couch to come within a tantalizing distance from her shoulder. "They won't get any other chances at you."

"Good." Rachel moved her own hand to take up his nervously, clasping his fingers tight. "There is a time and place for independence, and I don't think it's anything to be desired when you've got people gunning for you."

"You aren't going to put up a fight?" His eyes widened in mock surprise as he returned the pressure of her hand. "I didn't expect you to cotton to the idea of having some stranger sleeping on your couch."

"You're not exactly a stranger, Jake."

"I . . . I don't want to be," was his hesitant reply.

"Good." She moved slightly toward him.

"Rachel?" he said, smoothing her hair back with one strong hand. "Have I told you that I think you're one hell of a woman?"

"Not in so many words," she replied, enjoying the sudden rush of blood that surged through her head.

"You are, you know. And I'd love to get to know you better."

"I'd like that," she whispered. "I'm beginning to feel at home with you, and it's a feeling I don't want to lose." She pushed back to look at him as she spoke, trying to gauge the feeling in his eyes.

"I hope so." He spoke in a deep murmur.

"It's a rather cool evening," he said against her neck. "How would you like to spend it sitting before a nice warm fire with one of your friendly neighborhood policemen?"

"I'd love to." Rachel slid back slightly. "And I've got a bottle of wine downstairs someplace, too. It's just aching for an occasion worthy of opening it."

"It feels like a good occasion to me," he said. "I see you've got wood in here, already. I'll start the fire while you find the wine."

Rachel stood rather reluctantly, taking the tray with the coffee to the kitchen before going down for the bottle of rosé in the pantry. When she came back, he'd already lit a small pile of kindling in the grate. In only moments, they had a roaring fire adding its heat to theirs, and Rachel poured the wine.

"I'll bet you know all about me," she said, settling on the couch with her wine. Jake joined her there. "But I haven't gotten much beyond name, rank and serial number with you. It's only fair that you tell me something about yourself. Are you a local boy?"

"No. I was born in Philadelphia. My father is a lawyer."

"Large family?"

"Medium. I have two brothers and a sister."

"I'd often thought it would be fun to have a brother or sister," Rachel admitted. "I used to ask Santa Claus for a baby sister at Christmas."

"That's funny. I used to wish he'd take my brother, William, away with him." Jake laughed.

"Didn't you get along with your brother?" This was the Jake Connors she wanted to get to know. "I'd always imagined endless days of play."

"You can't go by my brother. He just didn't like me, and the feeling became mutual. I guess he didn't enjoy having a rival for father's time. We still don't get along."

"That's too bad. What about the rest of the family?"

"They hate William, too." Then he grinned and shook his head, squeezing her closer to him. "No, that's too strong a word. It's just that, well, Bill grew up to be about the shiftiest corporate lawyer our family has yet produced, and we've produced a long line of shifty lawyers."

"Come on, now, that's your family you're talking about!" The closeness of her family relationship didn't prepare Rachel for anyone who felt different. "Tell the truth."

"Truth? Let's see, my old man, William Sr., is the elder statesman at the firm of Connors, Connors, Goldblum and Harris. My older brother, William Jr., is the second Connors on the shingle. Then comes my dear sister, Caroline Honoria Connors Harris, whose husband is the Harris tacked onto the end of the firm. My younger brother, Miles Prescott Stevenson Connors, is currently attending Princeton. He's known affectionately as Skip. I'm afraid he's doomed to add his name to the firm, too, but for the time being he's majoring in sailing. Him, I like," he added with a wink.

"So that's where you got the Princeton sweatshirt. I hadn't pictured you as an Ivy League man," she told him.

"Is that good or bad?" He raised the brow over one amused, blue eye as she watched the fire.

"I don't know yet. How did you manage to fall out of the family tree? Shouldn't you be Connors number three on the letterhead?" Rachel lifted her glass and sipped some wine.

"I had better things to do," he told her. "I just didn't get into college fast enough for my deferment, so I got drafted into the army and did some time in Vietnam right at the end of the war. The old man was livid when I turned down his offer to get me out of the obligation. I figured that if I was dumb enough to get caught in the draft, I might as well take my medicine. After the war, I took my tuition money and attended Pennsylvania State as a law enforcement major. I had the feeling that I could do more good as a cop than a lawyer. Besides, I never did look good in a suit. It was at this point that William Sr. stopped talking to me. When I attended the police academy, he started telling his friends I'd died in the war. I joined the force, and that's about all there is to it."

"Why did you decide to come west?"

"I came out here because, well, because it wasn't Philadelphia, I guess." He spoke haltingly about his police service, his brow narrowing. "I was on the force there for a couple of years, but I started to get the itch to move along. I'd been through this area a couple times, and I liked it. Once I'd been out here a couple years, it became quite natural to call Tacoma home."

"Did you and your father ever get back together?"

"Yes. I think what annoyed him the most was that I never rose above corporal in the army. He could have accepted a career soldier, but he has no room for slackers at anything. My father is the result of too many years with too much money. He likes to brag about our ancestors fighting in the Revolutionary War, though I wouldn't doubt they bought their way out of that, too. Once he realized that I was serious about being a cop, he came around. He respects people who can make a commitment to something."

"He was just like any father worried that his children won't amount to anything," Rachel told him. "I'm glad to hear that you're back on speaking terms."

"Oh, yes, we get along remarkably well these days," he said, with a small chuckle.

"So, what do you do for fun, Jake? Or is following young women in your car your only hobby?"

"I hate to be a wet blanket, Rachel, but I've heard about Jake Connors before," he said, reaching over and squeezing her hand warmly. He spoke low. "He's rather a dull guy, once you get to know him."

"I hope you'll let me be the judge of that," she replied, snuggling in closer to him. He wrapped an arm around her shoulder. "He seems to have a few good points to him."

"Well now, if you think that, then I must be doing something right," he said, softly caressing her with the baritone purr of his voice.

They sat for a long time without speaking, each content merely to be close to the other. But the desire that flowed through Rachel as she sat within the strong arc of his arm far outshone the fire for heat. She couldn't help but look at him, studying the face in repose and trying to read the emotions within him.

His face was alive with the dancing orange of the firelight, softly illuminating the strong lines of his expression. It was such a caring face, seemingly untouched by the troubles that he must carry every day as part of his job.

"How can you stand dealing with things like this mess every day?" She lowered her head to his shoulder, resting her cheek there. "I get so frustrated with this lack of progress that I could almost scream."

Jake put his glass aside to slip both arms around her, kissing her cheek lightly. "I'm about ready to join you in that scream," he said. "And as long as I keep it impersonal it isn't so hard to take. That seems to have changed now."

Rachel felt a thrill at his words. "As long as we're in this together, it'll be fine, Jake." Then she gave up all pretense of carrying on a conversation and found his lips.

"How could we have missed each other this long?" he sighed, drawing back slightly. "I've heard your name many times, but I missed the music in it before. How could I have been so hopelessly tone-deaf?"

"Please, sir, you'll embarrass me with such talk." She spoke softly and laughed at the truth in her jest, for his words inflamed her as much as his kiss.

He smiled, stroking his finger across her cheek, and then made his reply without words. As she took his lips again, her tongue lingered on the edge of the kiss and she held herself against him. His hands worked like magic across her back, driving shivers of excitement to her core. Rachel held him desperately, returning the ardor of his lips while allowing her eager fingers to explore the thatch of his hair. Each touch of his lips and hands increased her desire, her primal need for him, building her throbbing emotions to the point of no return. This man and his influence on the long-dormant passion within her were all that mattered in the world at that moment, and Rachel longed to give in to him completely.

"I want you," Jake murmured, brushing his lips across her throat.

"We're consenting adults, aren't we?" she heard herself telling him. "And there isn't a person in sight to disturb us."

"Right, on both counts." His lips returned to hers and his hand moved lightly to cup one hot breast tenderly, massaging her lovingly. Rachel's breath shuddered out of her in a long sigh as his hand inflamed her already overloaded senses. This was the feeling that she'd been missing. This man was what her life needed.

Jake moved back, his eyes smoldering with emotion. "I...I can't right now, Rachel. I want everything to be right for us. And in a way I'm on duty." Then he pressed his hungry lips against hers, moving abruptly as though breaking free of some restraint. "Let's not rush anything."

"You're right," Rachel said, hoping the firelight would hide the impassioned flush of her cheeks. "We've both had a full day. The sensible thing to do is to get some sleep."

"Absolutely." He stood with forced resolve. "I'm going to camp out on the couch. And in the morning you'll get your chance to see the real me. If you can stand the sight of me after sleeping in my clothes all night, you can probably take anything."

"Don't worry, I'm tough," she said, standing. "There's another bed upstairs, you know."

"No, I'd better stay close to the main points of entry."

"All right, then, kiss me once more," she sighed, slipping her arms around him. "And then I'll get you some bedding."

He obliged happily, locking her in his arms and kissing her as though he might never see her again. Then, with regret-filled slowness, she went about her task.

The fire had burned down to glowing embers by the time she'd helped him put together a makeshift bed. They stood silently for a moment in the fading heat of the fire just holding hands and looking into each other's eyes. Soon, they would be alone with time and their passion together.

"Good night, Rachel," he said softly.

"Good night." And then she turned to go upstairs, unable to trust herself for another moment in his presence.

SLEEP WAS AN ELUSIVE GOAL that night. A car passed on the street, its headlights sweeping across the walls of her bedroom, and Rachel lay listening to the sound of its tires fading. Was Jake awake at that moment to hear it pass? The thought of the man downstairs only drove sleep farther away. It was as though every time she began to drift off her mind rebelled against losing its grip on the memory of their evening together. She bounced from lethargy to heady ex-

hilaration as she lay in her bed watching the blue shadows
of the trees moving on the wall.

All she could remember was his voice, like a cello playing
soft and low, and his eyes, holding her as though they were
afraid she'd disappear if he peered elsewhere. And the
memories flowed like a river, gaining depth and color as she
pondered them.

By two in the morning, when she realized the futility of
trying to sleep, she got up and belted her yellow robe over
the comfortable men's cotton pajamas she habitually wore.
She padded quietly through the silent house, being careful
not to wake him. Rachel was so sure of her surroundings
that she moved without turning on any lights until she
reached the kitchen. Once there, she filled the teakettle with
water and put it on the stove to boil while she busied herself
putting a couple spoons of herbal tea into her mother's tea-
pot. Tea and toast—perhaps with a touch of jam they would
be just what she needed to sleep.

She worked without turning on any lights, moving entirely by the bright glow of moonlight streaming in through
the windows. When the water came to a boil, she removed
the kettle from the heat before it could whistle. Then she
finished preparing her snack and took it back to the breakfast nook at the back of the kitchen, where she could look
out on the moonlit yard.

She didn't hear Jake rise in the living room, didn't hear
him come slowly to the kitchen to stand watching her from
the doorway. He stood for a couple minutes as though
fighting the impulse to join her, his face tight with yearning
for the beautiful woman sitting in the soft blue moonlight.
He turned away from the door for a moment, almost returning to his couch, but then reversed his decision.

"Can't sleep?" he asked abruptly, as he walked toward
her across the kitchen.

Rachel jumped slightly at the sound of his voice, then smiled as he approached self-consciously tucking the tail of his shirt into his jeans. "I was just enjoying the quiet," she said. "I did my best not to waken you."

"Light sleeper. I'd be a pretty lousy guard otherwise," he said. "You aren't in pain, are you?" He stroked her shoulder lightly, his concern written in the lines of his face. "That was a nasty ride you took down the hill."

"No, I'm a little stiff. That's all," she replied, smiling. "Would you like something to eat?"

"No, thank you. I'll just pull up a chair and watch. What's up?" He spoke calmly, but his eyes were narrowed with worry or concern.

"Nothing. I was just a bit hungry and thought I'd come down and enjoy the quiet."

"And now I've come and broken the spell."

"Not at all. It's always more fun to share the quiet with someone. And I'm glad I had the chance to see you with your hair all tousled from sleep."

"Great, there went my macho image," he groaned.

The fact of their being together at all was almost inconceivable, given the circumstances, yet here they were sharing a laugh over the awkward beginnings of their relationship. It seemed so natural, so perfect, that it was sure to grow into something lasting. Fate couldn't be so unkind as to create this feeling within her only to dash her hope to the ground. They had to have been brought together for some reason.

ON THE STREET in front of the house, a black car drove around the block. The three men inside sat in silence as they circled like vultures, waiting, watching. For now, they were kept at bay by the yellow Volvo parked in the driveway of the house on White Fir Drive. The reporter was nothing to them but a target, and she would be dealt with, but they didn't dare kill a cop. Not so close to D-day.

Chapter Eleven

"Nothing," Naomi said on Tuesday morning, her usually cheerful face downcast. "Bruce checked out two economics magazines with articles on the lumbering industry and one about Schofield Enterprises. He didn't check out any other research at all, as far as I could tell. Those articles were dry as dust. Certainly nothing exciting in them."

"That's all right, Naomi." Rachel smiled up from behind her new desk. "It was a long shot, anyway."

"But I did find out something interesting," the woman added, brightening. "Bruce's roommate called late yesterday. Scott wasn't in, so I took the call. The roommate said that the student union contacted him to see if we were going to renew Bruce's locker."

"What?" Rachel sat up in excited surprise.

"That's right, dear. He hadn't told the fellow he roomed with anything about it. He rented it in his name and listed *Banner* personnel for key privileges. I'd say he wanted to be sure we were notified about it if anything happened to him."

"When did he rent the box?"

"Last week. Wednesday. You can get the lockers for most any length of time up to a month. He only rented it for a week, so the rent is due tomorrow. I couldn't look inside the locker because the union was closed when I spoke to his roommate. It opens up at nine-thirty this morning."

Rachel glanced at her watch. Nine-twenty. "Why don't you get into that locker. Bring everything back here."

Naomi stood from her chair. "I'll be back in half an hour."

After she'd gone, Rachel sat back in her chair staring down at the gleaming new surface of her desk. This could be the break they were looking for. Finally, they'd have a solid lead.

Rachel had risen early that morning—barely after six—but she had felt refreshed by her sleep, the past day's experience firmly behind her. She enjoyed a hot, leisurely shower and dressed casually in jeans and a light sweater, then went down to greet the day. Jake was up when she came down after her shower, and the rich smell of coffee filled the kitchen. They made breakfast together, frying eggs and bacon and ignoring the questions that lay before them during the meal, sharing the heady joy of starting the day together.

When they'd finished breakfast, Jake drove Rachel downtown to the newspaper office, where Frank and his printing assistants were preparing the presses to get out that week's issue of the *Banner*. Jake went home to change clothes before returning to the task of looking through the bookie's captured betting slips.

Now Rachel realized that she hadn't given Bruce enough credit, assuming he'd been taken by surprise on the docks. It was obvious now that he was aware of the danger. He'd taken precautions against it. The fact that he only rented the locker for a week showed that he'd planned to alert someone at the paper about the locker before the maneuvers took place. If only he'd come to her, if only they'd been able to protect him in some way. But it was too late for recriminations now. All she could do was try to document the story after he'd done so much to start it.

At nine-thirty, with the presses rolling and the fate of the paper temporarily out of her hands, Rachel's anxious waiting for her reporter's return was disturbed by a call from the FBI.

"What can I do for you, Agent Fowler?" she asked.

"I am calling to say that anything you find in that locker will be regarded as evidence by this office. You'd best be advised to turn it over immediately."

"What locker?" she asked in shock. How did he know anything about the locker in the student union?

"Don't play coy with us, Miss Morgan," he advised, coldly. "I'm making the call as a friendly reminder. You should just give the evidence to me now and avoid trouble."

"If I come across any evidence, I'll give it to the proper authorities," she said. "You needn't remind me of my duty."

"Good. I'll be talking to you later."

Rachel replaced the receiver thoughtfully. The FBI investigation into Bruce's death must be more extensive than they had let on. Bruce must have been onto something very big, indeed.

When Naomi hadn't returned by ten o'clock, Rachel's anxiety soared. She called the student union at the University of Puget Sound and was told that Naomi had come for the locker key shortly after nine-thirty. She should have been back at the paper by now.

Before Rachel could think of where else to call for Naomi, her phone rang.

"Rachel? This is Jake." He sounded coldly official.

"Is something wrong?"

"One of your reporters had an accident downtown a couple minutes ago," he said, tersely. "It relates to our case."

"Was it Naomi? How is she?"

"Yes, and she's all right. Just a fender bender, really. But she said that they robbed her at gunpoint."

"What? Oh, my God, where is she?"

"She's here, at the station, making a full statement."

"I'll be right down."

"Good. See you in a couple of minutes."

Rachel hung up the phone and ran out of her office, grabbing her coat along the way. She pushed open the door to the press room, shouting, "Frank! Can I borrow your car? I've got an errand."

"Sure thing. The keys are in my coat pocket. What's up?" he replied, waving a folded section of newsprint at her.

"I don't know yet. I should be back in an hour or so."

"Okay. We'll hold down the fort."

Rachel got the keys from his coat, which was hanging in his office and rushed out to the car. Events had suddenly accelerated and she felt as though they were about to pull her off into a vast abyss if she couldn't get a hold on them once more.

"IT WAS A GRAY CAR. The right side was all banged up," Naomi said, angrily. "They rammed right into me at the intersection, and before I knew what was happening two big bruisers pulled my door open and shoved a gun in my face. They took the package. I'm sorry, Rachel."

"That's all right." Rachel clasped her hand and smiled across the interrogation table at her. "The main point is that you're safe and sound. We'll worry about the rest later."

"But there was a lot in there about Mr. Watkins."

"Do you remember what it was?" Rachel asked. "Anything?"

"No, I didn't try to memorize the information. I just glanced at it quickly and then shoved it back into the box to take to my car. I should have kept it where it was safe."

"You had no way of knowing anyone would be after you for it. I didn't know, either."

"So how did they know about the locker?" The woman regarded Rachel with cold wonder. "I only found out about it last night and didn't tell anyone till I told you this morning."

"I don't know. But I'm sure going to find out." Rachel stood. "How do you feel? Any bumps or bruises?"

"No, they didn't hit me that hard. But we'd just fixed the transmission, and now we'll have to take it back in for body work."

"The paper will pay for repairs," Rachel said, laughing. "That's the very least of our worries right now. You'd better go back to the office and type up some notes on the incident while it's fresh in your mind. Are you free to leave here?"

"Yes, I gave them my statement."

"All right, then. I'll see you at the office."

Rachel left her and hurried down to Jake's office. He was seated at his desk, just hanging up the phone.

"What is Agent Fowler's exact status down here?" she asked before he could voice a greeting.

"Fowler? Liaison, mostly. Why?"

"He knew about that locker this morning," she said, sitting in a wooden chair before his desk. "Did you know about it?"

"No, it was news to us."

"That's what I thought." Rachel paused, thoughtfully rubbing a finger against her chin. "When you told him about the papers Scott had found, did he act surprised?"

"Not particularly," Jake said. "Should he have?"

"I don't know. Did the information seem new to him?"

"No, come to think of it, he seemed more annoyed than interested. I just assumed that it was his natural disposition."

"I've got a very bad feeling about all of this Jake," Rachel said ominously. "Does the FBI have authority to bug my office?"

"Bug your office? My God, Rachel, you don't seriously suspect them of planting a listening device in a newspaper office, do you? I don't think they'd risk it. The press would have a field day if something like that ever got out."

"That's what I thought, but Agent Fowler knew about that locker. Naomi came to my office at about a quarter after nine to tell me about it, and he called me at nine-thirty to say that I'd better turn over the information to him as soon as I got it. Then about fifteen minutes later Naomi was struck by a gray car and the papers from the locker are stolen from her. She said the car was all banged up on the right side. It was obviously the same car that forced me off the road last night. How else could they have known about them?"

Jake sat for a moment drumming his fingers on his desk top. Then he stood resolutely. "There's only one way to be certain about this. We'll scan your office for electronic equipment."

RACHEL STOOD QUIETLY inside her door watching Jake sweep a long tube attached to the box he held in his hand over her desk top. A pair of slim headphones were clamped over his ears, connecting him to the box.

"So you don't have any idea what was in that locker?" he asked diffidently.

"No, she didn't read it." Rachel had a hard time adopting the same casual tone he was using as he did his work, but she managed to control the rage in her voice. "She just scanned it quickly."

"That's too bad." Finding nothing unusual with the desk, he checked the file cabinets and then moved to the walls themselves. "We can't help you get to the bottom of this without some concrete information."

"I know, and that's what has made me so mad," she told him. "They're always one step ahead of us."

"Something is bound to come up," he said. Then he paused, moving the device back over a section of the molding at the top of the wall. "Once the maneuvers are over, the FBI will open up."

"That will be too late, Jake," she said, with rising excitement. He had moved her desk chair over to the wall and stood on it to look closely up at the juncture of the wall and ceiling. "If they are spies, they'll be gone after the maneuvers."

Jake didn't say anything, but pointed up at the strip of wood along the top of the ceiling. It looked like one end of a section of molding was loose, hanging down a fraction of an inch where it joined a second strip. He got down from the chair carefully, saying, "Don't worry, we'll figure it out somehow. Do you have anything to do here?"

"Not really." She stood looking up at the ceiling as he walked toward the door. "We print today and deliver it tomorrow morning. I've got the next issue to start working on, of course, but I can't write anything till I know what's going on here."

"In that case, we should go rent a car for you."

"Good idea. Let's go." Rachel got her coat and joined him in the hall, closing the door solidly behind her.

"Definitely bugged," he whispered as he took his device apart and replaced it in the nondescript case it was carried in. "And I wouldn't doubt your house is bugged, as well."

"My house!" Rachel was barely able to keep her voice down to a whisper, her rage was so strong.

"Damn right," he whispered urgently. "And this is no FBI bugging job, either. The law requires that local authorities be notified about any federal investigations of that nature."

"My God, Jake, this is terrible."

"Come on," he said, standing quickly. "Let's get a car."

They met Naomi in the parking lot. She was just getting out of her compact car.

"Did you remember anything about the papers?" Rachel asked.

"They mentioned a building in Baker, California," the woman replied. "A hangar at an airport, I believe. Bruce's handwriting wasn't easy to read. I could be wrong about that."

"Anything else?"

"A telephone number. It was area code four one five, but I don't remember the rest."

"Good. You type that much up. There'll be a story in this yet. For the time being, don't talk of this in the office."

"Why ever not?"

"Rachel, let's go," Jake called from his car. "I've got to get back to work."

"I'll tell you later. Bye." Rachel hurried over to Jake's Volvo as Naomi strolled into the *Banner* offices.

"There's no sense giving them too much to talk about by telling them about the bug." He regarded her thoughtfully, the morning sun giving his face a rugged, ominous cast.

"For the time being," he said, "don't talk about it in my car, either."

"Your— Okay, let's get a new car for me." Rachel opened the door and got into the vehicle carefully, as though afraid it would swallow her up if she did anything too quickly. It was an unsettling feeling to realize that there was nowhere safe to talk. Not her home, not even a policeman's car.

It wasn't until they were driving the new Nissan sedan she'd taken a week's lease on that he opened up.

"It seems that the visit to your offices last week served a dual purpose," he said grimly. "They searched for past information, and also planted those devices."

"And they must have done the same in my home."

"I would assume so." He sat tensely beside her as she drove the car through the downtown traffic. "I don't think there's much point in checking your house for bugs. We can just count on their being there for now. I don't want to do anything that would alert them."

"Do you think we're being watched?"

"We'll just have to assume that, too."

"So what can we do?"

"It's going to be tough to do anything," he admitted. "I want to find out about the building in Baker, but anything I do officially will be reported to the FBI, and Fowler is obviously implicated in this whole mess. The next logical step would be for me to subpoena Watkins's telephone records, but that would take time. Fowler'd also be alerted. I don't suppose that you've got any contact in the phone company?"

"I might have," Rachel said, smiling. "But I assume that you, as a policeman, realize it's illegal to obtain information without a court order."

"Yeah, I know all about that." Jake grinned warmly. "But we need to find out if Calvin called a number in area code four fifteen, and I can't go through channels."

"Where is that area code?"

"San Francisco."

"Okay, I'll take you back to your car, and then I'll get in touch with some people who might give us some help. One of my friends from college works for the *L.A. Times*, and she might be able to dig up some information for us. And I might be able to get that telephone information, too."

"Great. If it proves helpful I can go through regular channels to get it stamped legal so it will stand up in court, but for now our priority is to move fast and quietly."

"What are you going to do this morning?"

"I'm going to find out if I'm being tailed or not, and then I'll see if I can put a tail on Fowler."

"What about those betting slips?"

"Fowler's been through them. There's probably nothing left."

"Damn," Rachel exclaimed. "Well, I suppose that can't be helped now. Take care of yourself, okay?" She steered the car back to the rental lot and stopped behind his car at the curb.

"Don't worry about me, Rachel. You just be damn careful not to get caught alone anywhere. You'll be safe as long as you're in a crowd. They don't dare try anything then. We've got to assume they're following you."

"I'll be careful. I'll pick you up for lunch," she said.

"Good. See you then." He started to get out but stopped, leaning over to kiss her cheek quickly. "Be very careful." Then he got out of the car and hurried up to his own vehicle.

The feeling of his lips on her cheek lingered, a spot of warmth growing to a blush as she savored the tingling sensation his lips left. Rachel drove to her lawyer's office with elation pushing her concerns into a corner for a moment.

"Is Len in?" Rachel asked, striding into the law offices.

"Good morning, Rachel. No, he's in court," the woman replied. "Can I help you?"

"Yes, you can. I need a safe telephone to make a couple of calls, and this is the only place I could think of offhand."

"A safe telephone? What's going on?"

"You'll read about it in the *Banner* next week, Judy. Do you think he'd mind if I used his phone?"

"Probably not. Go on in."

"Good. I've got one long-distance call to make, so I'll reimburse him when the bill comes."

"Oh, I think the paper's retainer is large enough to cover a couple of calls," the woman said. "But no snooping in his files."

"I promise." Rachel laughed, crossing to the inner office.

She sat behind the large mahogany desk and picked up the receiver of the telephone, dialing quickly.

"Wanda Clemens, please," she said, when she reached the switchboard at the telephone company. After waiting a moment, she said, "Hello, Wanda? This is Rachel Morgan. I've got a big nasty favor to ask of you, but I promise to return it someday. I need to know if a customer named Calvin Watkins ever called anyone in the San Francisco area. Yes, I need the numbers. No, that's all I need, just the numbers. I promise that not a word will be said about this. Okay, that's great. Yes, you can call me back." She gave the woman the lawyer's number and dialed again.

"*Tribune*?" she asked. "Connect me with the city room, please. Connie Wilson, please." She waited a long moment, drumming her fingers on the desk impatiently.

"Hello? No, I can't leave a message. I don't know where she can reach me. I'll try later, thank you."

She hung up the phone in frustration. Her friend was out, closing off that avenue of investigation. On a whim, she dialed another number.

"Is Mr. Schofield in, please?" she said, calmly. "This is Rachel Morgan."

"Miss Morgan." Schofield's voice came on the line. "What can I do for you?"

"I've gotten some new information, Mr. Schofield, and I don't have anyone to help me with it but you. That is, if your offer to help was genuine."

"It most certainly was," he said in a friendly tone. "I haven't been able to check with Mr. Watkins about his work with Pascal yet. But I assure you that if anyone associated with any of my companies is involved in illegal activities I want to know about it. And I certainly want him stopped."

"Good, because something else has happened," she said, urgently. "I've recently discovered that my office has been bugged, Mr. Schofield. I can't really go into details, but things point to Calvin Watkins as a culprit."

"Bugged? I find it hard to believe he'd be involved with something like that," the businessman said.

"My information is pretty reliable. But the point is that you might like to know as much about it as possible, yourself. So, it could be in your own best interests to check this out."

"Yes, it could very well be. What would you like me to do?"

"I want to know about the building in Baker, California, that North Chemical purchased from Death Valley Aviation. What is it, and what are they using it for? Also, I want to know who works for Pandora Exporting. You've surely got their employee records on file somewhere."

"I can certainly check into that," he said. "As for the building, it's a hangar at the airfield down there. We bought that property to service company aircraft when we're in the area."

"I wouldn't think you'd take many business trips to the desert. Who'd suggest purchasing the building?"

"I believe that Mr. Watkins did, but he had sound reasons. And the property also serves as a tax write-off."

"I see," she said, smiling. "So nothing in business has a single purpose, does it?"

"No, we've got to do everything we can to make a buck," he said, laughing. "Is there anything else?"

"Does Pandora have any business dealings in San Francisco?"

"Not that I know of."

"Well, I think he's—just a second, I'm going to put you on hold." The other line had begun blinking on the telephone, and Rachel switched on the intercom to ask, "Is the call for me, Judy?"

"Yes, it is," the secretary answered.

"I'll take it," Rachel said. Then she depressed the button on the phone. "Wanda? Yes, I've got a pad here."

She pulled a notepad over to her and quickly jotted down the two numbers that the other woman gave her. "Thank you, Wanda. Yes, I'll tell you all about it as soon as I can."

Glancing at the blinking light on the line where Schofield was waiting, she dialed the first number on the pad.

"Hello." A male voice answered.

"Is this Alberto's Pizza?" Rachel asked, quickly inventing an explanation for her call.

"No, this is the cultural attaché of the Union of Soviet Socialist Republics," he said. "May we help you?"

"Sorry, wrong number." Rachel hung up quickly. The connection was made, and she punched on the other line.

"Mr. Schofield? I'm sorry to keep you waiting."

"Not at all. I've sent my secretary to get that employment information for you."

"Good, but be very careful that no one knows why you want it. I think we can be fairly certain they aren't listening in at your office, but they might be keeping an eye on you."

"You make all of this sound very melodramatic."

"It is. And I've just found out that Calvin Watkins has called the Soviet embassy in San Francisco three times in the last month. Would he have any reason to call them?"

"The Soviet embassy? Are you certain of that?"

"Yes, sir, I am."

"My God," he said, as though her information had knocked the wind out of him. "Yes, I'll check this out right away."

"Be careful about it," she advised him.

"You can be sure of that, Miss Morgan. How shall I get this employment information to you?"

"I'll stop by to pick it up. It's reasonable enough that I'd stop by for a follow-up to the interview."

"That's fine. I'll be in touch later. Goodbye."

After hanging up, she dialed the second number on her pad.

"Parker residence," a cheerful female voice answered.

"Hello, is your husband home?" Why was that name familiar?

"No, Zack is on maneuvers this week," the woman said. "But he's not my husband."

"No, I should have known that. I'll call next week. Thanks."

Rachel hung up the phone and tore the top slip off the pad on the desk. Then she left the office.

"Thanks for everything, Judy. Tell Len I'll call later."

"What's wrong with your own phone?"

"It's a long story and I don't know the ending yet, I'm afraid. I'll sure fill you in when I know, though. Bye now."

She hurried out of the office and to her car. As she drove away from the curb, she took careful note of the nondescript black car that started its engine two cars back at the curb. It pulled away from the curb and followed as she joined traffic.

There you are, she thought. *You don't know I've spotted you, do you? You have no idea how seriously I've broken your cover. But you will. Soon, you'll know who really has the upper hand.*

Chapter Twelve

The black car followed her all morning, as she tried to go about her business as usual. It followed her back to the paper and then to the university campus, where she searched unsuccessfully for Scott Kirby, and it followed her to Schofield's office. She went in and found a spot in the lobby where she could see the car, waiting to see if anyone emerged to follow her up to the office. When nobody had gotten out after five minutes, she took the elevator up to the corporate offices.

"Mr. Schofield isn't in right now," his secretary explained. "But he left this package for you."

"Did he say when he'd be back?" Rachel asked, taking the thick manila envelope.

"No, he only said to give you this and tell you to call back if you want to know anything else. This must be the biographical data you wanted for your interview," she said, with a knowing smile.

"The—oh, yes. That's all I needed. Thank you very much."

Rachel left the office. Apparently, Schofield had felt compelled to give his secretary a cover story in case there was a bug in his office as well. And it would seem from the secretary's attitude that he'd let her in on the secret. In the elevator, she rolled the envelope and stuffed it into her large purse, emerging into the lobby looking no different than she had upon entering. Then she drove down to the police station to pick up Jake for lunch.

"I've got some people for you to check out," she said over their table in the Cliff House restaurant. They'd taken a quiet booth in the back, shielded by other diners if anyone had followed. "Can you run a check for criminal backgrounds without Agent Fowler knowing about it?"

"Probably. Though a complete check would involve FBI records, I don't see any reason for him to find out. I looked for Fowler this morning, but he hasn't showed up yet."

"Good. Maybe he'll give us some room to operate in." She took the envelope out of her purse and tore it open. "Schofield gave me a list of Pandora's employees. I haven't looked at it yet, but I assume it's complete."

"You're being careful, aren't you?" He clasped her hand protectively within his broad ones and studied her, concerned.

"Yes, I am," she replied. Her heart leaped within her at the contact of his eyes on her face, and she grasped his hand in return, smiling her assurance to those loving eyes. "I'm not about to do anything foolish now."

"Good. I don't want to lose you."

Those words, and the implication of permanence they carried, sent Rachel's pulse soaring. She knew that the commitment in his voice was sincere. This man wanted love to be forever.

But there was work to be done, and Rachel tore herself away from her thoughts to return her attention to the several papers that had been in the envelope, looking them over before handing them to Jake. Each one was a photocopy of the W-4 form filled out by the people working for Pandora.

"I managed to find out about those San Francisco numbers, too," she said with a triumphant smile, as he paged through the forms.

"You did?" He looked up from the papers, smiling broadly. "I don't suppose you got names to go with the numbers, did you?"

"Of course. I called them both, and I think they confirm all our theories." She gave him the slip of paper from her lawyer's office. "The top one is for the Russian embassy in San Francisco, and the second one is the home phone of a certain Zack Parker."

"The Russians. Well, I'll be damned. But who is Parker?"

"The name sounded familiar when I first heard it, but I didn't make the connection till I reread the *Banner* this morning," Rachel said. "Captain Zachary Parker is a navy pilot on the *Eisenhower*. He is most certainly participating in the maneuvers."

"He must be the guy the FBI is looking for."

"But now we don't dare tell them about him in case Fowler's entangled and gets them to abort their plans," Rachel said. "Bruce's killer will then flee."

"I can alert naval intelligence," he said.

"No, they'll ground Parker and that'll serve the same end. Besides, they probably won't be able to find any evidence against him unless he actually tries to carry out the plan."

"You're right," he admitted. "And we don't know what it is, either. Our best course right now could be to say nothing, but keep an eye on them."

"But there must be something else we can do." Rachel's voice was tinged with frustration. They seemed to be so close to some solution, yet they were so far away. And she still had no idea how Bruce Quinlan had stumbled onto any of it.

"Well, we can't do anything to raise suspicions here," Jake said, watching her with a gleam growing in his clear blue eyes. "But I need to get a look at that hangar in Baker."

"What? But Jake, what's the use in going to California?"

"Schofield said they bought the building to give them a place to service company airplanes in California. Right? That explanation just doesn't wash." An ingenious look stole onto the detective's features as he spoke, showing the progression of discovery as the puzzle began to fit together in his mind.

"It may be a bit out of the ordinary," Rachel countered, confused. "But, I'm sure they have a lot of aircraft."

"Yes, but Baker, California, isn't the business capital of the world. How much traveling do you think they do there? A hangar in L.A. would be better suited to their purposes."

"Maybe, but why do you have to look at it in person?"

"Because there's no one else I can trust to look at it. Come on. Quinlan thought that building was important enough to make note of, so it must be tied in. It's just a short trip. We could be back by morning."

"We?"

"We'll have to fly if we want to make it down and back in time," Jake said, taking her hand. "And you're the pilot on this team. Besides, I wouldn't leave you here unprotected."

"What if they see us fly off together? Then they'll know we're onto them. They could call the whole thing off."

"I think they already know that. Remember, we're assuming that your home is bugged. So they know we pretty much agree on how to investigate this case. But they also know that Fowler has us blocked on the FBI side. Just because we're working together doesn't mean anything will come of it.''

"Maybe," she said, thinking with chagrin of all that they would have heard by listening to their conversation the night before. "Yes, I suppose you're right. So, when can we leave?''

"I'll start a search on these names," he said, tapping the papers on the table. "And I should put in a request for a deep background check on Watkins, as well. I'll be on my own after that.''

"Okay, I'll go to the airport after lunch and rent a plane. Meet me at the Tacoma Aviation Systems hangar as soon as you can get away.''

"Are you really a good pilot?" Jake asked, with a sly grin. "Or was that landing the other day pure luck?''

"Just luck," she said, returning his smile. "You'll be lucky if you survive a flight with me.''

"You're the first pilot I've ever heard admit that.''

Spotting a movement from the corner of her eye, she turned to see a short man approaching them through the tables. "Speak of the devil," she said. "Here comes Calvin Watkins.''

Jake casually moved the papers from the tabletop to the seat beside him as he smiled across at Rachel. The business man walked up to their table wearing a friendly smile.

"Miss Morgan?" he asked, extending one hand. "I'm Calvin Watkins. I hear you've been asking about me.''

"Mr. Schofield said you were out of town." Rachel shook his hand lightly, drawing away from the moist grip he offered as if snake-bitten. "I would have come to talk to you, otherwise.''

"My meeting was concluded more quickly than I had planned," he said. "I don't believe I've met your companion.''

"Jake Connors." Jake shook the man's hand as well, eyeing him coldly. "I'm with the police."

"We don't often see the press being so cozy with the police force," the man said, smoothing one hand along the hair oiled back against his skull. His gray eyes had the deadly quality of a shark's eyes, seeming like holes cut in his face. "May I sit down?"

"Sure," Rachel said, and Jake slid over to allow him room on the end of his seat."

"What was it you wanted to know about me?" Watkins spoke in a quietly refined manner, but there was no refinement in the predatory gleam of teeth that passed for a smile.

"Pascal Semiconductor," Rachel said, keeping her eyes on his. "What did you do for them?"

"Bookkeeping." Watkins smiled. "They were operating in a very sloppy manner, and with the worldwide drop in memory chip prices they couldn't compete without drastic revision of their methods."

"You were hired to streamline the operation?"

"Yes, to suggest ways for them to cut their overhead."

"But you were let go after a couple months. Why?"

"I was never hired as a full-time employee," he explained. "My job was merely to suggest the changes, to act as an impartial observer, as it were. Is there something unusual about that?"

"Not that I know of. But it seemed odd that you'd be working for Pascal in that capacity, and then turn up as owner of Pandora Exporting. Especially since both companies have been purchased by Schofield Enterprises."

"That's not really unusual. I had always planned to start a business of my own."

"But you didn't start it. You purchased it from Mr. Carbellino and sold it to North Chemical for a large profit."

"Mr. Schofield wanted the company badly."

"No, he wanted your stock." Rachel gave the man an open, unsuspicious look. "Why did you insist that he purchase the whole company?"

"Simple economics," Watkins replied. "The more you sell, the more you can charge for it."

"It sounds like simple greed, to me," Jake said, appraising him coolly. "And what kind of salary are you pulling down as the head of this company of yours, Calvin?"

"That is between me and the IRS." Watkins smiled slightly. "I don't mind admitting that I'm greedy. I acquired the stock and saw a chance to make a profit on it. How I chose to make that profit is my own concern."

"Why did Mr. Carbellino sell Pandora to you so cheaply?" Rachel asked.

"Mr. Carbellino was in a hurry to divest." Watkins spoke with amusement, his smile seeming genuine for the first time as he glanced at Jake beside him. "But due to the nature of Mr. Carbellino's business, I'd rather not say anything that might increase his current legal difficulties."

"But the charges against him were dropped," Rachel said.

"Of course they were. But you surely realize that the only time the government drops their charges is when they want to go and get more evidence. If he did wrong in selling to me, I don't want anything I say to add to the evidence against him."

"I can see your point on that," Rachel said. "And that does seem to explain the discrepancy between purchase and sales prices. But why did you insist on staying on as company president if Schofield is going to phase it out of operation?"

"They have to have someone to continue operation while closing the books," he explained easily. "I saw no reason why it shouldn't be me."

"And you've kept twelve people on the payroll?"

"We have inventory to move. I can't very well do that without people." Then he glanced away, saying, "But I see that your meal has arrived. I'll leave you to your luncheon."

The waitress approached the table with a tray, standing politely to one side as Watkins stood. "It's been a pleasure speaking to you," he said. "Good day."

"Goodbye. Thank you," Rachel said, watching him walk away.

After the waitress had left them alone with their meal, Jake laughed, saying, "That boy is certainly a piece of work."

"Yes, he's an awfully forthright individual, isn't he?" Rachel agreed, smiling.

"I'll bet the man has a lie for every occasion. Did you look at those employment sheets? I only glanced at them, but it looked like they all said California for home state. He wouldn't have moved any of his employees up to Washington if the company is being phased out, would he?"

"No, I wouldn't think so. You don't suspect Schofield of lying about that, do you?"

"No, but I don't think he's aware of what is going on at Pandora. And I wonder about that timberland."

"Maybe I could do something to check on that before I go to the airport," Rachel suggested.

"Good idea. I don't want to start too many lines of inquiry or Fowler may catch on." Then he paused, looking into her eyes and said, "This is terrible, isn't it? Once you start looking closely at something you find that nothing is what it appears to be on the surface. Pretty soon you can't help but find ulterior motives everywhere. I wonder how long it will take before you see covert meaning in the things I do and say."

"I already have," she smiled. "I see through you, Jake Connors, but I think I like your ulterior motives. In fact, they match my own very closely."

"Do they now?" He took her hand in his soft, warm grip. "Then it shouldn't be too hard to sway your emotions. Pretty soon I'll have you right where we both want to be."

"I hope so," she said with a sigh. "And I hope it's sooner than we think, because the suspense is becoming unbearable."

RACHEL VISITED her lawyer's office again after lunch. Len Simpson was back from court, and admitted her with a curious look in his eyes.

"So, you stopped by to use the phone. Is it anything I should know about?"

"My office has been bugged," she said, sitting. "I needed a phone that wasn't tapped, and it had to be someplace where my visit wouldn't be viewed as unusual. I hope you don't mind."

"I don't mind." He watched her closely. "Are you certain about the listening devices?"

"Yes, completely. But it's under control at the moment. I wanted to know if you could check on some real estate for me," she said. "I could probably do it myself but, as before, I have to go through safe channels to avoid tipping off the wrong people. Could you do it?"

"Anything. What do you need to know?" He took his notepad and waited pen poised above the paper.

"North Chemical owns timber acreage just west of Rainier Park," she said. "It's here in Pierce County, near Ashford, but I don't know the exact location. I need to know where it is, exactly, how much land they own and how much it's worth."

"Where, how much and its worth. Is that all?" The lawyer put his pen down, looking at her expectantly.

"That should be enough. I'll be out of town for the remainder of the day, but I'll stop by first thing tomorrow. Is that too soon?"

"No, that will be fine. I have an investigator on retainer who could take a look at the land in person. Should I call him?"

"Yes, sounds good. If he can have the report by tomorrow morning, that is. Otherwise, it could be too late."

"We'll have it." The lawyer sat back with a conspiratorial smile. "Don't worry about a thing."

"Bill it all to the paper," Rachel said, standing. "And be sure to tell him to be discreet. I don't want to say too much about it, but it is a matter of national security. And, it has a bearing on the death of one of my reporters."

"You're telling me that someone is playing for keeps?"

"Yes, so your man had better keep his guard up."

"I'll pass that along."

"Good. Bye, now."

Rachel left his office in high spirits. It was only too bad she didn't have anyone in southern California whom she could trust. She'd rather not make this trip right now. But it was imperative that they find out why that hangar in Baker was so important, and Jake was right that they would have to do that in person. Besides, she didn't object to having a few hours alone with Jake Connors where there'd be no strangers listening in.

"THE FAA IS FINISHED with their work here, and I've got your plane put back together." Harry Peterson regarded her around the butt of his cigar with careful eyes. "I can have it gassed up and ready to go in an hour."

"I'd rather take a twin-engine today, Harry," she said. "I'm flying to southern California and need a bit more speed."

"We've got a Piper Navajo sitting out there you can use," he said, taking the cigar out of his mouth and using it to gesture toward the runway. "Just sign your life away on the insurance forms and she's yours."

"I'll take it. How soon can it be ready to go?"

"Ten minutes," he said. "So, how are you coming on finding out about your airplane? Any new clues?"

"Just that Chuck DeWitt was a couple thousand dollars in debt to a bookie. Did you know about that?"

"I knew he liked to bet on football, but I wouldn't have picked him for anything beyond a buck or two with the boys. What do you think, somebody bought his paper in exchange for a favor?"

"Bought his paper?" she asked, momentarily perplexed.

"Yeah, paid off his IOUs with his bookie so he'd be in debt to them instead."

"Yes, I guess that's what it looks like. You're not a gambling man, are you, Harry?" she said, grinning at him.

"Not me. I took my only gamble when I got married twenty-two years ago, and when that paid off I figured I wouldn't press my luck. Besides, after you've lived a few years, you realize there's no such thing as fast money."

"That's good to hear," she said. "Not that I didn't trust you before, but a person can never be too careful."

"That's right." He pulled out a couple thick forms with multiple copies and laid them on the cluttered desk. "Now just put your name and destination on these forms and I'll fill in the rest later."

"I'm going to put Portland down as my destination, Harry," she said, taking a pen and filling in the appropriate blanks. "But I'm going to go a bit farther than that. All right?"

"No problem there. You just sign your correct name and everything else is hunky-dory. And, if anybody asks, you went to Portland and took the Navajo because you don't trust your plane."

"Thank you." Rachel gave him the pen. "Could you gas my plane up and have it ready, though? I might need it."

"Will do." He took the forms back and creaked back in the old chair. "I'm keeping it locked up in the hangar for now, but if we get any repairs I'll have to move it out."

"That's fine. I'm sure you're keeping a good eye on it. I'd better go file a flight plan now so I can get going. If Detective Connors comes looking for me, could you have him wait?"

"You're flying with that cop, huh?" He smiled broadly at her. "Well then, I guess this is a pleasure flight."

"Yes, in a manner of speaking, it is," she said, coloring slightly as she walked out of the office.

When Rachel returned from filing her flight plan with the tower, Jake was waiting outside the hangar office. He greeted her with an enthusiastic hug.

"Not only are you the most beautiful woman in the world," he said, holding her close to him. "But you must be one hell of a reporter, as well, because you've got the instincts of a cop. Going after those employee records was a great move. I don't have complete reports back yet, but four of the twelve employees have local criminal records. I don't have the information from the FBI, so I can't say anything about the people who moved up from California, but I'd guess the pattern will hold. If the company had any official policy for rehabilitating convicts, we'd know about it."

"Everything is coming together, Jake. I just know we'll come back from this trip with some of the answers we need."

"We'd better," he said, as he accompanied her back into the office. "Because I'll need something concrete to justify leaving town without authorization. And especially for not letting the FBI or naval intelligence have our information about that pilot."

"They'll have it. I just know we'll come back with definite proof of our claims."

"Right," he agreed. "I don't want to take any chances that might let our murderer get away."

Jake opened the door for her and followed her into the hangar office where Harry Peterson had the keys to the airplane.

"Here you are, little lady," he said, giving her the keys. "She's parked out front. Now you try and put her down more gently than you did your plane the other day."

"I'll try, Harry, but you can never be too certain with us beginning pilots," Rachel told him, laughing.

"Beginning, nothing," the older man snorted. Then he looked at Jake, saying, "Pilots are all the same. Try to wish them luck, and they crack wise. You take care of this lady, boy."

"I intend to, Mr. Peterson. Though the only thing I know about flying is that it's all too easy to come down."

"She doesn't need help with the flying, it's on the ground where she has enemies. I'll see you two tomorrow morning."

"Right, Harry," Rachel called, walking to the door. "Come on, Jake. Daylight's wasting."

As they taxied out to the edge of the runway, Rachel couldn't help but notice that Jake seemed uneasy. The strong, capable man sat rigidly at her side staring straight ahead at the runway.

"Nervous?" she asked, idling the plane.

"Yup." He grinned at her. "To tell the truth, I've never really liked flying. And small planes are worse than airliners."

"There's nothing to worry about," she told him. "In fact, this size plane will coast better in an emergency than one of those big jets. An airliner would drop like a rock if the engines died."

"Great. Now I can be scared of them, too," he laughed. "But it's not the flying that I mind, it's the taking off that ties my stomach in a knot. I can never get used to leaving the ground. I hope you won't hold it against me."

"It's nothing to be ashamed of, Jake. Some of my best friends won't fly with me. Frank Ackerman, for one, is scared to death of flying." Somehow, Jake's fear of flying endeared him to her all the more. A man wasn't a complete person without fear of some kind, and she hadn't seen any sign of fear in the man till now. "I don't suppose you're scared of anything else," she said.

"Well, I'm not overly fond of spiders."

"Snakes," she told him. "I hate snakes."

"Good, now we're even."

"Navajo Zebra Zero Zero Delta Niner," the impersonal voice of the flight controller broke in over the radio. "You are clear for takeoff on runway three. Over."

"Roger, tower. Taking off on runway three." Rachel spoke to Jake as she pressed the throttle forward. "You just hang on and the worst will be over."

Moments later, they were airborne, and Jake released his grip on the edges of his seat with a relieved sigh. "All right, I can breathe again," he laughed.

"Look down there," Rachel said as she turned the airplane south. "My shadow is driving away."

"Going home to report on our departure," Jake commented, watching the black car drive away. "I wonder if they know where we're going."

"I logged a flight plan for Portland," she said. "We'll log a new destination when we reach that city."

"Good. You should know that I had Ron Jarvis, a buddy of mine on the force, run those names for me." Jake looked at her, a confident expression filling his eyes as he watched her fly. "I let him in on most of what we know just to play it safe. I know he's clean. It's probably best that someone on the force knows. After all, we're the only ones in possession of this information."

They flew swiftly toward the south, passing over the heavily wooded areas outside of Tacoma, and Rachel told him about her meeting with her lawyer. After several minutes of flying, Rachel pointed down at the forest below them.

"That piece of land is somewhere down there. I wonder if it has any bearing on the case, at all. I'm probably wasting money on an investigator."

"No, your instincts have been right so far, Rachel," Jake said, peering over at the trees below. "I wouldn't bet against you. Say, what do you think they're doing down there?"

"Where?" Rachel turned the plane slightly to bring the section of ground where Jake was pointing into view. A small, rectangular patch of gray showed through the trees, and it looked like several vehicles were moving across it. "I don't know," she said. "Probably someone clearing land to build a house. There's been a lot of people moving out to the country."

"Looks like pavement," he commented, turning his attention back to the open sky before them. "You know, a guy could get used to flying. Maybe it's all a matter of trusting the pilot."

"Of course you can trust the pilot," she told him, with an impish grin. "I haven't crashed an airplane in nearly four days."

Jake almost joined her in her laughter—almost, but not quite.

Chapter Thirteen

Death Valley lay in purple shadows when they crossed it. The hottest place in North America was settling down for the night in the shade of the Panamint Mountains as they continued south toward Baker and the mysterious hangar there. Moments later, they were given clearance to land at the small airfield adjacent to the modest desert town. Rachel landed expertly and maneuvered the airplane toward the fuel pumps.

"Can you fuel her up?" Rachel asked a young man in greasy jeans and T-shirt standing by the Chevron pumps near the taxiway. "We'll probably be taking off soon."

"Sure can, lady," he said, watching her walk toward him with obvious interest. "Cash or credit?"

"Credit. You take this one?" She handed him the credit card embossed with the newspaper's name.

"Sure do. Where you from?"

"Tacoma." And when he continued to regard her quizzically, she said, "Tacoma, Washington."

"Pretty long trip. In town on business?"

"Yeah, kid," Jake cut in. "We're supposed to look at some property here at the airport. You know which building here used to belong to Death Valley Aviation?" He crossed his arms and regarded the boy impatiently, his blue sport coat flapping in the light, desert breeze.

"Yeah, that one." The boy pointed toward the end of the runway. "But some chemical company bought it."

"Yeah, but they're looking to sell it now. Is there someone around who can let us in?"

"Not that I know of." The boy pondered the question for a moment, squinting into the light of the setting sun. "That side door should be open, anyway. It always is."

"Nobody works there?" Rachel asked, quickly.

"Hell no. Not in a month or so, anyway. It's just a big, empty building."

"Thanks, kid," Jake said. "You gas up the plane and we'll take a look around that old shack. Come on, Rachel."

They turned to the hangar the boy pointed out.

"Doesn't sound like this place is going to be much good for anything," Jake said as they walked across the tarmac. "A wasted trip."

"Looks like it," Rachel admitted. "But they must have had some plans for it."

The hangar, set slightly away from the other buildings at the airfield, was sadly in need of attention. The white paint had mostly flaked off and the old, weathered boards were warped out of shape. Happily they found the side door unlocked and they entered quickly, pulling it shut with a squeal of protest behind them. The interior was empty, echoing their footsteps as they inspected it. They noted a bench and rack holding a few tools against a far wall, and nearby lay other pieces of equipment, some of it tarpaulined and apparently designed to move aircraft parts around. Otherwise the place was empty. They walked across to the small office area and tried the door.

"This one's locked, anyway," Jake said, crouching to look at the lock. "Got another credit card?"

"Sure." Rachel found her library card and gave it to him.

"The wood is pretty dried out on this jamb," he said, as he slipped the card in between the frame and the strip of wood that hid the edge of the door. "There we go, instant access." He pushed the door into the office and handed the card back to her. She smiled, impressed.

"This office has seen a bit more use than the rest of the place," Rachel said, wiping one finger along the edge of the desk. "No dust."

"You're right," he said, opening the long central drawer of a metal desk. "And here's some of their paperwork."

Jake held up a flimsy sheet of pink paper that appeared to be from some kind of invoice form. Rachel took it and looked over the densely packed typing.

"What's this Nav Ops stuff?" she asked, reading the top line.

"Naval operations," Jake replied. "Third Fleet. This is apparently a fuel requisition form. Garbage really, but not the kind of garbage they should have here."

"They do seem to be interested in something more than civilian aviation."

"I can't make head or tail of these other papers." Jake had withdrawn a stack of papers from the drawer. They were similar to the one Rachel held. She took them from him and began to leaf through them. "They appear to be coded."

He crouched to pull open another drawer in the desk. It was empty, as was the one below it. "Nothing here."

"Look at this," Rachel said. "It was at the bottom."

She held the sheet up to the dying orange glow of the sun.

"It's written in clear enough English," she said, as Jake moved around to read over her shoulder. "Commander, Pacific Fleet," she read. "Alternative routes thirty-five latitude north and forty-seven latitude north approved for exercise of four sixteen. Flight at discretion of Blue Leader according to prevailing weather conditions. Land Three Fleet forty-seven north latitude one twenty-five east longitude as possible, else Edwards AFB.''

"I think we may have found our concrete evidence," Jake whispered, a triumphant gleam growing in his eyes.

"They're planning two flight routes for the exercises on Thursday!" Rachel exclaimed. "Four sixteen, that's this Thursday, the sixteenth! These must be the routes. Do you have any idea what they mean by this?"

"It's all secret, though I believe they're making some kind of transcontinental flight from the Atlantic to the Pacific. This would mean that they're planning to take either a northern or southern route depending on the weather."

"Forty-seven, north latitude would take them almost directly over Tacoma," she said.

"And thirty-five, north latitude? Where does that put them?" Jake spoke urgently as he read the paper again.

"Just south of where we're standing now."

"Let's take a look at this stuff out here." Jake left the office and walked quickly through the darkening hangar toward the equipment standing by the workbench. One of the machines attracted his attention right away. It was a forkliftlike apparatus with two sturdy arms reaching out four feet parallel to each other from an extendible post on a wheeled platform.

"That looks like a weapons rack of some kind," he said, examining the device. "You'd position those two arms beneath the missile or bomb you want to detach from the wing of the airplane, and then you can safely disconnect the weapon and wheel it away. Looks homemade, but it would probably do the trick. And over here is some kind of generator." He pointed toward a large hooded machine about hip level with a long, thick electrical cable coiled like a snake on the hangar floor beside it. "Judging by the type of connection on the end of that cable, I'd say that generator has been rigged to start a jet aircraft."

"What do you mean?"

"Not all jets are equipped with starters, so they give them a jump start of sorts, with an electrical generator. I don't know what kind of system navy planes, F-14s, use, but if they want to land a jet fighter here and take off again, they'd want to have something on hand to be sure it would start for them."

"Is that what you think they want to do? Land here and take off again? Why?"

"Maybe to take something off the plane," he suggested. "Hell, I don't know. If we knew exactly what they're testing on Thursday we'd be a lot closer to an answer to all of this. Unfortunately, nobody outside the fleet commanders knows what's going on. We can make a phone call to Naval Intelligence about this hangar, though. If nothing else, it sure isn't kosher for them to have naval documents on the premises. They'll send someone out to take a closer look."

"The paper said the route was at the discretion of the Blue Leader," Rachel said, as they walked back toward the bulk covered by the tarpaulin. "Could that be Captain Zack Parker?"

"Could very well be, though I'd expect the commander would at least be a colonel." Jake lifted an edge of the tarpaulin to reveal a wooden crate beneath. "Pull this up," he said, moving along to grasp the far end of the tarp on that side.

They lifted it up and over the top of what was revealed to be a stack of wooden packing crates. In the dying light, they could see that the crates were all labeled FARM MACHINERY: PANDORA EXPORTING.

"Pandora isn't shipping anything," Rachel said.

"They are now, but it isn't farm machinery." Jake tugged at the tarp, pulling it back down over the boxes. "Come on. We'd better get to a phone and get somebody down here fast."

But as they were walking across the empty hangar, headlights swept over the windows of the massive doors. They froze for a second, waiting while a car door slammed outside, then Jake was galvanized into action, pushing Rachel toward the office.

"Go through the office," he whispered. "There's an outside door. I'll play games with them while you start the plane."

"No, you come with me," she insisted urgently.

"Get the plane ready and leave the door open." He pushed her at the door again. "I'll join you as soon as possible." And he started walking toward the door they'd used to enter the hangar.

Rachel left him reluctantly, hurrying to the front of the hangar and peering around the edge toward the car parked before the large doors. Two heavyset men wearing cowboy hats were standing looking across at her rented airplane.

"You guys work here?" She could hear Jake call out from the other side of the building. The two men turned toward him in surprise and walked around to the side door.

"What you doing in there, buddy?" one of the men asked.

When they'd gone to talk to Jake, Rachel began walking rapidly out toward the plane waiting by the fuel pumps. Glancing quickly over her shoulder, she could see the men entering the hangar behind Jake. Then a light came on within the massive building. Rachel walked across the cracked concrete, her heart fluttering like a hummingbird within her chest.

"All set?" she asked the kid by the pumps.

"Ready to go," he answered, holding out a clipboard with her credit card and the gas receipt clipped onto it. "Just sign here."

She took the board and a pen and hastily scribbled her name on the slip, then took her card and turned toward the plane.

"Didn't like the building?" the young man asked, watching her step up onto the wing and open the door.

"It isn't really what we're looking for," she called, slipping into the pilot's seat. "But my associate is talking to a couple of gentlemen about it now. Maybe they'll make a deal of some kind. Stand back now. I'm going to power up."

Rachel turned the key as the boy walked back around the gas pumps. First one engine and then the other shuddered to life on either side of the cockpit, and she pressed the throttle ahead slowly. The airplane rolled forward toward the lighted hangar where she could see the dim forms of Jake and the two men standing inside. At the sound of the engines, they turned toward the windows that ran in a row across the large doors.

One of the men pointed toward her plane, and Jake nodded, moving toward the side door. One man grabbed his shoulder, and Jake shrugged him off while walking openly toward the exit. Then the two men moved swiftly, leaping at Jake as he spun and ran. Jake emerged from the hangar just ahead of them, lashing back as one caught his jacket, breaking free and propelling himself toward the plane with long, powerful strides.

His two assailants weren't up to the task of catching him, giving up to return to their car and throw open the doors. Jake leaped up to the wing behind the left engine and jerked the door open, jumping into the plane to fall heavily behind the seats.

"Get a move on!" he shouted, half laughing. "Those idiots recognized me!"

"What?" Rachel pressed the throttle forward, turning the plane away from the hangar toward the runway.

"They knew who I was! It took them a minute to realize it, but they knew all right." He pulled himself up into the seat beside her, struggling to catch his breath. "Let's go!"

Rachel gave the plane more power, sending them bumping along the concrete taxiway toward the main runway of the small airport. It was nearly twilight and the runway lights looked faint.

Something pinged beside her window, followed by a loud splintering sound as a web of small cracks formed in the tempered glass.

"They're shooting at us!" she exclaimed. "My God, they're shooting at the airplane!"

And then she could see the car driving up beside her left wing, stopping, and the men jumping out with rifles. The sound of the shots was almost lost in the drone of the engines as Rachel turned onto the runway and sent them racing along the stretch of concrete.

Seconds later, they were airborne and flying back over the field where the two men stood watching them soar overhead.

"This is too much excitement for a plain old ordinary newspaper editor to handle," Rachel said, laughing with relief. "What did you tell them in there?"

"I tried to carry on with that story about buying the building, but they didn't buy it for a minute. Then one of them remembered where he'd seen me and that was the end of our party." Jake sat looking out into the night sky before them, raking a thatch of hair off his forehead with one hand. "That was close."

"Too close."

"Can you get military frequencies on this radio?" he asked, looking at her with eager concern. "We've got to call someone about that place."

"I wouldn't know who to call. We're near Edwards Air Force Base, maybe we can raise them," she said, turning the radio dial. "Except, of course, I don't know their frequency. I'll have to contact a civilian tower first, and—"

The plane shuddered hard, wobbling slightly in the air, and Rachel scanned the gauges before her urgently. Then the plane shook again, and the starboard engine began to sputter noisily.

"It looks like those cowboys were lucky with that rifle," Rachel said calmly. "We're losing fuel."

"What?" Jake turned in his seat to stare at her gravely. "You can't be serious, can you? He actually hit us?"

"More than once, I'd guess, by the rate the gas gauge is dropping. And he must have hit the starboard engine, too. It's not going to keep running for long."

Jake turned to look at the struggling engine on the wing to his right, laughing ruefully. "This is what I get for flying."

"We'll be all right." Rachel adjusted their speed slightly as she spoke, calmly slowing their fuel consumption while piloting them through the fading strawberry-orange glow of the sun setting beyond the Pacific. Once again, the routine of flying came to bear to calm her at the controls. "I hope there will be enough fuel to get us to Fresno, but I doubt it. There are a lot of small airfields in the desert, in between. So we should have no problem finding a place to put her down."

As if to refute her optimistic words, the starboard engine choked violently and then fell silent, the propeller turning uselessly backward in the wind.

"Okay, that's it," Jake said. "Let's get back on the ground and sort things out down there."

"Not that I disagree with you, Jake, but we've got to get to a runway first. I'm not about to bust up a rented plane."

"Sounds fair. Do you know where we are, exactly?" Despite his professed anxiety over flying, Jake looked calm in the soft yellow glow of the instrument lights filtering up from the console. It was as if he became more coolheaded as the seriousness of the situation increased and didn't allow personal feelings to hinder his professional performance.

"Judging by our air speed and direction, we should be approaching China Lake and Westend. There they are." She pointed toward two small clusters of light far ahead to the right and left. "I've done quite a bit of flying down here in the past few years, so I know the area pretty well. There's a dandy little landing strip at Little Lake. That's about another thirty ground miles farther."

"Can we make it that far?"

"No problem." Watching the fuel gauge, she could see it move slightly down from half full, losing fuel at a much faster rate than she'd thought at first. "Fresno is definitely out, I'm afraid. I wouldn't want to try going over the Sierra Nevadas in this condition, and we're losing gas too fast. So I guess we're going to be stuck for the night."

"Can we rent a car in whatcha-callit? Little Lake?"

"Nope. No car rental, but there's a motel and I know that there's a mechanic there. Maybe he can patch us up overnight."

"It's worth a try. Head her into Little Lake. At the very least, we've got to get to a telephone."

By the time they got to Little Lake, the fuel gauge had dropped to about an eighth of a tank, a loss of practically their entire fuel supply in little less than an hour in the air.

And by the time they landed on the airstrip the gauge read empty. So when Rachel and Jake stepped out of the plane, they did so with extreme gratitude.

That was when Rachel's emotions caught up with her and she threw her arms around Jake in relief, letting his strength reassure her as she clung to his warm chest.

But their relief faded fast after Jake got to the telephone. While Rachel contacted the local mechanic, he called Tacoma with their news.

"Are they going to do something about that hangar in Baker?" Rachel watched him approach her from the pay phone outside the small steel building that served as rest area for the pilots.

"Yes, they'll alert the L.A. office of the FBI and have some people out there by morning." Jake looked shaken, almost ill, as he leaned against the side of the building. "Agent Fowler moved fast after we left town," he said.

"What do you mean?"

"He's requested a federal warrant to search and seize the contents of the *Banner* offices on suspicion of espionage. And for good measure he's asked for arrest warrants for both of us on the same charges."

"He what? He can't make those charges stick!" Rachel glowered at Jake in dismay, her eyes flashing with defiant fire. "He's the one implicated in this! They've got listening devices in my office! My home!"

"You're right," Jake said, throwing up his hands. "The charges won't hold up. And I doubt any judge will let him search the paper. But it'll keep us busy for a couple days, and that's all they need. And with us out of town they'll probably pull those bugs. We won't have any proof that they were listening."

"What about the navy? They won't let Parker fly!"

"I don't know if they will or not," Jake said in resignation.

"What do you mean, you don't know?"

"Fowler is the bureau liaison to the navy as well, and from the sound of it, he's built up enough of a paper case against us to kill our credibility."

"Who did you talk to?"

"The duty sergeant at first. Then I called Ron Jarvis at home. He filled me in on it." Jake slipped his arm around Rachel's shoulders, holding her closely to his side. "They'll move on the Baker airfield because they can't afford not to, but they aren't about to assault the reputation of a naval captain on the word of two suspected traitors. Besides, it sounds like Fowler has fabricated evidence to finger a different flyer."

"This is sick." Rachel willed the tension out of her shoulders, allowing a small laugh to escape her drawn lips.

"That's for sure. While everyone is running around arresting the wrong people, the bad guys will run free to complete their plan. And the sickest part is that we're still not entirely sure what that plan is."

"Or how any of it relates to Schofield Enterprises." Rachel laughed. "How on earth did Bruce dig up so much trouble doing a financial story about the lumber industry?"

"Those college kids." Jake sighed. "You just never know what they'll be up to next."

She embraced him and lingered, to savor his warmth and comfort as long as possible.

"WELCOME TO THE BATES MOTEL," Jake said quietly as they entered the dark motel room.

"Quit that," Rachel said, searching the wall by the door for a light switch.

The floorboards creaked under the pressure of their feet. Turning on the light didn't change the empty feeling. The room was clean and neat, showing the care directed it in the tightly made bed and dusted surface of the bureau. But the wallpaper was old and yellowed in the corners, and the faded curtains were as dated as the furniture.

Despite this, there was something comforting in the fastidiously clean face this motel had put on.

Jake threw himself down on the bed, which creaked loudly in friendly protest. "For some odd reason, this place reminds me of my grandmother's cabin in the Adirondacks," he said, contentedly. "Her place is a bit larger, but they had the same decorator."

"I suppose I should have held on to some sense of decorum and insisted on two rooms," Rachel said. She stood uncertainly beside the closed door, watching the reclining man as he laced his fingers behind his head and closed his eyes. "But I didn't want to spend the night alone."

"Me neither. Besides, we've got to think of some kind of plan." He sat up with a good-natured groan, swinging his feet back to the floor. "How long will it take to patch the plane?"

"He promised to have it back in the air by noon tomorrow. That's why he's draining the rest of the gasoline out overnight. He wants the tanks aired out as much as possible in case he has to do any welding, but temporary patches will probably do till we get home. At least the engine doesn't look like a serious problem. A stray bullet nicked a wire and it came loose."

"He knew where to aim, that's for sure. When I saw all those holes in the wings, I couldn't see how we made it this far."

"Our problem now is making it till Thursday." Rachel walked over and sat beside him on the bed. "Did Detective Jarvis have any news about Pandora's employees?"

"Yes, he did." Jake slipped his arm around her shoulder, smiling. "Every single one of them has a criminal record in either California or Washington. A couple of them were convicted of fancy crimes like forgery and embezzlement, but most of them were in for robbery or assault. But what's more interesting is that they all have some construction experience."

"Is that odd?"

"It seems odd to me that he'd collect twelve men together, all of them with records, and all of them with construction experience." Jake spoke thoughtfully as he massaged her shoulder lightly.

"I think I'd better try to get hold of Scott Kirby," Rachel said. "I couldn't find him this morning, and if I know him at all he's been up to something dark and mysterious. Maybe he got some evidence we can use."

"Good plan," Jake said, standing. "As long as we're here for the duration, I'll take a shower. See if you can find him."

It took a couple of calls to locate the intern reporter, but she finally reached him at Naomi's house.

"I'm hiding out, boss," he said, cheerfully. "I spotted a couple gray suits outside my dorm, so I came to play houseguest with Naomi. I knew you'd be able to find me here."

"What on earth is going on up there?"

"They haven't gotten any kind of warrant yet, but Len Simpson figures it's only a matter of time before they put a lock on the whole thing. You should have told me you were a spy, Rachel," he said, laughing. "Is there any money in it?"

"None yet, Scott. Where were you this morning?"

"I spent most of the day following that Watkins guy around. Did you know he keeps a second house in town?"

"No, I didn't."

"He's got a fancy apartment on the bay, but he is also renting a broken-down ranch house near the military housing in town. He went there twice today. And he met a couple dangerous-looking types who pulled up in a black Lincoln. They were carrying briefcases when they went in, but didn't have them on the way out. Looked like a payoff."

"Has there been anything on the news about us?"

"Nothing yet, but I got a tip from one of the guys at the *Tribune* that they're investigating some fly-boy named Medvid for possible involvement with the Ruskies. Is he the right man?"

"No, but I'm sure there's plenty of evidence against him. You were right to stay away from the FBI, Scott," Rachel told him, thinking of their next move. "Agent Fowler is working for the other side, so he's got the deck stacked against all of us. I want you to keep an eye on Watkins's house. Did you have your camera when you were there earlier?"

"Of course. Got some clear shots of the three of them."

"Good, we'll need all the evidence we can compile. Keep an eye on them, but don't try anything dangerous. And make sure Naomi knows how to reach you. If you get into trouble, call Detective Ron Jarvis with the police. You can trust him."

"Will do, chief. When will you be back?"

"Tomorrow evening, some time. Bye now."

Rachel hung up the phone feeling somewhat hopeful. If nothing else, they'd have some documented evidence to refute the case against them. It was too late to call Len Simpson and he hadn't expected to have the report from his investigator till morning anyway, so she had to content herself that they were doing as much as possible for the time being. A hot shower and a good night's rest were what she needed the most.

When Rachel came out from her shower, Jake was sitting up against the headboard of the bed wearing his jeans and with his shirt open. He had been watching television, but walked over and turned it off when she came out.

"How do we do this?" he said, opening his arms in a questioning manner. "I mean, there doesn't appear to be more than one bed."

Rachel laughed. She, too, had felt awkward, and she'd dressed herself completely again after her shower rather than break the ice herself. Neither of them had taken time to pack for an overnight trip. Now she stood uncertainly admiring the broad expanse of chest his open shirt had revealed. "I don't know what to do," she admitted. "Do you have any suggestions?"

"Which side of the bed do you want?" he asked, walking toward the light switch.

"The right side is fine."

"All right, then. Let's just turn off the light and get some shut-eye. We can worry about being embarrassed in the morning." He snapped the light switch, and the room was cast into darkness.

Rachel slipped out of her jeans and sweatshirt and pulled down the covers on her side of the bed, feeling a small, involuntary thrill tickle her spine as she slipped in. A moment later, the bed creaked again as he got in beside her. She lay on her back for a moment looking up at the unseen ceiling and savoring his warmth beside her. Outside, the desert wind sifted around the old building.

"Can you hold me, Jake?" she asked.

"Of course."

He slipped his arm around her, and she snuggled in against the side of his body, nestling her head into the hollow of his throat. The feel of his well-muscled torso against her, his chest rising and falling in long, comfortable breaths, made Rachel feel so safe it seemed incomprehensible that she could have gone so long without someone like him in her life before. If nothing else came out of this mess, at least she had found Jake Connors. Moments later, warm and safe in the arms of the man she loved, she fell blissfully asleep.

Chapter Fourteen

To awaken in a man's arms was a pleasure like no other Rachel could remember experiencing. For the first few moments of the day, everything was right and proper on that beautiful Wednesday morning. All things were possible and no hope was too great to hold in her heart.

Rachel turned slightly, sliding under the protective covering of the arm he'd casually thrown over her in his sleep to kiss him lightly on the cheek.

"Wake up, sleepyhead," she whispered.

Jake twitched slightly, his eyes flying open, but then he smiled and returned her affection with a light kiss on the lips. "Good morning," he said, kissing her again. "Sleep well?"

"Wonderfully well," she sighed, snuggling against the pillow of his arm beneath her. "Can I make an arrangement to always have you there to guard me in my sleep? I like it."

"I think we can make arrangements."

He kissed her again, holding her close against him, savoring this moment free of care and obligation. And his kisses sent explosions of heady excitement tingling through her that threatened to destroy the little resolve she had to get out of bed and face the day, as she slipped her hands lovingly over his strong back. But she broke off the contact with a lusty laugh.

"Don't tempt me," she said, rolling to her back and stretching the night out of her body. "We've got work to do."

"Yes, we're about to be labeled fugitives from justice if we aren't already. I suppose we should do something about that."

Rachel slipped out of bed and walked to the bathroom heedless of her state of undress. The night had taken away her shyness, and she felt totally comfortable crossing the room in her underthings. She couldn't be shy with this tender man again.

After they'd freshened up as best they could, they stepped out into the glare of the desert sun and hurried across the highway to a café that served the small, sunbathed town. Rachel went to use the pay phone while Jake ordered breakfast.

"Don't tell me where you are," Len Simpson warned when Rachel reached him. "As an officer of the court, it's my duty to tell the law of your whereabouts, so I don't want to know."

"You're sounding awfully official this morning," Rachel said brightly. "Have I been charged with anything yet?"

"No, but they're looking for you as a material witness. That's the next best thing." The lawyer sounded tired.

"What about the paper? Do they have a warrant to search it?"

"No, and they probably won't bother if it isn't absolutely necessary. It's one thing to accuse a reporter of treason, but an entirely different thing to start searching newspaper offices. All right, then, let's get down to business. I'm not foolish enough to think there's a shred of truth to the charges, so I won't waste your time with stupid questions. I assume you're calling to see if we had any results on that property down south."

"Exactly."

"I've just been going over his report," Len said. "The land in question is only about twenty acres. It's a narrow strip of land right against the border of Rainier Park. Heavily wooded, but according to the report there just isn't enough land for it to be viable for commercial logging."

"Did your man get on the property? Did he see it?"

"No, he couldn't get onto the property itself. There's a chain across the road leading in and there were several men there all day. He could hear machinery running beyond the trees. And a man living close to the property says they've been in and out of there with heavy machinery for the past couple months. They poured a lot of concrete, judging by that man's statement."

"Any ideas what they've been doing in there?"

"No. And nobody has gone out of his way to explain the construction, either."

"What kind of terrain is it?"

"Fairly level. It's just below a finger of high lands sticking out of the Cascades. The trees are fir and cedar with some maple thrown in. That's about the extent of it."

"Thank you, Len," Rachel said, warmly. "If you can keep the law from confiscating my business for another day, I think we can have the whole thing cleared up."

"But you aren't going to tell me what's going on?"

"I only have suspicions now, Len, so I can't tell you much."

"Have it your way. Take care of yourself, now. And don't go getting arrested for anything. I'm not a criminal lawyer, and I hate to lose a paying customer."

"Thanks, Len. I'll take care."

Rachel hurried back to their table and relayed the new information to Jake.

"You think they've built a runway in there?" he asked.

"I can't think of anything else requiring a long strip of land and a lot of concrete. They'd need something to cover the possibility of the planes choosing a northern route."

"We've got to try and get this information through," Jake told her. "Maybe I can relay it through Ron."

"It's worth a try." Rachel grasped his hand tightly as he stood, looking up into his eyes. "Our best defense will be to see that they are caught," she said. "Fowler probably has every other angle covered to cook us good."

Jake squeezed her hand gently and winked as he turned and walked over to the pay phone. Moments later, he was back with an annoyed expression clouding his features.

"The arrest warrants just came through," he said, sitting. "We're now officially accused of espionage. He planted some military papers in my desk at the station. They've got warrants for our homes, too, and I wouldn't doubt he's salted them with all sorts of incriminating evidence."

"How can they do that? I mean, how could they have convinced a judge that we'd have access to any secrets?"

"He's probably established a solid paper trail linking us to their scapegoat, Captain Medvid. Remember, Pandora has a couple pretty good counterfeiters working for them. It wouldn't be hard to forge our signatures to some correspondence tying us all in with communist agents. And, after they've pulled off their plan and it's obvious that Captain Medvid wasn't the traitor, they'll turn up a safety deposit box or something filled up with papers indicating that we were in league with Captain Parker to make Medvid look guilty. They'll have us blocked no matter which way the wind blows. Stopping these people is like trying to put out a forest fire with a squirt gun.''

"Can Detective Jarvis get the information about the landing strip through to them?''

"Maybe, but he's got no evidence to back him up. We don't either, for that matter—not concrete evidence, anyway. All we really have is rumor and supposition. And if we came forward to present our ideas, they'd throw us in the brig along with Medvid and worry about sorting it out later.''

"But all they have to do is send someone out to investigate that land,'' Rachel insisted.

"Sure, but even if anyone is willing to accept any information that came from two fugitives, it will take time to put anything through channels. First, Ron has to get someone to take him seriously, and then they've got to get the county sheriff to go out and look. And he'll have Fowler running interference all the way, so the chances are damn slim that anything will get done in time. Even if they did get anything done today, it wouldn't make any difference from the naval point of view. The whole fleet will be operating under radio silence from noon today till eight o'clock tomorrow morning.''

The waitress brought their breakfast orders, and they both dug in hungrily, precluding talk for a moment. Finally, Rachel said, "Okay, we'll have to see if we can sneak back into Tacoma some way. We can land in Olympia and have Scott meet us with his car. Unless they've got someone following him, that is.''

"Not enough manpower to follow everybody,'' Jake commented, over his coffee. "Besides, they've certainly got Medvid locked up by now, so they think the maneuvers are safe.''

"I just wish we knew more about the maneuvers," Rachel said. "What are they testing? Is it some kind of missile or ray gun or some other Buck Rogers contraption? What is so damn important that Watkins would work so hard to get it?"

"Whatever it is, I'm sure the Soviets would gladly pay a king's ransom to get their hands on it. It beats developing the technology themselves."

"And they'll get what they want if we can't get around Fowler." Rachel scowled out the window of the café, watching a swirl of dust twisting along in the hot breeze.

"Cloak and dagger games," Jake said bitterly. "They've done all they can to keep this whole thing in the dark, and now all that secrecy is working against them. One crooked FBI agent has been able to mess up the whole thing by feeding everybody the wrong information. We can only guess that there's something on the plane that they can re-move quickly and package for shipment. Most probably a missile of some kind."

"All right, then. I'll find Scott somehow, and we'll get back to town. Then we'll play it by ear. If we knew when the operation was going to take place, we'd be ahead of the game."

"It's possible that we know more than we think," Jake said. "They're breaking radio silence at eight tomorrow."

"Is that significant?"

"Probably. Listen, all we know about this business is that it apparently involves a flight of navy planes that are flying cross-country from one fleet to the other. They wouldn't maintain radio silence after the operation is complete, so I'd guess the flight will be coming over just after dawn, which would put them down on their carrier in the Pacific around eight."

"So we've got to get their hidden runway closed down before eight tomorrow morning. That's about twenty-two hours from now."

"Twenty-two hours, and we're stuck on the edge of the Mojave Desert with an airplane full of holes and prices on our heads."

"You have a way of putting things that really inspires confidence, Jake," Rachel laughed. "Do you think we should just fly off to Mexico while we're this close and be done with it? This may be our last chance to take it on the lam."

"That's an intriguing idea." Jake laughed, taking her hand across the table of their small booth. "But I left my favorite sneakers at home, and I can't flee to Mexico without them."

"Okay, if that's the way it is, I'll see if I've got enough change to get in touch with Scott Kirby. And then we'll see how the repairs on our plane are progressing."

THEY WEREN'T AIRBORNE until nearly one o'clock, but the fuel tanks were patched and the starboard engine was running smoothly. Rachel had finally managed to track Scott down, instructing him to get to the airport in Olympia and wait for their arrival. So, for better or worse, the stage was set for their return.

"Scott said that Willis Schofield has been trying to get in touch with me," Rachel said as she sat at relaxed attention behind the controls of the plane. "Scott's going to see if he can find out what he wants."

"What could he want?" Jake watched the ground roll beneath them, rising from the gray-brown expanse of desert sand to the evergreen-covered peaks of the Sierra Nevada mountains. "Our problems have moved beyond the area of business concerns."

"I don't know," Rachel said. "But he's been very helpful so far, so I don't see any problem in meeting with him."

"Well, if you trust the guy, I will, too. But I'm not sure it was a good idea to tell him so much about all of this."

"I trust him," Rachel said, but her brow was knit with concern as she thought about the industrialist and his relationship with Watkins.

Jake continued watching the terrain below them as it built to rocky peaks that reached up toward the plane like eager monsters hoping to pull them down from the sky. "Can you get a little more altitude out of this thing?" he asked. "Mother Earth looks a bit too close for comfort."

"I'd rather not waste fuel climbing," Rachel told him. "We'll use it for speed, instead. Besides, we're at least a thousand feet above the mountains."

"That's easy for you to say." Jake sat back, resting his head against his seat and closing his eyes. "Tell me when the scenery is a little more friendly."

Rachel smiled lovingly, saying, "Why do you think Watkins sold his company to Schofield, anyway?"

"Probably because he wanted to put some distance between himself and Arnold Carbellino. Investigators looking for dirt on Arnie would have come around sooner or later, but with the company safely tucked under the Schofield umbrella it might get ignored. We're assuming that he was using the company to hide his preparations for his big stunt with the maneuvers. He could lose his whole plan within the mass of corporate paperwork and nobody would pay any attention to what he did. And getting Schofield to foot the bill was probably a big part of his reasoning, too. It's a case of hiding in plain sight. He's right out in the open, but nobody pays any attention."

"Until Bruce Quinlan got a bit too nosy."

"And his lovely editor backed him up."

"But I would never have suspected anything if they hadn't searched my home or done any of the other things they did."

"Watkins must be getting nervous. He didn't dare leave you alone if there was any chance that you knew anything. And I don't imagine that he believed for one minute that Quinlan was doing his investigation without your supervision."

"He was audacious, but let his own insecurities ruin him."

"He isn't ruined yet, Rachel," Jake reminded her, turning his head to look at her seriously. "Not by any stretch of the imagination."

BUT NEITHER WERE THEY RUINED, and they landed at the Olympia airport shortly after eight that night without challenge, finding Scott Kirby waiting for them in the terminal.

"I'm parked in the lot out front," he said. "Any bags?"

"No, we didn't have time for that," Rachel told him as they hurried through the scattered people waiting for incoming flights. "Let's get out of here before somebody spots us."

"You weren't followed, were you kid?" Jake asked.

"No way. I took busses around town for a while and then borrowed a friend's car to come here. We're all clear."

But, as they went out to the waiting car, Rachel couldn't help feeling conspicuous, as though everyone they passed was turning to watch them, talking about them, moving toward a phone to call the police. Merely walking across an airport lobby, even in a town where the chances of anyone recognizing her were slim, was an almost intolerable ordeal. She wanted to be out of there and hidden in the vehicle outside, safely anonymous.

"You drive, Scott," Jake told him as they got to the dusty old Plymouth sedan in the lot. "I'm the one the Tacoma police are most likely to recognize, so Rachel will sit up front beside you and I'll sit in back where I can duck down if need be."

They got into the car, and Rachel turned on the radio, adjusting it through the static on the AM bands till she found a station broadcasting the news. After several local stories the announcer began a story of immediate interest to them.

"In an announcement this afternoon, a navy spokesman said that certain conventional weaponry would be tested as part of a larger exercise designed to test what he termed as 'the navy's inter-ocean capabilities.' Though no details were released, our information is that the primary test of the maneuvers involves a flight of F-14s leaving a carrier in the Atlantic and crossing the continent to land on the carrier *Eisenhower* off the coast of Washington. Though they haven't said what the exact purpose of the flight is, the navy has issued a statement that the test is in strict compliance with all treaties in effect between the United States and the Soviet Union. Meanwhile, in other news—"

She switched off the radio and sat back tensely.

"That confirms it," she said. "Their pet pilot is going to land his plane so they can strip it and ship the important parts to the Russians. Now, if we only knew which route they'll be taking, we might be able to stop them."

"We'll just have to work under the assumption that they'll be taking the northern route since the fleet is waiting for them there." Jake leaned forward in the back seat to watch the road ahead of them. "But there aren't enough of us to do it right. We've got to cover that airfield and still maintain contact with Watkins. That's a tall order when we are fugitives, ourselves."

"They should have moved on the airfield in Baker, right?" Rachel turned to look at him closely as the glare of roadside lights swished over the serious set of his face. "Or do you think Fowler stopped any bureau action in that area?"

"I don't know." He stroked her hair lightly, letting his fingers linger there. "But then we don't know their criterion for choosing the route of that flight. That airfield may not have ever been a serious consideration. We've got to worry about getting ourselves out of this mess. And to do that, we need to do more than stop them in the woods. We've got to catch Watkins and Fowler, as well."

"I contacted Willis Schofield's office," Scott told them. "The guy wouldn't even talk to me, but his secretary gave me a number for you to call. Any time, night or day, she said. Do you think you'll get any help out of Schofield?"

"We won't know until I talk to him," Rachel said. "He was checking on Watkins, and he might have found out something."

"We can't afford to turn down help from anyone," Jake said, grimly. "Even though I don't trust Schofield very far."

"You can sure count on me. Say, I wrote down the address of that house Watkins went to," Scott said, pulling a slip of paper out of his pocket and handing it to Rachel.

"Good work, Scott." Rachel patted his shoulder. "You've been a lot of help."

"You'll have no choice but to put him on Watkins's trail," Jake said. "He can't fly, and that's probably the only way to get into that airfield. They're sure to have the road guarded, and we don't have time to try sneaking around them."

"What are you going to be doing?"

"I'm sticking with you," he said, with a loving smile. "That's my primary assignment."

"We've made a good team so far." Rachel spoke with
heartfelt thankfulness, and for a moment she felt a spark of
communication that was wordless. They were there for each
other, now and forever, and words could not make the
commitment more complete.

"This is great," Scott crowed, breaking the mood with his
enthusiastic exclamation. "A firsthand account of two cit-
izens breaking a spy ring that had the officials stumped. The
story will have everything; murder, blackmail, treason, organized crime and a crooked FBI agent. It's a reporter's
dream!"

"And it could be a reporter's nightmare if we don't manage to catch them with their hands dirty," Jake said grimly.
"You could end up writing this story from behind bars."

Scott laughed. "The good guys always win, don't they?"

"Bruce Quinlan didn't win," Jake said. "So don't get
cocky."

Scott returned his attention to the road, a look of concern darkening his eyes. For now, they all settled back to
watch the dim passage of scenery as their car took them
closer to their destiny in Tacoma.

"I'LL MEET YOU IN MY OFFICE after ten o'clock."

"But why? What is so important?" Rachel stood in the
phone booth, struggling to hear over the rumble of a truck
waiting at the diesel pumps. They had stopped by at a gas
station on the outskirts of Tacoma. "What do you need to
tell me, Mr. Scofield?"

"There's too much to go into over the phone," he said,
nearly shouting. Even over the telephone, and covered by
the bellowing truck, the anger in his voice was clearly evi-
dent. "I know what he's up to," he said hotly. "I can't even
start to explain over the phone. You've got to come for it in
person."

"You should call the police with any information."

"No. There's a federal agent involved. I can't take the chance of my information getting to him. You come here."

"Fine. We'll be there just after ten."

"Yes. Hurry, please."

"Keep your information safe. We'll be there."

"Good. I'll leave one of the lobby doors unlocked. There is no watchman, so you should be able to get in and out undetected. Come right up to my office." He hung up with a decisive click, and Rachel replaced the receiver of her phone with thoughtful slowness. He had the evidence on paper. Their ordeal would be over soon. Or would it?

She hurried back and slipped into the car with an increased sense of urgency. "Schofield says he knows what Watkins is planning, and he wants us to meet him at his office after ten."

"Does that change our plan?" Scott put the car into gear and drove back onto the highway.

"No," Jake said. "We'll meet with Schofield, and you go ahead with your end. If he can give us something concrete, it may help stop them, and there's no time to go through channels."

"Find Watkins," Rachel told Scott. "Stick close to him and keep your camera handy, and use a long lens. Got that? I don't want you getting too close."

"I wish we had a better idea of where to pick up Watkins, kid, but we don't," Jake said. "You'll have to check out his apartment and that house, as well as the warehouse."

"I'd expect him to lay back tonight," Scott commented, driving through town. "He's got a big day tomorrow."

"Which is exactly why he'll be on the move. He's got to stay on top of things tonight."

"And we'll be on top of him." Scott stopped on a dark street near the university, parking in the darkness beneath the sighing fir trees and out of sight of prying eyes.

"You'll be careful, won't you?" Rachel grasped his sleeve lightly as he opened his door.

"Don't worry. I'm on the job, boss." Scott grinned with excitement as he slipped out of the car. "I'll be careful."

"If something happens that you can't cover, call Ron Jarvis at one of the numbers I gave you," Jake told him as he took the boy's place behind the wheel. "Don't let Watkins skip town."

"I won't." Scott stepped back and turned to run into the shadows toward the campus.

"I hope he knows what he's doing," Jake commented grimly, as he put the car in gear and turned back toward town. "For that matter, I hope we all know what we're doing."

"You're not worried, are you?"

"Me? No, as long as we're not flying, I'm not worried at all." He patted her knee affectionately as he spoke. "All we need to do is foil a well-planned and still unexplained conspiracy. It sounds like a snap to me."

Rachel didn't feel cheered by the light tone he affected. There were still immense barriers to overcome.

"Schofield sounded angry on the phone," Rachel said, as they drove toward the bay. "I hope he waits for us. It would ruin everything if he decides to take matters into his own hands."

"He's a businessman," Jake said, looking around warily as they neared the office building. "He knows enough to go through proper channels with something like this. I don't expect he'll start doing his own work after years of delegating authority."

Jake stopped on the street before the building. The small plaza in front of the entrance was deserted, looking cold and lonely in the glare of streetlights. They sat for a moment watching the building, waiting for something that never happened. There was a light in a window on the executive floor—a small rectangle of light near Schofield's corner office, though the industrialist's office itself was dark.

"Is the car too conspicuous sitting in front?"

"They won't know this car." Jake craned his neck to search for any sign of company on the street. "I'd rather have it handy."

"Will we need to make a quick exit?"

"I don't know." Jake opened his door and swung his legs out. "But something doesn't feel right about this. You should have asked for a different meeting place."

"I thought about it," Rachel said, as they both stepped out onto the dew-wet pavement. "But he'd already hung up."

"We've got ten hours till they break radio silence. Let's get his stuff and see if we can do anything with it before then."

They hurried across the open plaza and into the lobby through the door Schofield had left open. As if to reinforce her optimistic feeling, the elevator doors opened immediately upon request with a cheerful ding, and they stepped inside. They pressed the button for the fifteenth floor. The elevator took them up in ominous silence as Jake removed his police revolver from its holster beneath his jacket and stood ready before the doors.

The executive floor was dark and silent. The sound of their footsteps were swallowed by the thick carpeting covering the floor as they approached the doors to Schofield's office. Jake waved her off to one side of the double doors and took the handle in his hand, turning it slowly. The door opened with a small click that sounded like a gunshot in the silence, and Jake pressed it in. Then he leaned in to survey the reception area, squinting through the gloom to distinguish the shapes of the furniture inside until he was satisfied that no one was waiting for them.

"Come on," he whispered, motioning to her as she stood against the wall beside the other door.

Rachel entered carefully, and followed the detective to the inner office. As with the last door, he opened this one slowly and peered inside cautiously. Someone was seated behind the large desk, the dark form standing out in relief against the backdrop of lights on the bay through the window behind him.

"Mr. Schofield," Rachel said, following him into the darkened room.

The man didn't move, but a voice answered, "Come right in."

And then there were lights and a flurry of movement as two men rushed in to club Jake on the back of the head and pin him to the floor. Rachel stopped awkwardly, turning to run as Calvin Watkins rose smiling from the chair behind the desk. But a blond man caught her with one thick arm, throwing her back toward the office wall like a doll. She was caught by a second man, larger, stronger.

He swung a folded handkerchief over her mouth and nose. She fought against him as he pinned her arms to her sides and held the handkerchief to her nose. Then the will to fight drained away and her limbs became leaden, too heavy to move, her eyelids too heavy to hold open.

Chapter Fifteen

The room Rachel awoke to was small and dirty and bare of furniture, save a bed and a plain steel chair. She lay bound to the bed, and she was vaguely aware that Jake was seated in the chair. There was a humming sound in her ears and her head ached. It took long moments of dazed concentration to become fully aware of where she was. She lay on her back, her head resting on a hard pillow that smelled of mildew. Her wrists were bound together, and her arms had been stretched over her head and secured to something above her. Her legs, however, were free, and she was not gagged or tied in any other way.

Panic surged through her in the first minutes of consciousness, but she forced herself to breathe deeply and examine her predicament as closely as possible. Looking slowly around the room, she could see that they were alone in the small room. Jake was propped in a chair against the wall. He was straddling the back of the chair, his forearms bound tightly to the steel back and his legs tied to the legs. He was still unconscious, his head hanging down on his chest and moving slowly with his tortured breath.

"Jake," she whispered, anxiously, but he made no response.

She moved her aching legs experimentally. They were all right, but her shoulders ached horribly from the restricted position of her arms above her head and her arms felt swollen and numb as the strands holding her wrists sent stinging needles of pain through her fingers.

She appeared to be tied to the headboard of an old bed in a long-neglected bedroom in a small tract house. The paint on the walls was chipped away in several places to reveal faded, floral wallpaper. A window on the wall to her right was covered with heavy curtains that admitted no light. She could see two doors, one gaping open to reveal the dusty interior of an empty closet.

She dropped her head to the dirty pillow, blinking against the incessant pain. Why had they brought them here? If they were anxious to have them out of their way, why didn't they take the simple step of removing them permanently? And what were his ultimate plans for them? Would they be spared or dealt the same fate as Bruce Quinlan and Chuck DeWitt?

But the plans and motivations of her abductors weren't her immediate concern. She had to get to Jake.

Rachel took a deep breath and threw her right leg up and over the left, slipping her hips around and twisting her torso in the same direction. Her hands were tied too close to the headboard to allow her to flip easily over to her stomach, but she continued to twist until she'd finally managed to achieve a prone position. Then she grasped the wooden post and pulled her knees up till she was kneeling on the pillow with her forehead pressed against the dingy wall. Her shoulders throbbed, and it felt as though shards of glass were passing through her veins as blood began to resume its normal course in her arms.

She slid around to sit with her feet off the side of the bed. She studied the bedroom door from her new position, taking note of the old knob and fittings on the door. It didn't appear to have any kind of lock on it, though, from that distance, she couldn't be sure.

She had no idea how long they'd been left in the dismal room. It could have been days, for all she knew, though her lack of hunger told her only a couple of hours had passed. Her headache had faded quickly since waking, and she was able to move about with less pain. She no longer felt afraid of the men who had imprisoned them—that emotion had long since hardened into anger, and every moment she spent in the room, her determination to exact a stiff price for their invasion of her life increased tenfold.

Rachel twisted herself back to a squatting position, and was about to push against the old wood holding her bonds when footsteps sounded outside the door.

She didn't have time to move before the door was flung open. A tall man, bloodlessly blond with eyes the color of dirty ice, stepped into the room and crossed to the side of the bed, glowering down at her. Behind him, a stocky fellow with lank black hair stood indifferently in the shadows outside the door.

"A commendable effort, my dear, but useless." Calvin Watkins walked in regally, swaggering to the side of the bed. "You're far too late to do anything now."

"It's not over yet, Watkins!" Rachel snapped.

"No, certainly not," he agreed, smiling broadly. "Not in the broadest sense anyway, but, for you and your slumbering friend, it is most certainly over."

"What time is it? Where are we?" Rachel sat glaring up at him.

"It is three o'clock on the glorious morning of Thursday, April Sixteenth." He stopped smiling, watching with empty eyes. "And this is just a little house I maintain for meetings that I'd rather not hold in my office."

"So why are we still alive?" She returned his gaze with cold fury. "You'll have to start cleaning up your loose ends if you want to get away with it."

"Get away with what? Am I doing something illegal?"

"Quit playing coy, Watkins! What are you going to do with us?"

"I would gladly cut your throat for the trouble you and your newspaper have caused me," he hissed, leaning down close to her face. "But I don't think my clients would like more bloodshed. So we will keep you out of the way until everything is finished. After that . . ."

"After that?"

He just laughed.

"I'm not worried, Watkins. What did you do with Schofield? Or was he in on this kidnapping?"

"Willis? I believe he's safe enough. He should have known better than to start calling up all those company files. My people took note of his interest, and we kept an eye on him. He's safely out of the way now."

"So, what is it? What are you going to take off that plane that is so damn important?"

"Nothing." Watkins stood, folding his arms regally before him, smiling victoriously.

"It's all going to come out anyway," she said. "Why not gloat a little bit while you've got a chance? What is it, some kind of bomb? A missile?"

"We wouldn't think of taking anything off that airplane," Watkins repeated. "Nothing at all."

"They're going to steal the whole plane."

Rachel turned her head quickly, startled by the new voice, and she saw Jake sitting up resting his head against the wall working his tongue over his dry lips with an unfocused look in his eyes. "Should'a known all along," he said, his voice a rasping hiss. "Just refuel it and fly it out. That's why you had a starter unit in Baker, and why Pandora bought a fuel truck. Not a bad plan. An F-14 can fly itself out intact faster than you could ship the parts by themselves."

"Of course," Rachel said, watching Jake as the life came back to his eyes.

"Well, aren't the two of you smart." Watkins rocked contentedly on his heels, laughing quietly. "Yes, my dear, we'll need to refuel the aircraft in order to keep its rendez-vous with a Russian carrier. There's far too much equipment in the airplane specific to the weapon for anything but the sale of a total package. That plane was simply going to disappear, presumably into the ocean. But as I said, your investigation has alerted too many people. I can't kill everyone who might know, so I'm afraid that my buyers will be stuck in a rather embarrassing position. By then, of course, I shall have collected my fee and left the scene."

"Pandora didn't ship any of that equipment overseas, did it?"

"Of course not. Pandora Exporting is only a paper company. The majority of the equipment was always on the site in the woods. There was much work to be done."

"How can you be sure they'll take the northern route?" Jake asked. Fully alert now, he watched the two men with Watkins as he talked, sizing them up even though he was bound to the chair.

"The weather is cooperating very nicely with our plans," Watkins gloated. "The northern route has priority in all but the most adverse weather conditions, and this morning will be calm with a light overcast."

"What the hell are they testing, anyway?" Rachel asked. His offhand, confident manner eroded her anger some-what, leaving her with a feeling of futility that ate at her heart.

"What does it matter?" Watkins laughed. "My clients are willing to pay handsomely for it. That's all that counts."

"Yes, that's all you'd care about, isn't it?" Jake said. "Business as usual. Right?"

"Of course." Watkins stepped back toward the door. "And I will receive the remainder of my fee when the airplane lands safely on the carrier. At which point, of course, I'll be off to a more hospitable climate. My men will…uh…clean up here. They'd do it now except we don't want to alert neighbors who'll steal the show. But now I must leave you. It will be dawn soon. I've got a flight to catch."

Watkins turned and walked quickly out of the room, leaving them with the two silent men.

"We're right outside," the blond man broke his silence, speaking in a flat, unaccented voice. "And the window is nailed shut. You should relax. Don't make any loud noises. My friend out here is a rather nervous individual."

He paused in the doorway to study each of them closely. He said nothing more, expressing himself eloquently with his determined scowl and cold, glaring eyes. Then he walked out, leaving the door slightly ajar behind him.

"I'll bet you're glad you had a cop along for protection," Jake whispered ruefully.

"Don't be hard on yourself. How's your head?" Rachel regarded him warmly, wishing to hold him in her consoling arms more than anything else.

"I'll live, I guess." He pulled against the rope holding his arms to the back of the chair. "If this was a wooden chair, I might have a slim chance of breaking it and getting free. They didn't miss a trick, did they. Tying me backward in the chair makes it rather hard to walk with it."

"There isn't any use anyway, Jake. They'd hear you no matter what you tried to do." She pressed her feet against the bars of the headboard and pushed, slowly increasing the pressure.

Jake worked his arms around in their bonds, managing to gain a bit of slack but not yet enough to slip his hands free. "We've got to get out of here, first of all. And then we've got to stop that plane from landing."

"All of that without being seen by any law enforcement officers," Rachel whispered, straining against the bars. "Where the hell is the cavalry when we need it?"

"I've been wondering that myself." Jake grinned at her. "And I wonder if perhaps it isn't time for your strapping young reporter to come blundering in."

"Scott?" Rachel relaxed her legs, leaning her head against the cross bar of the headboard to catch her breath. "If he did manage to find Watkins at any time tonight, he probably stayed with him. They're driving down to the air-strip now. Dammit! I'm the one who told him to quit pulling foolish stunts, to follow instructions from now on. We told him not to lose Watkins, and he'll stick like glue now."

"We can't afford to wait for him, anyway." Jake leaned to tip onto his feet to stand precariously straddling the steel chair. He hopped forward about two inches. "I'm afraid it's going to be a damn slow escape." He hopped again.

"Oh, Jake, we'll be tied here until his lease is up."

"Don't lose hope now. Hope is what's left over when all else fails." He hopped again, reaching the foot of the bed.

"You sound like a greeting card," she said. "And you look like a damn fool."

"Yes, but if I can get that far without making any alarm-ing noises, I might be able to untie your hands." Another hop, and he caught his balance leaning against the bed. "I'll have to come all the way around in order to reach you, however."

"Okay, it's not impossible." Rachel's spirits lifted a bit. His arms were bound to the chair, but his hands were free. If he could reach her, he might untie the ropes holding her in place. "But please be quiet. I'd rather let them have their stupid airplane than see you get shot. I just want us to be together."

"I appreciate the sentiment." Jake continued hopping around the foot of the bed, panting heavily from the exertion. "But if we don't stop them, we stand a good chance of being separated anyway. I hate to break this news to you, but they keep men and women in separate prisons."

"Good point. Hop faster."

Jake made his way around the bed slowly, reaching the headboard in about five minutes. "Twist your hands out of the way," he said, leaning the back of the chair against the side of the bed and straining his hands toward her. "It doesn't look like you're tied too tightly."

"Can you get it?"

"I think so. Give it some slack if you can."

With his arms crossed atop the chair, he could only work on the knots with one hand, but he started working it loose.

"A couple minutes is all we need," he whispered, leaning close to her as he worked on the cord with his left hand.

Slowly, with awkward care, he undid the knot, but his progress was so painfully slow that Rachel despaired of ever gaining their freedom. The bedroom door stood half open no more than five feet from his back and all that was needed was a quick glance around the door to end their actions. And maybe their lives.

He'd almost freed one wrist when a board creaked in the hall. Rachel stared over Jake's head at the doorway while he tugged the last loop out of the knot restraining her right wrist. Two men were speaking quietly beyond the door, but she couldn't tell what they were saying. *Please keep talk-*

ing! Don't come in yet! And then her hand was free, and she turned her attention to the remaining wrist while Jake tilted back and turned to face the open door. He was standing behind the door in his forced crouch when Rachel released her other hand and the heavy tread continued in the hall.

The blond man stepped into the room, stopping abruptly when he saw that Jake's chair was gone from the wall beyond the bed. One more step, turning to look at Rachel on the bed, and Jake threw himself forward hitting the door, knocking it shut and bouncing toward the man's knees. They tumbled to the floor as Rachel threw off the last rope and ran to help.

She pulled the gun from its holster beneath his jacket as he tried to pin Jake down.

"What's happening in there?" The door at Jake's back sprang open, hitting the front legs of the chair.

Rachel jumped back and aimed at the man who now lay very still and staring up at her in fear. "We've got your friend covered in here!" She shouted angrily, as she tried to hide her trembling. "Don't try anything!"

Jake struggled to push himself farther back against the door, using his body as a barrier to assault as he held the gun cocked and pointed awkwardly at the blond man's head. There was a moment of silence from the hall, then footsteps moving away. Still trembling, Rachel stepped around their blond captor and knelt to work on Jake's bonds.

"Keep an eye on him," Jake whispered. "You'll have to be ready to use that gun, Rachel."

"Oh, God, Jake, I could never shoot anyone." The knots on Jake's arms were tighter than the ones that had held her, and her fingers felt thick and clumsy. She'd never get him untied in time. What was the other man doing? Were there others beyond the door? The questions taunted her, fought for her concentration as she struggled to untie the ropes and watch the blond man at the same time.

"Almost home free," Jake said calmly. "Take it easy and don't rush. All I need is one hand free. Just one—"

Rachel heard a muffled click just a split second before the door exploded above them, showering the room in splinters of wood. Then, she heard another small click.

Chapter Sixteen

A short scream burst from Rachel's lips as the sound of the shotgun continued to reverberate in the small room. Then she scurried back just as the second blast tore another hole the size of a softball in the door and the pellets snapped into the far wall. The blond man leaped to the other side of the door, pressing himself against the wall.

The muzzle of a double-barreled shotgun slid through one of the holes in the door, swiveling, seeking aim blindly. "Slip that gun out here, lady." The gunman spoke smugly.

"I'll shoot your friend!" Rachel pointed the gun at the blond man's face, breathing deeply and evenly as she held the heavy revolver in both hands.

"So shoot him," the man said, laughing. "He's not my friend." The gun moved toward her, aiming at her voice.

"Maybe I'll shoot you." She stared down at Jake, hoping to find instructions in his anxious eyes. He rocked himself tighter to the door, holding it with his weight.

"You'd have done that by now, lady. Now give me the gun or I'll have to take you out."

"She'll give it to you!" Jake shouted out, trying to rock over to his knees. "Just a second."

"No!" Rachel knelt quickly, touching Jake's leg softly.

"Listen to him lady. It's your only chance." The voice was gloating, triumphant.

"Jake," she hissed. "What are you thinking of?"

"My hand is almost free. Pull me out of the way and untie me," Jake commanded, in a heated whisper. "Hurry!"

"Don't be stupid, lady," the gunman called. "Your reporter was stupid and look where it got him."

"What do you want?" Rachel grasped the leg of the chair and pulled Jake toward her, keeping her eyes on the man seated across the room from her.

"Untie me," Jake's voice was harsh with hurried authority. "We've got to let him in."

"You ready yet?" The man sounded more cautious now, wary of the time it was taking to open the door. "We don't have all day."

"We can't let him in," Rachel whispered as she fought the knots. "We'll never get out of here."

"We won't anyway," Jake whispered, squeezing his hand through the loosened rope. "Not if he gets the gun."

"But if we—"

The doorknob turned and the door swung in slightly, without resistance this time. Suddenly, the shotgun disappeared and the door burst open, the gunman right behind. Jake pulled his hand out and grabbed the gun from Rachel.

He fired without hesitation as the shotgun roared at the far wall like a cannon and the gunman screamed in pain.

The room fell eerily silent. Then the man moved, groaning, and Jake took a deep breath. "That was too close," he said. "Rachel, see if one of them has a knife and cut my other hand free. Careful now."

Rachel kicked the shotgun away from the fallen man and studied him for a moment. He was the man with the birthmark that she'd seen at the paper, but he didn't look so dangerous lying holding his wounded shoulder.

"I have a knife," his blond companion offered, before she could ask.

"You're a lot of help, Alex." The wounded man twisted to glare at his companion. "One hell of a lot of help."

"My knife won't change anything, Louie." He held his jacket out wide on one side, exposing the empty holster as he reached his other hand in toward the pocket of his pants. "I will get my knife out for you, Miss Morgan," he said, keeping his eyes on the bore of the revolver Jake trained on him. "It is most certainly too late to stop them from taking the airplane now, and I assure you that I have no desire to get shot."

"I hope you don't."

He removed a penknife from the pocket and slid it across the floor to her. Rachel knelt and grabbed it, using it to slice through the rope holding Jake to the chair.

"What do we do with these guys?" she asked as she cut the ropes holding his legs to the chair.

"Tie them up and call the police," he said. He stood and picked up the shotgun, breaking it open to pull out the two spent shells. "We've got to move fast."

Rachel crouched beside the wounded man. A great deal of blood had soaked into his shirt around the bullet hole over his left shoulder, but the flow seemed to have slowed considerably. "He isn't going to bleed to death before they get here, is he?" she asked Jake anxiously.

"No, he'll be fine. They can be here with an ambulance in five minutes. Take a look for my handcuffs, won't you?"

Rachel went out and moved quickly through the nearly empty rooms in the house. Jake's police revolver and handcuffs were lying on a counter in the kitchen, and she brought them back to where he stood guard over their captives.

"Okay, boys, I don't have time to be as fancy as you guys were, but I think I can keep the two of you in one place long enough for reinforcements to show up. You, Alex, put this on your left wrist. And, as long as you're being so helpful, you'd better give me your car keys." Jake threw the handcuffs at him. "Call the police, Rachel. Tell them the circumstances and who you are. We can't wait around to explain things."

Rachel made the police emergency call in the kitchen. Her eyes caught sight of a briefcase on the table, but she dismissed it. She didn't have time to comb through the case. After she dialed police and recounted what had happened, she scurried back to Jake, upstairs, watching as he secured the handcuffs.

"I'll leave the key on the kitchen table," he said. "See you bums in court."

Neither man made a reply as the pair left the bedroom and descended the stairs. Jake immediately headed to the kitchen, tossing the key onto the table there, next to the case. "What's that?"

Rachel, right behind, said, "I saw it earlier, but left it alone. There's no time."

Jake lifted a hand. "Just a second, Rachel. It may be relevant to what's about to happen." He began to look around for a tool. He grabbed a knife from a knifeblock, and began to pry open the clasps. In seconds, the lid popped open. Inside, money and papers spilled out.

"My God, look at that," she said, taking one of the papers, a sheet from a yellow legal pad. "Say, this looks like Bruce's handwriting."

"Are you sure?"

"Yes, and that's definitely his style of scribbling in the margins. These must be some of the papers from the locker that were stolen from Naomi. Why on earth would they have kept them around?"

"I don't know, and we don't have time to figure out much more. Take the papers, and we'll put the case back into as much of its original condition as possible."

Out on the front stoop, the two stopped to survey the small cottage that had served as their prison. Rachel immediately recognized the neighborhood. It was old, middle class and dated. "Their little headquarters, I'd guess." Jake spoke disdainfully.

"It's a dismal spot for it."

"The place has seen better days, that's for sure. They didn't leave much behind."

"No, but we'd better be on our way if we don't want to be among what they left behind."

"IF YOU CAN THINK OF ANY WAY to stop them short of taking flight, speak up," Jake said, as he piloted the criminals' car through the quiet streets.

They were driving toward the airport in a black Ford that had been parked in the driveway of the house. The battered gray sedan that had forced Rachel off the road and stopped Naomi Aaronson to steal Bruce's documents was locked in the garage.

"Never get there fast enough any other way." Rachel felt more optimistic now, with the cool wind rushing in through the open window and the lights of the sleeping city rushing past the car. It was still possible to prevail, still possible to triumph as long as they were free. "Did they have anything to say while you were tying them up?"

"No, their information has a price, I'm sure. It's time for the bad guys to start bargaining for immunity."

Nearing the airport, Jake slowed the car and scanned the road carefully.

"You're sure your plane will be ready?"

"He said it would be when we left. I only hope it's out of the hangar. I'm not sure if they keep anyone on at night to help us taxi it out."

"We'll just have to cross our fingers on that score. What worries me is whether they've put out any bulletins on us with airport security. You'd think that someone on the force would consider the necessity of guarding your plane."

"But they don't know we're back in town. Didn't, anyway, before I called. Why guard my plane when we've already got one?"

"Good point." He turned in at the private aviation entrance, driving along the hangars to the one belonging to Tacoma Aviation. "Okay, you check out the plane while I call the station. If I can't convince them to send out the troops to bust that air strip, they'll at least send a couple squad cars down to arrest us. One way or another, I'll get someone down there."

He stopped the car by the office door. A dim light shone from within. They got out quickly, and Rachel ran around to look at the planes parked on the concrete in front of the hangar. "It's out there," she called. "I'll check it out." She ran out to the plane as Jake went to the pay phone.

Harry Peterson had promised that the plane would be ready and waiting, and he was as good as his word. Rachel turned the key and was rewarded by the confident purr of the engine kicking to life. Moments later, Jake came running across the tarmac and jumped into the seat beside her.

"We'd better get into the air," he said, slamming the door behind him as he looked out toward the runways. "Agent Fowler just called with a tip that we have been spotted heading toward the airport. We should have company any minute now."

"How did he know?"

"I'd imagine he heard the radio call when they sent an ambulance out to the house. If we escaped there, our only logical destination is the airport."

"Are they going to send anyone down to the strip?"

"I talked to Ron Jarvis," he told her. "He's arranging for a reception committee at the airstrip. If they can find it."

"They'll find it," Rachel said, confidently. "It will be the stretch of woods with a jet fighter plane circling overhead."

"We'd better get a move on. I think I see some rather official looking red lights approaching now."

Rachel could see the vehicles turning in toward the private hangars with the familiar glow of red lights flashing on top.

"Tacoma tower, Tacoma tower." Rachel called the tower as she powered up and started the plane moving out toward the runways. "Tacoma tower, come in, over."

"Tacoma tower, over."

"This is Piper Cherokee Delta Niner Zero Three Zero Charlie requesting immediate clearance for takeoff."

"Negative, Cherokee. You've been denied clearance by Tacoma police. Please hold position, over."

"Negative yourself, tower. Give us clearance, because we're going up." The police cars had passed the last hangar and were skidding to a halt behind the car in which they'd arrived.

"Please hold. I'm in communication with the police now."

"Give me a runway!" Rachel shouted in to the microphone. "Give me a runway or I'll take the first one I come to!" Uniformed officers had gotten out of two of the cars with guns drawn, while a third car followed them onto the taxiway. Rachel increased their speed.

"Negative, Cherokee, please hold."

"Give me a runway!" She could see Fowler standing among the officers waving his arms, apparently exhorting them to fire. But the policemen, who had assumed the firing position, were returning their weapons to their holsters as the plane drew farther away. "Okay, then, I'm taking runway seven. You'd better not have any jets coming in!"

The police car had drawn up beside them on Jake's side of the plane, the driver motioning for them to stop.

"Okay, Cherokee." The air traffic controller spoke in tired resignation. "Nothing coming in. You have unlimited ceiling, so get out of here."

"Thank you, tower. Cherokee out."

"That was close," Jake said. "Another couple minutes and they'd have had us in cuffs."

"Is that car clear?" Rachel turned off the taxiway onto the main runway.

"Yeah, they stopped short of the runway," Jake said, turning in his seat to watch behind them. "I'm going to owe those guys one hell of an explanation."

"We just saved them from the embarrassment of arresting the wrong people." She gave them full power, sending the plane bouncing down the runway in a sudden burst of speed.

"Easy now!" Jake snapped around to face forward, gripping the chair tightly. "Don't rush on my account."

"Just one more trip and I promise to never make you fly with me again." Rachel laughed as the plane lifted off the concrete and rose rapidly into the sky.

The hazy clouds overhead were just beginning to turn pink in the east, a faint intrusion of color into the black sky. As they gained altitude, the color deepened, filling the eastern sky with the red fire of a new day. Rachel turned the plane south and began adjusting the dial of the radio as Jake released his grip on the chair and took a deep breath.

"I'm not getting anything on the military frequencies," Rachel said. The radio hissed with empty static as she turned the dial.

"Radio silence. Whatever they're simulating, it probably extends to the air as well."

"Wait a second." She turned the dial slowly back through the fluctuating static hiss until a short squeal burst through. Then there was the faint sound of someone talking. "Affirmative," it said. "All but one."

"One what?" Jake leaned closer to the speaker. "Who are we listening to?"

"I don't know, but I can usually pick up air force pilots at this frequency."

"Blue Three experienced electrical malfunction." The words were clear and sharp, then faded again.

"It's got to be them."

"Next, he'll drop out of formation," Rachel commented, grimly. "We should be over the runway in about five minutes."

"He hasn't broken ranks yet, or they'd be yelling about having a plane down." Jake scanned the horizon for any sign of an airplane. "They're probably above the clouds."

"Blue leader, blue leader, I have a mechanical malfunction!" The voice shouted, fear propelling the words from his throat. "Losing altitude! Repeat! Losing altitude!"

"There he goes!" Jake shouted. "Can we get there before him?"

"I don't know where he is. We're still three or four minutes away, and then we've got to get into position to land. If he drops fast, we'll never beat him."

"Damn! We'll never stop him once he's refueled."

"Blue Three, what is your status?" There was no reply but static. "Blue three! Come in! Blue flight, I've lost sight of my wing man. Can anyone get a visual on Parker?"

"Negative," someone responded. "Nothing here."

"Blue three, come in, please." And the static began to swallow the voices again. "May Day. We have a pilot down. No visual." That was it, the static took over the frequency again.

"He's at the strip, for sure," Jake said. "How fast can they refuel an airplane?"

"I don't know. Did that check of Pandora personnel turn up anything on military backgrounds?"

"No, we didn't have time to request that. How far to the airstrip?"

"We should be over it now, but I can't tell." Rachel put the plane into a long, banking turn as she scanned the ground for any sign of activity. "It's still dark on the ground and the sunrise is blinding up here. I'll take us down low."

"Not too low, please." But he laughed as he said it, his normal confidence returning to his voice as he concentrated on the job at hand.

Moments later they were flying close to the treetops, skimming along at the base of the mountains looking for the lighted strip of concrete that had to be below them somewhere. After completing one pass of the likely area, she turned and flew over it again.

"How long have we been looking?" Jake asked.

"Nearly ten minutes. This is the right place. It has to be. But I don't see anything."

Below them, the forest continued in a seemingly unbroken carpet of green rising and falling with the terrain and swaying in the light morning breeze. Then Jake turned his head quickly, scanning the forest to their left.

"There," he said, pointing. "Lights coming on."

Rachel turned the plane and the patch of light came into view just ahead of them.

"They killed the lights to refuel!" she exclaimed, dropping them lower to the trees as they approached the strip. "They're all ready to go!"

The runway was clearly visible now, a rectangular patch of concrete lit with floodlights along its entire length. At one end, the airplane was moving slowly around away from the fuel truck and the crowd of men who were already scattering toward several cars parked beyond the concrete.

"Damn!" Jake slapped the door with his fist in frustration. "We blew it!"

"Not quite," Rachel admonished, breathlessly. "Maybe if he sees us up here, he'll sit tight. Hold on."

She flew low over the clearing, mere feet above the fir trees. The aircraft was nearly in position, pointed back in the direction from which they'd come. Once they'd passed the runway, Rachel twisted the plane through a steeply banked turn, coming back at the runway behind the powerful military craft.

"What the hell are you doing?" Jake shouted, laughing in anxious disbelief as they approached the rear of the runway. Below them, a line of headlights moved quickly along a narrow road away from the site.

"He won't take off with us overhead."

"You want to bet?"

The jet lurched on the runway as they passed over it, and then it began to roar along the concrete. Jake twisted to watch the plane below them gain speed on the ground and begin lifting slowly as they flashed overhead.

"I don't think he knows we're here!"

"Oh, God, no! Hold on!"

She twisted the controls sharply to the right, trying to pull them out of the path of the rising aircraft. The jet leaped into the air, rushing toward them like a bullet that was too fast for them to avoid. Then, as quickly as it began to lift, it nosed down roaring beneath them with a blast of thunder.

Suddenly, something slammed into their plane as a dark object shot up before them. Rachel fought the controls, struggling to gain altitude even as the fighter roared into the trees with a splintering crash. Then the forest erupted in a orange and yellow cloud of flame that burst and faded behind them as the jet fuel exploded.

They spun, nearly catching the treetops with a wing before Rachel regained control of the pitching craft and lifted them in a long, slow turn. They rose up into the light of dawn just beginning to break over the mountains.

"Oh, God," Rachel said breathlessly. "I never thought he'd try taking off. He must not have seen us till after he started."

"You're lucky I didn't have breakfast," Jake said weakly. "What hit us?"

"The pilot ejected," Rachel said, feeling calmer. "There, you can see the chute just going down in to the trees. The canopy over the cockpit must have struck us."

"He's lucky he didn't strike us, too." Jake brushed one hand over his brow and sat back in the seat watching the blur of white dropping into the trees west of the strip. A long gash of dying flames the warplane had made when it crashed marred the forest below. "You know, after living through your aerobatics, normal flying isn't half bad at all."

"I'll make a believer out of you yet," she laughed. "All I need is time."

"I'll give you all the time you want," he said, reaching out to slip his fingers softly through her hair. "Just get us down on terra firma first."

She turned the plane back toward the runway, putting them down gently on the tarmac and stopping near the abandoned fuel truck. They both climbed out of the plane as soon as the propeller had stopped spinning and stood regarding the trees around them.

"The forest is too wet to burn," Jake said. "The few flames left won't last long when the remaining fuel has been used up. Let's look for the pilot. He wasn't far off here."

"Wait! Someone is coming." Rachel pointed toward the intermittent flashes of headlights approaching through the trees.

Jake drew his gun and stood before Rachel as they watched the car approach. A moment later, the car came around the trees and entered the airstrip clearing. Friend or foe, they were ready to face the intruder.

Chapter Seventeen

"It's Scott!" Rachel cried out in relief. She ran out toward the car that rushed up and skidded to a halt.

"This is going to be great," the young reporter called as he jumped out of his car with his camera. "The story of the century! Pulitzer prize time! We'll all be famous!"

"Slow down, kid," Jake laughed, putting his gun away. "Help us find the pilot."

"The pilot? Damn, this gets better all the time! Who is he?"

"Unless I'm way off base, it's Captain Zack Parker," Rachel explained as they walked into the woods. "Calvin Watkins made several calls to his number in San Francisco."

They skirted the area of splintered, still smoldering trees marking the trail of the downed plane, and found Captain Parker unconscious and still strapped into his ejection seat. The low altitude at which he'd ejected hadn't allowed enough room for his parachute to slow his descent enough, and it was obvious that he'd broken his leg in the fall. But he was breathing normally, and the seat had protected him from any more serious injury. They cut him out of his harness and carried him back to the strip after Scott had snapped several pictures for their coming edition.

"How did you get here?" Jake asked Scott as they placed the injured flier on the soft earth near the runway.

"I followed Watkins out. He was at the house for a while, then he came straight down here."

"Where is he now?" Rachel put in.

"I don't know. He left with the rest of them while the plane was trying to take off. He's probably headed back to Tacoma."

"Why on earth didn't you stay with him?" Jake scowled at the reporter as he stood above the airman.

"Are you kidding? The government will have the crash site sealed off as soon as they arrive, and I wasn't about to miss out on firsthand photographs. Get real, officer, this is a scoop!"

"Reporters are nuts," Jake stated with an incredulous laugh.

"Maybe, but we've got an exclusive," Scott replied easily.

"What do you propose we do now?" Rachel asked Jake.

"Well, as much as I hate to say this, we've got to fly back to Tacoma."

"Do you think we can catch Watkins?"

"I don't know," he admitted, leading her by the hand toward the plane. "But somebody left a briefcase full of money in that house, and I'm sure not going to let him go without a fight. Hold down the fort, kid," he called to Scott. "There should be someone from the sheriff's department out here soon."

"What about this guy?"

"He's all right. If he wakes up, sit on him."

"Are you ready, Jake?" Rachel called down from the plane as she slipped through the door.

"No, but that hasn't stopped me yet."

THEY WERE AT THE HOUSE no more than twenty minutes later, well ahead of anyone leaving the woods by car.

"Ready?" Jake took her arm on the front walk, standing close to her side.

"No, no, I'm not ready." A short sigh slipped unbidden from her lips, and she turned to bury her face in Jake's shoulder. "The past few days have gone by so fast that I never had time to think until now," she said. "I feel like I'm on a roller coaster that just left the track, and I don't know where we'll come down."

"Don't worry." He held her gently, stroking her hair with one strong hand as he nuzzled his cheek against the top of her head. "I'm here to catch you, Rachel. I'll always be here."

"I know." She lifted her head to meet his steadfast gaze with loving admiration. "You've been my rock through all of this, and I've relied on you being there for me."

"I just went along for the ride." He smiled down at her with devotion, his attention dancing across the soft contours of her face. "And it was one hell of a ride."

"But it's not over yet, is it? We've got loose ends to tie up." She dropped her head back to his chest, listening to the steady throb of his heartbeat. "We'd better get in there before he shows up."

"He may not come here, you know." Jake looked toward the house, looking from one blank window to the next. "He might not come back to Tacoma at all."

"No, I can't imagine him leaving without that briefcase." She turned to look at the house with him. "If it was important enough to hide here, it must be important enough to come back for. I wonder if the police found it when they came for the two in the bedroom."

"I doubt it. There's no police barrier across the door, no officer on duty. Fowler must have pulled some strings to cut off any investigation and keep the site clear."

"In that case, it's up to us. Let's get it over with." She marched resolutely beside him to the door.

They entered the dark living room and turned on a light. "Give me a chance to check the place over," Jake said, walking through to the small kitchen in the back of the house. Then crossing the living room, he looked into the meager bedrooms and the bathroom that opened off the short hall.

"There's no one here," he said, coming out of the hall. "And the briefcase is still in place."

"It's even a dreary place in daylight," Jake commented.

"And sad," she agreed. She felt a sudden need for his touch and put her arms around him and kissed his cheek.

"Now, we wait," he said, returning her embrace. "Someone should be here soon."

They turned out the lights and sat on the couch in the living room to wait. Outside, the morning sun was bringing the street to life. A screen door slammed, and they could hear a car driving away as one of the neighbors left for work.

Twenty minutes later, there was no sign of anyone coming to claim the briefcase.

"I don't think he's coming," Jake said, wearily. "He must have figured on a trap."

"He'll be here." Rachel stood, stretching. "He won't leave anything behind. Wait a second," she whispered quickly, rushing to the front window. "There's a black car parked at the curb across the street. I don't remember it being there when we came."

"Probably a neighbor working a night shift." Jake had just begun to rise when a voice from the kitchen froze him.

"Sit down, Connors," Agent Fowler commanded from behind them. "I've got your friend covered."

Rachel spun to stare at the weapon in the FBI agent's hand. It was pointing right at her stomach.

"And I've got you covered, Fowler," Jake said, calmly. He held his weapon steady in his right hand as he lowered himself back to the couch. "We seem to have a standoff."

"But I'll shoot Miss Morgan." The agent's voice faltered slightly, unsure of himself with the bore of Jake's gun trained on him. "You wouldn't want that to happen, would you?"

"I'm a cop, Fowler," Jake said. "And a good cop never gives up his gun if there's any alternative. In this case, I don't expect either one of us to live very long if I put my gun down. So, I'm content to leave things as they are. At least, this way, I'll get you."

The dead seriousness in Jake's voice startled Rachel at first, but his logic was faultless. Fowler's mistake had been in not shooting the policeman as soon as he'd entered the room. Now it was too late to correct his error.

In fact, it could be later than any of them thought. A movement outside had caught her eye, and she'd been able to steal a glance through the front window to see a man approaching the front door. She wasn't able to see who it was before he was obscured by the window frame, but any intrusion would be welcome at this point.

"I don't think you've killed anyone in this deal yet," Jake was saying. "You don't want to start now."

"Don't be so sure of that. There's a lot of money involved," Fowler said.

"Finally going to get your share of the pie, Fowler?"

"Damn right. I'm sick of watching the criminals living high while we eat dirt on government wages," he said bitterly. "I'm getting old in this dead-end job, Connors, and it just isn't worth it anymore. I came for my money, but maybe I can get away clean by getting rid of the witnesses, too."

"So, that's your case hidden in the kitchen," Rachel said, loudly. No more than five feet to her right, the knob of the front door was turning slowly. "How did you get in?" she asked.

"You neglected to check for a basement entrance," the man said, smiling. "And, since I knew you had taken the car, I felt it was wise to—"

The front door flew open and Calvin Watkins entered with a gun in his hand. In one move he was in and holding one arm around Rachel's throat while pointing his revolver at Jake. When Rachel fought against his strangling grip, he pulled back tighter and moved the barrel of his gun to her right ear.

"Your little standoff has changed drastically, hasn't it?" Watkins said, his voice a silken purr. "I think you should drop your weapon and slide it over to me, Connors. Do it now, please."

Jake dropped his gun to the floor with a resigned smile on his face. "Well, Calvin, how's business these days? Aside from blowing your big sale this morning, that is." Jake spoke calmly as he pushed the gun across the floor with his foot. "Everything going on schedule?"

Fowler stepped forward eagerly, stooping to pick up the gun.

"Of course." Watkins smiled, showing his teeth. "It is no longer any of my concern. And if I hadn't decided to pick up some extra traveling money, I wouldn't be bothering you good people. It is extremely unfortunate that I happened to run into Agent Fowler again," he added. "Extremely unfortunate."

Without warning, he swung his gun and fired twice, knocking the startled FBI agent off his feet and back over a cushioned footstool. He rolled up against the wall and lay still.

Rachel's scream died in her throat as she watched the smoking revolver in Calvin's hand swing back and take deadly aim on Jake's face.

"Why? Why did you do that?" Rachel asked, her voice creeping back slowly.

"You can never trust a rogue cop, my dear," he said easily. "If they are willing to betray their oath, they will betray anything. Besides, it's his money that I came for."

"And you're prepared to do anything, aren't you?" Jake spoke calmly, as if nothing had happened, keeping his eyes on the gun in Calvin's hand. "But what will they say when you get to the motherland?"

"Russia?" Watkins laughed harshly. "My dear boy, I'm no Russian, and certainly not a communist. Just an old-fashioned capitalist out to make a quick million or two. I don't care if they get their merchandise or not, as long as they can't blame me for the loss."

"You really are vermin, Watkins," Jake sneered, watching the gun in the other man's hand. "I can understand doing this out of some ideological passion, but to betray a country for money alone puts you in the lowest class of rodent."

"A wit, aren't you, Connors? Well, I can afford to let you laugh."

"How did you get the others into it?" Rachel asked, fighting to calm her voice. "How did you buy Captain Parker?"

"The captain is a gambler, my dear," Calvin replied, hot against her ear. "He felt the chance to earn a large fee and eradicate his volume of debts was vastly superior to the alternative he was offered."

"And you have the connections to take advantage of a gambler's weakness," Jake said. "Did you buy up their debts, along with the other favors provided by Carbellino?"

"Yes, of course. My criminal friends thought they were helping to set up a sting of Schofield Enterprises. They are expecting a large payoff for their help."

"They'll be waiting a long time, won't they?" Jake smiled.

"A very long time, yes. But now I must take leave of you. If you, Sergeant Connors, would be so kind as to retrieve my briefcase, I'll depart."

"No," Rachel shouted, suddenly, heedless of the arm around her throat or the gun at her head. "This man has been trying to run my life all week. He's done everything he can to make me feel afraid and weak, and now he wants us to help him escape, too. Don't help him, Jake. I'm tired of the whole thing!"

"Bravo!" Watkins laughed. "That was a very good speech. I could tell it came from the heart. For my part, I assure you that I had no intention of disrupting your life, but I couldn't afford to take chances. Your reporter, of course, was an inconvenience that simply had to be dealt with, and that led to more problems. Your own inquisitive nature is at fault, my dear."

"I'd prefer to blame you," she spat.

"I don't doubt that."

"Was it all your idea, Watkins?" Jake asked quickly.

"For a healthy fee." The man laughed. "I obtained a firm commitment to six million. Half in advance. After all, I was the one who orchestrated everything. Of course, I don't expect to get the rest of it now. But enough small talk. If you will consent to getting my case, Sergeant Connors, I can leave you alone."

Jake moved slowly, obviously unwilling to leave them alone together. He stood and walked past the silent body and disappeared into the kitchen.

"Hurry!" Watkins snapped. "I'm trying to be a nice guy, but if you try to delay me I'll be forced to deal more harshly with you than I'd like."

"Get off it, Watkins! You aren't really planning to leave us alive," Jake called from the kitchen.

"I'm not a murderer by nature," Watkins stated. "Fowler's death was a necessity. He knew too much about my plans for the future. But I need only to restrain you to get away clean. I can't expect to pull this off without the authorities finding out I did it. It's gone beyond that. But I know a place where neither the United States, Mother Russia, nor the mob can find me." He spoke with the ease of a man well in charge of the situation and arrogantly at ease with himself. To hear him speak, you wouldn't think he had a care in the world. "My flight leaves soon, and I plan to be traveling with a clean conscience. As well as an assumed name," he added, with a cold laugh.

"It's too bad things didn't work out properly, isn't it?" Jake said casually. He walked through the kitchen doorway holding the briefcase up before him. "Your name would go down in history if you'd managed to organize the theft of a fully loaded warplane."

"I did well enough," Watkins answered. He began walking sideways, taking Rachel toward the door. "I will admit, however, in retrospect, that, I should have left Miss Morgan alone. Without her help, you'd never have caught on."

"You win some, you lose some." Jake forced a laugh. "It was an awfully complicated plan to expect everything to work perfectly."

"There might have been easier ways, but this one suited my purpose nicely. The hijacking of an F-14 would have been the crowning achievement of a long and illustrious career. Especially when it was carrying their new heat-seeking missile system. And now I shall be on my way," Watkins said. "Bring the case over here."

"Get it, Calvin." Jake swung the case out to the side, sending it flying at the couch.

Calvin's eyes followed the movement, and Rachel took that chance to twist down and away from the gun. Jake leaped forward, breaking them apart and slamming Calvin back against the wall. He grasped Calvin's throat tightly in one hand and pinned the gun against the wall above his head.

"Drop the gun before I choke you, Calvin," Jake commanded.

The man did as he was told, and Jake kicked the weapon away as he whirled Watkins around to face the wall and hold his arm up behind his back.

"Okay, Mr. Watkins," Jake said. "You are under arrest. Anything you say can be used against you in a court of law—"

"Shut up!" the man cut him off. "I know my rights!"

"I guess you'll have to miss your flight, after all," Rachel said.

Calvin Watkins didn't find any humor in that at all.

Epilogue

Journalist thwarts sky pirates.

Jake laid the stack of newspapers on Rachel's desk so she could read the banner headline and stood back with his arms crossed over his chest. "I'll bet you'll be nearly impossible to get along with for the next couple weeks," he said, grinning crookedly.

"Me?" Rachel looked up, a demure smile lighting her vivacious features. "What ever do you mean?"

"You're a heroine from coast to coast this morning. Most people I know would be unbearably proud of themselves if they were in a similar situation." He pulled a chair up and sat across from her, his smile spreading into an expression of all-consuming pride and admiration.

"I might as well admit that I do feel pretty good about it," Rachel said, rocking back and forth in her chair as she waved her hand at the papers on her desk. "But it isn't what all those headlines say that pleases me, it's the fact that they're saying it two days after the *Banner* broke the story. We scooped them all by two days! Can you believe that?" She let out a whoop of pure delight and shook back her auburn tresses.

"Journalists!" He laughed. "You get more excitement out of a couple inked pages than being kidnapped, shot at, or anything else you went through."

"Now, Jake, I—"

"Wait a second." He grabbed the newspaper from the top of the pile and scanned down the first column. "Here it is. 'She took her single-engine propeller craft and prevailed in what amounted to aerial combat with a fully armed F-14 Tomcat fighter plane.' 'I hadn't planned things to work out like that,' she said, in a telephone interview.'" He dropped the newspaper on the desk. "Not only are you a hero but you're modest, as well," he said, laughing.

"Modest, nothing. I wouldn't have been over him if I thought he would still take off." Rachel hid her eyes behind her slender fingers, shaking her head.

"The *Los Angeles Tribune* calls you a national heroine."

"Oh, please." Rachel moaned, laughing.

"Has it been rough being on the other end of the newspaper game?"

"Not too rough. But I am getting rather tired of telling the same story over and over again, and I'll be more than happy for things to get back to normal around here."

But it wouldn't be normal for awhile yet. After the *Banner* story had broken in the Wednesday edition, the national press had been quick to pick it up. Rachel had suffered through two days of questions so far, and it didn't look like the weekend would be any better.

Many of the other papers simply took her story just as she'd written it, but the larger dailies sent reporters to inundate the paper's small offices. After them came the television reporters, and stringers for news magazines. A secret plan to steal American military technology, coupled with the abduction of a reporter and a nationally prominent businessman, was a major event.

The Department of Defense hadn't wanted to say too much about the weaponry that was the target of the whole operation, but once the story broke they released information about their new, lightweight missile guidance system. The computerized heat-seeking hardware would allow American aircraft to more effectively aim the missile at enemy airplanes and avoid the possibility of it homing in on the wrong craft. Officials admitted that an expanded system based on the same principles could be programmed for use against either incoming missiles or Soviet satellites. The test itself had been a total success, with the six missiles that were launched striking three of the four drone aircraft over the Pacific Ocean, more than twenty miles from where the jets were flying when the missiles were fired. The only weapons that weren't fired were the two on Captain Parker's airplane. But that was the only information they were willing to release about the test itself.

"So, what could the *Banner* possibly have lined up for this week to rival last week's blockbuster?" He leaned forward, lacing his fingers together on the desk as he gazed across at her.

"We've still got our report about the lumber industry to write up. And then there's the garbage collection schedules for spring cleanup, and much more that needs to be reported. And, of course, I've got an exclusive interview with Willis Schofield. He's got quite a tale to tell of being taken at gunpoint from his own office. He's granted us the exclusive interview."

"Maybe that will keep you from bothering the police department from now on," he said, smiling.

"I doubt that." She pulled a notepad across her desk and sat with her pen poised above it. "Have there been any new developments?"

"Watkins still isn't talking," Jake said. "But we've got solid evidence linking Louie Hunt to Bruce Quinlan's murder. It's only a matter of time till someone breaks down and gives us witness confirmation. A gun we found in his apartment has been confirmed as the murder weapon, so they're about ready to go forward with an indictment."

"What about the federal case against Watkins?"

"Our friend, Alex, has been very helpful about that. He's eager to avoid prosecution, and we need an inside witness."

"I take it that it was meant to work pretty much the way we'd figured it out."

"Exactly that way. Watkins found out about the defense work they were doing at Pascal Semiconductor. He managed to get copies of some of the plans and peddled them to the highest bidder. When he got wind of the maneuvers, he figured out a way to parlay a few gambling debts into a major payoff. That's when he convinced his pal Carbellino that he needed a dummy company and a couple other favors in order to pull a scam on Schofield. Watkins and Carbellino bought up Schofield stock as fast as they could, and then let it be known that it was available. Captain Parker was his major find. He was about fifty grand in debt to mob gambling organizations, and Watkins bought up his debts."

"Wait a second. Captain Parker would rather betray his country than find a way to pay his debts?" That was something Rachel still found hard to believe.

"It's not so unbelievable. His naval career was ruined if the debts were discovered," Jake explained, leaning back in the chair. "Ruined either way, for that matter. Basically, he chose to live in freedom with a hundred thousand in pocket rather than face court-martial from the navy and a couple leg-breakers sent by his bookie. Fowler was working for the Russians on the deal. He just got tired of being a poor public servant, another sucker looking for fast money. So, with a fed and a pilot in his pocket, Watkins had everything covered. All he needed was some men to build a runway on land that Pandora already owned. It's all over now but the shouting."

"There'll be quite a bit of that. Schofield was nearly incoherent with rage when I saw him," Rachel laughed. "He just can't believe they were taken in so completely."

"He should have kept better tabs on Pandora once he'd been forced to buy it. The deal was so insane to begin with that he should have known there were ulterior motives behind it. I suppose he was so happy to have fought off the takeover he didn't examine the deal.

"Has his information about the company helped?"

"Yes, he's got all the purchase orders and pay slips for Pandora, as well as copies of company papers showing how Watkins received his payment from Russia. They simply paid Pandora for that equipment he was supposedly shipping overseas, and Watkins funneled it over to a Swiss bank account. He used most of Schofield's payment for Pandora to pay his bribes and operating expenses, and kept the rest for himself. The briefcase in the kitchen contained money he'd withdrawn from the company account that afternoon to pay off Fowler. But after the plane went down, he knew he wouldn't be getting the rest of his Russian payment. He needed that for travel expenses."

"If Bruce hadn't gotten curious about the sudden trading in Schofield stock, none of this would have come to light until it was too late," Rachel said. "It's strange to think that after all of the moves they went through to avoid official attention, it was a young man researching a story on an unrelated subject that did them in.''

"But how did he find them out?'' Jake asked. "We've been concentrating on building our case and haven't had time to trace Quinlan's story."

"It was the stock.'' Rachel rocked back in her chair contentedly. "As you know, Bruce was doing a piece on the lumber business, and he was a very meticulous reporter. When he started looking at the health of the industry, he happened onto all Schofield's companies since Schofield owned major lumbering concerns. He found out that there'd been unusually heavy trading in Schofield stock, and all in one direction—toward Calvin Watkins. Then he found out that Watkins wasn't in the financial position to be purchasing blocks of Schofield stock without an unseen backer, so he went further and found Carbellino putting money into the project. He established a paper trail between Watkins and Carbellino simply by digging into financial records, then apparently he began working forward from there until he found out that Pandora never intended to sell equipment overseas.''

"Clever boy,'' Jake mused. "At that time, Watkins still expected to be able to pull off the deal with the Russians, so he couldn't have Bruce wandering around with evidence linking him to a mobster. That would have ruined his planned life of luxury. So he had Bruce killed.''

"Yes, but he went too far and ruined his own plans with his paranoia. What a tangled web.'' She dropped the pen and stood, stretching. "At the moment, I want to quit thinking about it. Do you think it's possible to escape my hot story?''

"After you did so much to find it?" Jake stood, too, walking toward her around the desk. "I thought reporters lived for the chance at the big story."

"The *next* big story," she corrected him. "Always the next story. This airplane thing is old news now."

"And what will the next story be about?"

"Us." Rachel slipped her arms around him, nestling her head comfortably against his chest. "The two of us being together is the biggest news I've ever had."

She raised her face to meet his, as he lowered his lips to hers. The feeling of his arms around her was natural, so obviously right. All Rachel wanted to do was stay there in his arms letting the wonderful fire of their love spread through her.

But her office door opened to admit Scott Kirby, bearing a handful of notepaper.

"Rachel, you've got to hear this!" he exclaimed, oblivious to the embrace he'd interrupted. "I just got off the phone with—"

"Get out of here, Kirby!" Jake commanded.

"What?" He stopped short, staring in incomprehension.

"Yes, Scott." Rachel turned him gently toward the door. "We're in conference right now. I'll look at that later."

"Turning down a big story?" Jake asked, when Scott closed the door and she'd returned to his arms.

"There's a time for everything." Rachel sighed. "And, after all, it's only Friday and our deadline isn't until next Tuesday."

The only deadline that concerned her now was the time till their next kiss.

 *Harlequin Intrigue·*

COMING NEXT MONTH

#109 EXPIRATION DATE by Aimée Thurlo
Andy O'Reilly was dead . . . and no one knew why.
His partner, private investigator Melanie Cardenas,
was desperate for answers. His estranged son,
Patrick, was out for revenge. They had a common
quarry—Andy's killer—and working together was
their only hope for success, for justice, for love.

#110 STRANGER THAN FICTION by M. L. Gamble
Claire Kennedy couldn't believe her bestselling
writer's latest mystery was plagiarized. Was the
accusing Tony Nichols just masterminding a vicious
hoax? But then evidence disappeared, people
vanished—and a corpse appeared. Now more than
just Claire's reputation was threatened—her life was
at stake.

Harlequin
Superromance

MORE THAN
A FEELING

A powerful new Superromance from
ELAINE K. STIRLING

Andonis Sotera was the kind of man a woman might encounter in a Moroccan café after dark, or on the deck of a luxury cruise ship. In short, Andonis was the kind of man a woman like Karen Miller would never meet.

And yet they fell in love. Suddenly the civil servant from a small Canadian city was swept into the drama of Andonis's life. For he was not only her passionate, caring lover, he was *The Deliverer*, the one man who could save a small Mediterranean country from the terror of a ruthless dictator.

But Andonis needed Karen's help. And she was willing to risk her life to save their love....

MORE THAN A FEELING...
Coming in February from Harlequin Superromance

Harlequin Temptation dares to be different!

Once in a while, we Temptation editors spot a romance that's truly innovative. To make sure *you* don't miss any one of these outstanding selections, we'll mark them for you.

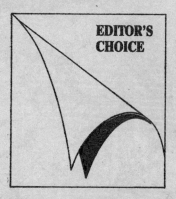

EDITOR'S CHOICE

When the "Editors' Choice" fold-back appears on a Temptation cover, you'll know we've found that extra-special page-turner!

THE *Temptation* EDITORS

Spot-1B